MW00343310

Praise for

THREE BODIES BY THE RIVER

"John Kralik's suspense novel, *Three Bodies by the River*, is a rich and thrilling read. Set in 1990s LA, innocent, inebriated lawyer Sam Straight is almost killed, then wanders into Wonderland—or is it the Dark Empire? The characters are bigger than life and unforgettable; the writing is tight and punchy. Kralik has won this case."

—MARY LOGUE
Author of the Claire Watkins Mysteries and *The Streel*

"John Kralik has crafted an amazing first novel filled with the grit and grime of the underbelly of 1990s Los Angeles. Writing in a style reminiscent of Thomas Wolfe, Kralik's characters have depth and authenticity that will draw in every reader. And the story continues to build until the crashing conclusion!"

—KERRY ROSE
Author of the Lenny Clapton mystery series

"Half the lawyers I know want to be writers. Most should stick to litigation. John Kralik is the exception. In his new book, *Three Bodies by the River*, with its wild cast of characters and a plot to match, Kralik uses his legal background to produce a first-rate contribution to the docket of great LA crime fiction.

—EDWARD GRINNAN
Editor in Chief and Vice President, Guideposts, and Author of *The Promise of Hope*

"John Kralik has delivered a gripping page-turner that reveals his deep sensitivity to his lively characters. *Three Bodies by the River* moves at such a fast pace you don't want to put it down. A must-read for any thriller aficionado!"

"A brilliantly paced crime story, transitioning seamlessly from legal thriller to Los Angeles noir in the '90s. Kralik has written a first-rate characterization of criminal investigations and the legal system in general. His character stumbles but is surefooted in his assessments of who and what is good and who and what is evil. Best to start early in the day, as it is easy to stay up all night reading this book."

Three Bodies by the River

By John Kralik

ISBN 978-1-64663-335-7

Cover design and illustration by Skyler Kratofil.

Published by

köehlerbooks™

3705 Shore Drive
Virginia Beach, VA 23455
800−435−4811
www.koehlerbooks.com

THREE BODIES BY THE RIVER

JOHN KRALIK

VIRGINIA BEACH
CAPE CHARLES

To every lawyer who has ever wished he was asleep,
And it was all a dream.

PART ONE:
SAM AND JOEL

CHAPTER ONE

I look south from a window on the thirty-third floor of the Library Tower, hypnotized by the slow progress of the jets lined up in the airspace above Century Boulevard. The jets float patiently west, magically equidistant, like a floating string of Christmas lights traveling to the ocean.

Awake, I dream. My dreams medicate the pain of a life I have grown to hate. Perhaps you are surprised that a partner in an international law firm, successful enough to have risen above the anonymity of the crowded Los Angeles legal community, is a man who hates his life. Perhaps you yourself are a member of the Los Angeles legal community. In which case you are not surprised.

In my dreams, I fly, just as you do in your sleeping dreams. It's probably all that sitting on the freeways, but in LA, everyone flies above the city in their dreams. Now I fly south towards the string of jets. As

I draw close, I see the passengers trapped in their seats, staring out at the endless expanse of the crowded, dirty neighborhoods of South Los Angeles. I fear for them. I become the Catcher in the Smog, an angel come to warn them, crying out, "Turn back, go home. Go back to a flat, right-angled state where life makes sense."

Floating into the white smoke circling up from the refineries of Torrance and Carson, my soul projects into the orange and purple swirls painted by the early-evening sun refracting through the complex, chemical smog, then touches down at the airport, watching the new ones step off the plane. I have failed to catch them.

My dreams of being the Catcher in the Smog do not sufficiently distract me. My mind drifts, to memories, painfully real. Memories of Alberta Emerald—not her real name: the client who started me on my way to this thirty-third floor. My partner Joel Green claims I fell asleep during her cross-examination in the trial that got me an offer of partnership here. My story is that I only closed my eyes. By the time I opened them, Alberta had lied her way to a stunning eight-figure victory over an insurance company that had enough money to pay.

Closing my eyes now, I am again with Alberta at a "gentlemen's club" outside LAX on the notable night we first met.

"You're too drunk to drive" was the excuse I gave myself for driving into a parking lot I had passed many times in my younger and prouder days. The neon sign promised women who were completely nude, which I somehow inferred would be better than the women who were just totally nude, or even the "Live Nude Nudes," which were among the Inglewood options I had passed up by that time. I went in to have another drink, telling myself it would clear my head from the three gins I had on the flight.

There is very little good alcohol in the gentlemen's clubs near the airport, but whatever I was drinking numbed my embarrassment at paying to see female nudity. I stood up from the bar stool, belatedly realizing I had only a fraction of my sense of balance, fearing the refuse in the dark, stale carpet coming up to meet me, and then wondrously appreciating the marvel of being stabilized when my elbow became wedged in the valley between Alberta's breasts. She caught me in her arms and reset me on my feet.

Looking up from my elbow in drunken amazement, I gazed into Alberta's wide blue eyes, highlighted by dime-store glitter.

"First time you've been in here?" she said.

"Been here a couple of times." No percentage in being a rookie at anything. Especially not this.

"Why don't you buy me a drink?"

Based on her pupils, I didn't think she needed a drink any more than I did.

Alberta turned to her left, sweeping her vast red hair into my eyes with the power of Dr. Faustus's red cape, and commanded a paunchy, dazed bartender to serve us.

"Two martinis up—and, Barry, give us real Bombay," Alberta commanded.

"What have I been drinking?" I'd been asking for Bombay.

"Safeway Select. Not bad, but not Bombay."

"I'll remember to ask for the real Bombay next time."

"Can you really tell the difference?"

"Not anymore."

"Me neither."

"Lately everything tastes like black licorice."

"You'll be able to tell the difference tomorrow morning."

"Why did you catch me?"

"I was headed your way. You're the only one tipping right now."

It turned out I had tipped her twenty minutes before when she was dancing on the bar. Her hair had been tied up then, and I didn't recognize her now that it was flowing over her shoulders. She was draped in a white gown, made transparent by the spotlight trained on the dancer on the bar above us. Beneath the veil, she wore only the couple small pieces of lingerie she had removed on the bar a few minutes ago.

"The guys who come in here are kids. Most of them sit up here at the bar all night without leaving a dollar."

She paused. My mind, in blankness, could not formulate a response. "This is my last night here."

I guess I looked like the kind of sap who might leave a really big tip if I believed it would help a young lady reach for a more heavily clad future.

The dancer above us on the bar was trying hard, but her movements seemed painful. Even watching her was excruciating. Some of the less desperate were ignoring her, declining to participate in the agony. Her hair smelled of stale hairspray and sweat when she hung it down near our drinks. Alberta and I moved in unison to cover our glasses with our fingers. The real Bombay seemed worth protecting. The dancer spread her legs and pumped them outward, but the movement caused her weakened stomach muscles to collapse, revealing the stretch marks.

I took out a couple of dollars.

"Give them to me."

I did.

"More."

I gave her a couple of fives. Seemed appropriate. When I finally gave her everything left in my wallet, Alberta stepped firmly onto the bar, planting her heels. With authoritatively swinging hips, she strode over to the hapless girl, who looked up, letting the spotlight accentuate the pockmarks in the skin stretched over her cheekbones. Once sharing the spotlight, Alberta threw off her veil, folded the bills twice lengthways, and appeared to swallow them with greedy aplomb. Alberta was a great show, and now everyone was watching. Alberta drew the dollars back out of her mouth slowly, with appropriate drama. Alberta knelt between the scrawny girl's legs, ran her tongue along the marked belly, and lovingly inserted the money behind the tiny triangle of cloth covering the girl's pudendum, a crude gesture that somehow radiated love: as if Jesus' good Samaritan had come back as a stripper. I would later learn that Alberta liked young girls compulsively, and without discretion.

The scrawny girl's acne-marked face had been concentrated on a far-off, and far more just, place, but it opened just then, and her smile made me see the braces, and then the child in her. Despite the wear and tear, she was about nineteen.

Alberta picked up her veil and swaggered back to me. The boys at the bar cheered and threw money at the feet of both dancers. Alberta retrieved some of the money and gave it to the teenager.

Alberta hopped off the bar and fit herself under my shoulder. "Let's go in the back. I'll give you a dance."

"I don't know."

"Come on. This will be good for you."

"Don't know if I can afford it now," I said to remind her she had cleaned me out.

"You've got a credit card."

The last thing I wanted was to let the greasy-haired, pony-tailed guys behind the spotlights have my credit card number, but she put her hand in mine and dragged me after the louche swagger of her bared gluteus muscles and into the darkened back room.

As my eyes adjusted, I saw about ten corner booths stripped from a 1960s-era steak house and placed at odd angles around the room so that they did not face each other. In a few of them, one or two partially clad girls fawned over the semicomatose bodies of the maimed, the stupid, or the unlucky—in all events, the profoundly lonely.

In the dim light you could almost not notice the stained and threadbare sections of carpet, the tears in the red faux leather, the blotches of unblended patches on the wall. But the smell of dust, stale beer, and ashes dating back before the California ban on smoking in public places let you know you were not in the Ritz-Carlton. The smoking police were doing a good job that night, though they were apparently willing to overlook the action in the booth where three girls were pleasuring a vast expanse of a man in a shapeless brown gabardine suit. Two were doing their best to fawn over each other—thereby distracting from the third one's head, buried deep in the gabardine crotch.

Alberta used my credit card to get us two more real Bombays and a stack of pseudo poker chips redeemable for dances. I thought the chips were in denominations of ten, but later (when I looked at my credit card bill) they turned out to be twenty-fives.

The bored waitress said it was the usual policy to keep the credit card on file until the guest left. Even through the deadening force of Alberta's charm and the gin, I had enough paranoia to demand it back. Alberta nodded to the girl, and the credit card returned. The stereo played a deafening thing sung by a metal band. It started out like music, but then became too weird for me to follow.

"Some real music is coming," Alberta whispered in my ear. She was used to the sensibilities of those twenty years older than she. Despite the surrounding dank, her perfume was sweet, her skin soft, and her touch gentle. And then came the beat of John Hiatt's "Real Fine Love."

Her dancing was insistent, languorous, and perfectly in time to the music, which was, thankfully, real. She hooked one leg, then the other, over my shoulder, pushing her pelvis into my face with every slap of the drums. She tumbled off me onto the floor, leapt up, hooked her thumbs under my underarms, elevated my arms over my head, then grabbed my wrists, pinning me to the sticky old leather of the booth.

"I went looking for a fire just to burn it all down," Mr. Hiatt's gravelly voice rang out. Alberta's bra flew off as she thrust her chest into my face, first one, then the other, and everything in between.

"Your breasts are beautiful." I sounded like an idiot.

"The best money can buy."

Alberta aroused and scared me. I had only enough pride left not to get off in that disgusting room, just a couple booths over from the moaning of the man in gabardine.

Alberta pushed aside the fabric in her crotch an inch or so, and I could see the downy sheen of her pubic hair.

"You wanted to know, didn't you?"

"I guess, but I'm still not really sure."

She rolled her eyes as if to say "oh, you." I was getting the feeling I often get when I'm with a woman and I've had too much to drink. It was what has generally passed for love in my life. I summoned the brain cells to try to say something deep, something that would impress Alberta, make her love me back.

"This is like sliding down a long muddy hill in the rain. Completely alone."

"Don't worry, I'm sliding with you," she said. There was something evil in my stomach, rolling around and telling me to leave or puke. Alberta told me there were four dances in an hour. Whether or not she danced, in an hour, all the chips were gone.

By that time, I'd had another couple of gin and tonics to settle my stomach and help me fall in love, so I said, "I'm not sure I've done enough for you."

"Don't worry," she said. "You will."

I suppose I did give Alberta the pleasure she was looking for when she took the witness stand a year later, against the insurance company denying her a payout on the death of some decrepit dude she had married a few weeks before he died. I think I only asked about six questions on direct, allowing only the barest rubric of Alberta's claim that she had suffered severe emotional distress at the denial of the claim. During cross-examination, I became paralyzed. All I could think of were the cases I had researched the night before about my duty as a lawyer not to present perjured testimony. *You can't control the cross-examination*, I kept telling myself. Sure enough, the insurance company lawyer gave her the openings she needed, and she blasted through with an unstoppable recitation of her love for the old guy and the depth of her emotional distress at losing him.

Alberta could dance around a leading question as well as she could dance around sodden patrons at a gentlemen's club. The lawyer for the insurance company kept digging, and she covered him up with her dirty comebacks. She made him seem like an abuser as her eyes welled with tears. I closed my eyes and tried to forget the string of profanities that had rung through our conference room as she demeaned an old fart she barely knew and denied her involvement in the process whereby she was named as his only beneficiary just before his death. For the record, she denied it again on the stand.

I don't know how long it was before Manny Wu, the sheriff's deputy filling in as the bailiff that day, dropped a book on the floor to wake me up. I startled and looked over at him. He rolled his eyes. Manny would become my friend in the next couple years. It never hurts to be friends with the support staff in a courtroom. Manny was already watching out for me.

The jury, at least the men on the jury, did not seem to notice the book drop. Actually, Alberta could have admitted she was a pathological liar, and the men would not have heard it. They were drowning in thoughts of the liquid softness of her skin, and the creamy fullness of the flesh bursting from her tightly fitted dress. Sex had been my only criteria during jury selection, and I succeeded in getting a jury that included ten men without the tactic being noticed.

Eyes closed, I did not want to compare the insurance fraud Alberta was committing on the witness stand to cruder but more honest forms of crime, and so I let my mind drift to the back room of the gentlemen's club and dreamed of my hands pinned overhead by Alberta's athletic arms and smelled her perfume once more. I know my eyes were again closed when the judge called my name loudly: "Mr. Straight, redirect?"

"No, Your Honor." The jury appreciated that. I could see the relief and pleasure in their faces. They were ready to issue their verdict.

By a vote of ten to two, the jury awarded Alberta forty-seven million, partly for her severe emotional distress, but also to punish the insurer for daring to deny the claim. The judge reduced it to fifteen million. I convinced her not to run this by the court of appeal. The men on the jury waited in the hallway, and Alberta obliged with her autograph. The women jurors rushed from the courthouse with tight, straight mouths, and without meeting my eyes.

It was enough to change Alberta's life. Changed mine too. After more than a decade of seemingly pointless struggles, I had a tiny claim to a tiny fame, something to distinguish me in this town of people dying to distinguish themselves before they become just so many ashes, so much garbage to be washed into the vast sewers leading to the ocean.

In this way, the lies of a stripper allow me to live in a paradise I thought I wanted. Alberta even introduced me to one of her friends from her days at the gentlemen's clubs, a tall girl with exotically short hair, and an exotic name: Xanthe. Alberta's case put me in the office where I now sit, lights off, looking out at the first darkness of South Los Angeles, wondering whether there is anything left of my marriage to Xanthe. There is a bottle of the real Bombay in my desk, and I consider pouring some into my coffee cup.

I remember the fires I saw from this window the night after the Rodney King trial ended. I knew the city would burn down, but mainly I was thinking of how I would finally get a day off from work.

It is dark now. I truly long to sleep, and to dream I live somewhere else, and that I am anything but a lawyer. I feel fatigue in every cell of my body. Tonight, there are no fires burning in LA. No going home: there is still work to do. A new complaint has been filed against Oddyssey. That's right, this company calls itself "Oddyssey." With two *d*'s. It's Joel Green's client.

Joel asks me to come to his office to discuss what he calls "this deeply disingenuous lawsuit."

CHAPTER TWO

"**W**ake up, Sam. I need you with me."

I turn my head back in answer to Joel. Joel knows when I've drifted out to become the Catcher in the Smog or flashed back to the night I met Alberta.

Joel and I are sort of partners in the Los Angeles office of a big New York firm named Cohen & Cranston.

Someday, I think, I will look back at the 1990s as the unhappiest decade of my life. Perhaps it will just be the final decade.

It has been more than twenty years since Joel rescued me from a lake in Northern Michigan where we worked together one summer. We're moving well into our forties now, and Joel is no longer rescuing me; I rescue him. I rescued him when I got him a partnership at C&C two years ago. He doesn't know that I gave up some of my compensation to make the numbers work.

Joel didn't shave today, and as his wife, Ellie, has recently reminded both of us, he is no Don Johnson. Tonight, he has the look of a man in a cage. The refulgent array of smoggy sunset colors in the window encircles his head, setting it ablaze.

Joel has a half-gallon bottle of Trader Joe's "Vodka of the Gods" on his desk and is drinking from a water glass filled with the stuff. His muscular arms have gone flaccid over the years. His two sad chins and the directionless spreading of his gut seem normal to the people he deals with these days. Only I remember the powerful young man and the easy confidence with which he strode the world back in Michigan. His hair is all gone now, save a few wisps on the side of his head that connect above his neck.

I have the feeling he is going to ask me to rescue him again.

Joel rocks forward in his big chair and shoves a crisp new Xerox copy of a superior-court complaint forward on the desk. Like all superior-court pleadings, it has twenty-eight numbered lines on each page. The lines reaffirm that the world can be ordered after all, that even the evil of a lawsuit must be fit into an obedient arrangement. The good people in the file room have installed crisp, plastic exhibit tabs. For good measure, they've added a blueback cover.

On the first page, a box at the left shows the name of Laurilee Geller as the plaintiff. The defendants are listed as Caleb "Kid" Cauer, an individual; Oddyssey, Inc., a Delaware corporation; and "Does 1 through 100 inclusive."

"Why did they have to use two *d*'s?" I say. "It just makes them look like they can't spell. Opens them up to people who want to say they're odd."

"It's the internet. You need an odd spelling or you just get lost. A search with the right spelling of Odyssey would have turned up a lot of pointless analysis of Homer," Joel says.

"I guess spelling isn't that important anymore," I say.

I read the causes of action, the building blocks of a lawsuit. *Assault and Battery (Sexual), Intentional Infliction of Emotional Distress.* Normally, it would be pretty simple to plead those claims, but there is more than eight pages of detail about how Kid Cauer, the sixteen-year-old CEO of Oddyssey, Inc., Joel's new internet client, raped—yes, raped—his fourteen-year-old girlfriend, the aforementioned Ms. Geller, on numerous specific occasions. There are dates, times, locations throughout the Southland.

I flip to the one exhibit, denominated with a shiny plastic *Exhibit A* tab. It is a large, hand-drawn penis. Hair flowers everywhere in angry pencil strokes. "Oh, Jesus," I say.

"I know. There's no decency anymore, is there?"

"I guess the legal purpose of this is to show she was at least pretty close to the Kid's naked body, but really, is this necessary?"

"I think the answer to your question is yes."

"Is it accurate?" *Why do I think Joel knows this?*

"Well, there was no *forced* rape. They rely on her age—but he was a kid too."

"I mean this," I say, pointing to Exhibit A.

"I suspect it's not far off. Of course, I haven't personally looked."

"So, you're telling me this is all true? How am I supposed to defend that?"

"Sam. I don't remember you ever being intimidated by a complaint just because it was true. They were kids. For fuck's sake. Come on. You remember when we were kids. When did you get so moral on me? The president can't even control his dick these days."

"It was different when we were kids. That was love. This is just . . . disgusting. Perhaps what's most disgusting is that it's a lawsuit. That I have to read about this kind of trash in a legal document."

"You're always so concerned about the dignity of the law. Look, we have to do something, or Oddyssey's public offering is gonna get cancelled. Then I'll be really fucked."

I am quiet. If it were anyone else asking me to get involved in a case like this, I would tell him to go to hell. I'm a litigator, not a corporate lawyer, so to me, all these new internet companies look like they will end in a hurricane of litigation when everyone figures out that they can never make any money.

But this is Joel. Joel is desperate. His billings have been down, and he's in danger of getting cut loose by the partnership.

About a year ago—and seemingly by chance—Joel formed an unlikely father-and-son bond with this Kid Cauer, the juvenile founder and president of Oddyssey.com. Cauer and Joel have now brought Oddyssey to the brink of a second public offering. This is going to be the big one, the one that will make them a real LA company, with a fancy office building in the marina and a corporate jet sitting in the Santa Monica airport.

Joel takes another swig of his vodka. It seems to ignite him. He gets out of his chair like he wants to go somewhere. But there is nowhere to go. As he reaches the door, he realizes this office is the only safe place in the world for him right now. He deflates. His shoulders are hunched over by the fat on the back of his neck. At forty-six, he is an old man.

Without turning back, he says, "Come on, Sam. I need this."

I feel embarrassed. Joel only ran across Cauer because he was living in the crummy apartment where Cauer's juvenile friends were hanging out, and he was only living in that crummy apartment because his wife, Ellie, had thrown him out of the house he was still paying for. Ellie said he was drinking too much. *Sure he was, Ellie. You would too if you were married to you.*

Cauer is still only eighteen, but he's been in the news for almost three years, having become something of a media sensation when he appeared on the *MaryLee Lacy Show* last year. Stuff like this always starts on TV.

"You're seventeen, and you run your own successful company. You're thinking about going public and selling stock on the NASDAQ. I've heard you're even employing your parents. How do you do it?" MaryLee had asked, looking at him with those big, adoring television eyes.

"Actually, MaryLee, my parents are terrific employees. I couldn't do all this without them."

"They are here in our audience tonight," said MaryLee. The Kid's parents seemed smaller than the audience members around them. They looked down, as if afraid to meet even the inert eye of the camera, as if they were hiding something.

"Have they asked you for a raise yet?" MaryLee asked.

"No, but now that you mention it. . . "

MaryLee and the studio audience tittered with appropriate humor.

Taking charge of the interview, the Kid went on: "They told me to clean up my act, and I did. No drugs, no alcohol, no extramarital sex. Like I tell other kids, the success just comes natural when you're living clean."

The camera focused on his eyes in one of those moments that transforms ordinary people into powerful electronic spirits. Tears turned the Kid's blue eyes into deep blue lakes of emotion in which all viewer rationality drowned.

"Such a message for young people," MaryLee had said. "So different than the messages they get from our popular culture."

And that was all it took to make Kid Cauer into LA's celebrity business boy of the decade.

I have lived in LA long enough to know that no one in this town has a completely clean act, but that hardly keeps them from using their publicist to proclaim their latest regimen of virtue as one of the endless, fleeting redemption sagas designed to regain the public's ephemeral grace.

Looking at what my friend has become makes me want to suspend my own disbelief. Oddyssey could be just what Joel needs to get his life back to respectability.

For one thing, Cohen & Cranston, eager to be part of the new information age, is all in on Oddyssey. The New York partners' greedy appetite has been awakened for even bigger chunks of money: the firm has taken part of its fee in the stock that will be issued with the second public offering.

The billing machine is in motion. Back at Cohen & Cranston's 200-lawyer New York office, tired young associates are staying up all night writing the offering circulars, finding ways new and old of delivering deadening detail without providing even the basic facts to the SEC.

"Unlike other internet startup companies, Oddyssey has audited financials showing it makes money, lots of it," Joel says, repeating a statement I've now heard from at least a dozen lawyers at C&C.

I suppose he's right. It can't be all smoke and mirrors. Still, I have yet to find a human being, including Joel, who can describe clearly for me just what it is that Oddyssey actually does.

Everything was on track to make the firm's, and Joel's, cash-filled dreams come true. Then, just last week, three lawsuits were filed in federal court against Oddyssey. The alleged facts were stark and scary: that Oddyssey itself was nothing but a big fraud, and that the financial statements were fiction.

But those complaints quickly lost their momentum. After all, a Big Six audit firm had signed off on the financials. Richard Total, a litigator in C&C's New York office, quickly filed his usual Rule 12(b)(6) motions in response. Federal judges hate these kinds of cases, so everyone assumed the suits would be quickly dismissed.

But now there is this crazy Laurilee Geller thing with the Kid's penis as Exhibit A. This is the kind of case that could have implications far beyond any money damages. No one is interested in financial statements, but everyone is interested in sex. A case like this could totally undermine the whole premise of the offering: the Kid's squeaky-clean image.

"Why don't you get Total to take this on?" I say. "He's doing the other three."

"This is different. Total will use any problems with this to get me out of the partnership. Maybe you too. Besides, this is state court. He doesn't know anything about state court—he's not even a member of the bar out here."

I'm still not buying. So Joel digs deeper. "Look, if what Laurilee is saying is true, I'm going to need someone really good. Someone who can do the impossible."

The problem with doing the impossible, I have learned, is that someone will want you to do it again. While you can sometimes do the impossible in state court, the judges are so unpredictable that something impossibly bad could also easily happen. And it is very hard to get state court cases summarily dismissed in the way they can disappear in federal court.

"Total's a good lawyer," I say. I no longer underestimate the predatory viciousness that has served Richard Total so well in his career as a litigator in the New York office. "Although, I suppose I mean that in the same way I would say that Beelzebub would be considered a good lawyer."

About five years ago, the C&C associates had performed a skit at a firm outing in which they portrayed Total as Dorothy's little dog Toto, hopping along after the senior partners. Every associate connected with the sketch was fired within a year. The other associates call the lawyers who work with Total—and fawningly obeyed him—the "Total Assholes." Total himself is known as "*The* Total Asshole."

"He's not like you." Joel knows I don't want to be anything like Total.

But what is unique about me? My biggest verdicts came from the era when you could sue insurance companies directly. Jerry Brown's Rose Bird court allowed that sort of thing. And then there was Alberta.

After the Alberta Emerald case, the *LA Daily Journal* did a profile of me that made me look like an insurance company killer. C&C brought me on to help corporate clients who needed to sue insurers for environmental cleanup damages. They made me a partner, even let me bring Joel in. I won those cases, but most of them were done now, and Joel and I needed something new to do, or else we would be out. You can't be a partner this year on last year's billings.

I'm tired of helping corporations. I want to go back to representing clients who are real people, with real needs, whose lives I could really improve. C&C doesn't like representing those kinds of people. I've started representing pro bono clients to have a few real people to help, but I worry the executive committee will soon focus on how little of my time is actually being billed to paying clients.

Joel realizes I am dreaming again. I do this a bit more than other people. Perhaps I should also mention that sometimes I see people who aren't really there. I have conversations with them, sometimes lengthy ones. Most of the people I talk to are dead now, but some are still alive. I've never told anyone about these voices. Sure, it's a bit unusual, but this is LA. It's what I do to get by.

"Look, little brother, I am really exposed here."

I motion to Exhibit A: "You're not the only one."

"I don't feel like jokes, Sam. We can't let this get to a deposition. Just letting the Kid talk about something like this on the record can destroy the company. I need you to do what you always do. I need you to make it go away."

I remember I am his only friend.

"Okay, on one condition. I need to meet him face-to-face. I need to figure out exactly how much of this is true. I don't want to make the wrong move and get both of us thrown out of the firm. Or into jail."

Lately, I have begun to worry that Kid Cauer has disappeared or is hiding out in some foreign jurisdiction. His publicist puts out lots of pictures, and arranges for phone interviews, but no one has actually seen him for almost six months. Even Joel has only been talking to him by phone. There are rumors he's doing some kind of business in China.

"Of course. I'll set it up tomorrow." Joel rustles some papers as if he is searching his desk for the number. I get the feeling this is all for show. "I'll get you the number tomorrow," he finally says.

"Do we have any help on this?"

"You can use Valerie Huxtable," he says.

"I was hoping that we could get somebody who could actually get something done."

"The New York partners have all those people tied up. You know that."

"Well, I better get started." I pick up the freshly Xeroxed copy of *Geller v. Cauer*. Joel empties his glass as I gather myself to leave.

"Thanks, brother," he says.

"Tell me something, Joel. What do you think Oddyssey does?"

"You know. . ." He thinks for a moment, hoping I don't really want an answer. But I do. "You ask them a question and they find the answer. They're starting to call these things 'search engines.' People are putting the answer to everything on the internet, and eventually it will just be there. For now, they find the answer and send it back to whoever asks. But they're trying to develop computers with the answer, so no humans will be needed."

"That sounds like what all these other crazy phony companies do already. And why is that any better than what Lexis Nexis is doing?"

"Lexis Nexis costs money. This is free."

"All these companies are going to make money giving things that cost money away for free? It doesn't make any sense, Joel."

"You have to meet the Kid, Sam. You'll get an idea of how he can make it seem magical. All of these things are a certain percentage of flash. And don't you watch television? The slogan? *Not just answers, Action.* Oddyssey promises action. How can you miss with a slogan like that?"

"What kind of action?"

"Whatever people want."

"For free?"

"No. Presumably they charge for the action, if not for the answers. They're showing actual profits, more than a million a month. Huge profits for the internet."

"How are they making that money if they haven't started charging for the service yet? And even when they do, that service is going to be free, right?"

"They're offering the service on a prototype basis. The money comes in each month like clockwork. You saw the press releases they've been issuing. It's amazing."

"Maybe too amazing."

"Big Eight financials." The audited-financials line again. It's actually the Big Six now, but Joel lives in the past a lot. So do a lot of the New York partners. He goes on: "I went with the audit partner to view their building. You never saw so many computers and cubicles. The people talking on the phone sounded like a crowd at Dodger Stadium."

"Where was it?"

"Compton."

"You could rent a building in Compton for almost nothing."

"There was an employee gym, a kennel for pets. They had a little restaurant where the employees could get lunch, for free, a place where they could leave their laundry, and it would be done for them, for free. Everyone seemed happy about working overtime. Setting up all that as a show would cost millions."

"Which you got for them with that first debt offering."

Back when Joel and I were in our thirties, and we had a little office in the Bradbury Building, we used to sit around drinking like this. We talked a lot about why we had gone out and started our own firm, about why we would never be like everyone else, like all those guys we hated in law school, the ones who came to class in their three-piece suits because they were interviewing with big firms.

We used to have a simple way of assessing whether we were making progress. One of us would say to the other, "Are we good lawyers?" It was a tradition that we dropped after joining Cohen & Cranston, but I feel like asking now.

"Are we good lawyers, Joel?"

Joel looks upset. He drinks the rest of the vodka in his glass.

"I know this much, Sam: You are a good lawyer. You can make this go away. And I want you to do it. Not for the damn Kid. For me, brother."

I have an urge to say something that will acknowledge our closeness in this moment, that we could actually be brothers.

"You remember that place in Mexico where we went surfing after the bar exam?"

"The guy with the old hands. Cutting up the limes for the margaritas."

"We were just going to stay there if we flunked the bar exam."

"But we passed," Joel notes morosely.

"Yeah, dammit, we passed."

I've let too much happen to us. I never should have brought him to this place. We should have stayed in our own little firm, where we were happy making much less money.

Something tells me he is lying. Not about everything. But he's definitely lying about something. I've been a lawyer for a while, so I'm pretty used to being lied to. By other lawyers, even by judges. By clients. Especially by clients. But I never thought Joel would lie to me.

I need a cigarette. These days, that means the stairwell. Although the nineties are an increasingly unhappy decade, people have decided to make it worse by denying themselves and others the comfort of a cigarette.

CHAPTER THREE

In the stairwell, I feel safe from code enforcement and unwanted company. The menthol tang from the Kool cigarette mingles with the taste of the Bombay Sapphire from the bottle back in my office. I drop some ashes on the stairs and smooth them into the corrugated metal. There's a bunch of old cigarette butts out here, mostly from me.

My guess is Joel is still getting drunk on the cheap vodka in his office down the hall. I'm not like Joel. I still drink gin, and good gin at that. I light up another Kool. "Come on up to the taste," I tell the empty floors below me. "Yeah, okay, it can possibly kill you. Very, very slowly. Sometimes that feels like the whole point. If you're afraid of that, you might as well stay in bed in the morning because there's a lot of worse things out there."

I stamp out the end of the butt and come back to the office hallway.

I do not turn on the lights in my office as I come in. My saliva tastes like the cold bottom of an ashtray as I spit into the trashcan under my desk.

I look out my window at the blank Los Angeles sky. How wondrously different the Upper Peninsula sky over the lake had been on that night twenty years ago when Joel saved my life. Here the dirty sky has no stars, only the lights of the city flashing a gray wall back at you: light with no source, no life.

A sound comes from the hallway. The closing of the heavy double doors that seal off the firm from the elevator lobby. Then the loud rhythmic clicks of the door lock falling back into place. The glass windows throughout the office shudder in their glazing from the force of the door settling heavily into place.

That double door opened in an orderly way. It has to be someone with a key. Maybe one of the lawyers forgot a file needed for court in the morning. Nothing out of the ordinary.

I don't call down the hall. But Joel and I are no longer alone.

I start to pull off the gloves I wear when no one is around. My hands, cracked from psoriasis, have been bleeding on the files lately, and people have complained about the blood stains.

Another sound. This one comes from inside Joel's office at the other end of the hallway. I can't define it, so I keep listening. There is a bang, like metal. Then, a thud. A rapid scuffling of sounds and grunts. And then an urgent voice.

"What? No. Stop."

The desperate voice is Joel's. Each of Joel's words starts loudly but cuts off quickly. I stop taking off my gloves.

"Joel," I try to yell. My voice is strangely small—like I'm dreaming, and my mouth won't move.

There is a muffled banging, like sandbags being thrown against a wall. The windows of my office and the glass hallway walls rattle as they do during earthquakes. My fear of heights surges in my stomach—the awareness of suspension in the Los Angeles sky perched on a bunch of steel held so loosely together that the floors can be shaken by nothing more than the harsh, sharp movement of the door, or a human body.

A thud. Somebody throwing Joel's body against the wall?

"Ahhhh. Sam." His voice is filled with pain and wretched pleading now.

Without thinking, I rush out my office door, my shoes gaining traction on the short blue carpet.

"Help." A tone I have never heard in Joel's voice. It scares me.

"Coming." It's all that comes out.

By the time I reach Joel's office on the other end of the hall, I am running as fast as I can, lungs burning from the caustic tar remnants in my throat. To the left is the glass wall into Joel's office. Behind his solid, block wood desk, I see the top left side of a head, covered in a black leather mask, smooth and shiny.

A flash of bright metal rises. There is red on the knife. It comes down hard and fast, and I hear the sound of it entering something below the desk. A dull swishing sound follows.

For a moment, nothing seems real to me, and then I think I need to do something. Now. *Do something. Now.*

"Stop," I yell with all the force of my body.

But I am stopped. Every muscle in my body refuses to move. My thoughts revolve in a pointless pattern of lawyerly thinking. *Is this really happening or am I observing only circumstantial evidence of an assault? How would this come out in the testimony?*

A rasp of Joel's voice ends the loop in my head. Joel's body on the ground behind the desk.

"Sam, get help."

Still I don't move. I realize someone is killing Joel. And he could kill me too.

Joel is your brother. He would die for you. Go. You must go.

I rush through the door, launch over the desk, and try to grab at the intruder. I go for the knife as it rises above for another plunge. He swings the knife back towards me. The knife cuts into the side of my abdomen, but I manage to push it away before it tears too deeply. Not satisfied, he draws it back for another slash.

Grasping the neck below the slippery black leather, I try to drag the attacker's head towards the rectangular metal casing of the heating-and-cooling system by the window. There is a sharp metal edge there. I want to split his skull with it.

Each second has slowed into two. I rush, but he ducks and my body sails. The wet, smooth leather on top of his head glides down the middle of my sternum. I smell sweat. Like that of a young athlete, new and clean and salty. I fall onto the floor, the hard, industrial carpet burning my face.

You need to see his face, to memorize it. When he attacks again, I try to tear off the mask, but he flips me around on the ground. Now he controls me from behind. I feel his knee in my spine. The force crushes the breath out of me, and then he takes back his knee. He lifts me like dead weight by my belt and the back of my shirt.

I feel myself flying towards the window and the empty thirty-three stories of air outside and below it. Fragments of night rush to my head. "Die, you fucker," he grunts.

I hear the window's dull bang as my head sails into it. The blood freezes in my veins with the fear of the sailing and falling that will surely follow. But the glass is stronger than my head, stronger than the force of my body behind me. My head bounces. The impact twists my neck. I fall back.

My body falls to the floor by the window. Next, I feel a long surface of new pain in the back of my thigh. He has found his knife. I feel metal tearing through the surface of my leg, swishing inside the muscle tissue. I try to scream the pain.

I try to form a thought. *A terrorist? Deranged or angry client?*

His voice has a mechanical sound as it ticks off the words. "You. Stupid. Fucker. You should have stayed in your office." The knife comes from the side now, aiming for something vital, cutting my side, into my gut. The pain shocks me. I feel the scream exit my mouth. Flipping over, I kick him with my good leg, and he falls back towards the hallway door. The knife drops to the floor, and he leaves it there.

He turns away, running out Joel's office door. *Notice, notice everything you can.* The skin is splotchy and spotted on the back of his neck. His spine is erect, with big shoulders held back by a set of muscles no one is born with. Looking down, I see his bare back and jeans, a thin-waisted torso with the legs whipping out ahead. I try to run after him, but the pain in my leg stops me.

I look for Joel. He is facedown on the floor behind the desk. He doesn't seem to move. His eyes are tired, but open, still with some life force behind them. Blood has clotted in the fleshy crevices of his neck. Joel's mouth opens and closes slowly. He is trying to say the same word, over and over. His bottom teeth disappear behind his front teeth, but he can't enunciate the beginning of the word. "UhUHuh, UhUHuh," he repeats.

What is he trying to say?

A repeating sound. Gentle. Coming from the carpet near his waist. His hand is on the floor, and he is drawing a circle. An *O*.

"Oddyssey?" I say.

He nods, and now I understand what he is saying. He points at the *O*. Am I imagining him saying "Something. Wrong"?

Not thinking clearly. Looking towards the door, I see the knife, some kind of military surplus blade, brutal and ugly with intent to cut human flesh. Dragging my leg, I move over and reach down, touching the thick metallic webbing of the knife handle. The knife is slippery with blood. Stupid. Why would I want to touch the knife? I push it away, suddenly revolted by the wetness of Joel's blood, my blood, soaking into my cloth gloves.

My field of vision becomes dominated with black. And then it is all black. I feel my head hit the floor. *What is he trying to say? Is something wrong with his darling client? Something wrong with Oddyssey?*

I hear Joel's voice as I heard it so long ago in Michigan, the voice of an older brother telling me in the plainest words, "Just let it go, Sam."

And so I do. There is calm in blood loss.

My last thought is one of relief. Tomorrow, I will finally get a day off.

CHAPTER FOUR

Dirty white walls rush by. Metal railings. As I try to inhale, my whole chest aches. I am surprised by the effort it takes to fill my lungs with air. I try to shake my head free, but my nose is filled with a tube that extends down the back of my esophagus. My lungs pull to get the air around the tube and through to my lungs.

Gathering my energy, I take a second breath. Why do I need all available strength just to breathe?

Try to talk: "Where. . . Joel. . . " is all that comes out. I can't seem to finish my words. My lips smush together like so much papier-mâché.

A man with a neat black mustache stands at the foot of my bed, staring at me. His shaved head shines against the backdrop of the white ceiling and the unforgiving fluorescent lights. He wears a green paper shirt and baggy, green paper pants. A stethoscope is hooked around his neck. *Do they still use those things?*

Then I say, "Where's Joel?" I've relearned how to talk. A little. Perhaps there is a way out of this mess. I am not dead. The young leather-head stalker has not killed me.

"How are you feeling?" he asks.

How the fuck do you think I'm feeling, is what comes to mind. "Huh?" is what comes out, sounding like a question.

"I'm just the orderly, Mr. Straight. You're in post-op. I'm going to get the doctor."

"What?"

"You're lucky you're alive, Mr. Straight. Your doctor will tell you."

He looks around to see if anyone is listening. "Doctor Mendoza came in for you. Classy lady. Don't usually see her around here. I would have noticed her." He stops to ponder Dr. Mendoza a minute. "She'll be here in just a minute. I'm just spos'd to make sure you're awake. You have pain?"

"Yeah. Yeah, pain." My leg hurts and my whole left torso is throbbing. It's hard to form thoughts. "Am I with you now?" I try to say. I'm making words, but my voice sounds like grunting.

"Don't talk now. You're going to be fine."

Fine. Really? I locate each wound by memory, seeing again the image of the blade plunging into my body. Each location responds with dull pain, which then comes alive to snap and hiss. I fear I have lost the diaphragm muscles I need to breathe.

"I was hoping not to see you till next year," says Dr. Rosa Mendoza gently, as she strides into the room. Confident, in a pin-striped business suit, as if she owns this place. No paper garments for Rosa. The way she looks is a talent in itself.

I am still afraid of not breathing, but I feel calmer now, just seeing her here. A woman this beautiful will not let me die.

"You've some nasty knife wounds, Sam. The one in your leg wasn't too bad, but the one in your ab is pretty wicked. Luckily, they're not too deep.

Nothing vital hit. You just need to heal. You may have had a concussion too, though not a big one. Your Glasgow Coma Scale was good today."

Dr. Rosa knows I've worked enough injury cases to know the Glasgow scale. "Where's Joel?"

"On the other side of the floor. No visitors right now, Sam. You're going to have to wait to talk to him. What happened?"

"I tried to stop some kid from stabbing him. The guy was just pounding the knife into him, Rosa."

"Did you get a look at this guy?"

"Some. It happened so fast. Maybe there was more than one."

"Okay, look, Sam, I've been holding off some aggressive cops here, and they've been telling me that they need to talk to you."

"Can't you keep holding them off?"

She shakes her head. "Not these two. I'm going to stay here, though, and make sure it doesn't get too off track.

"I think I'm about ready for another shot."

"I'll get you one, Sam, but it hasn't been that long since the last one. In the meantime, let's try to talk to these cops while you're awake enough. And then maybe you can get some rest."

"But I can't breathe, Rosa. I can't rest if I can't breathe, can I? What if I stop breathing?"

She smiles and takes my hand. She reaches with her other hand to my face and wipes away my hair. She holds me for the next few minutes, just smiling. I see her chest rise and fall below her shirt. My breathing seems to catch its rhythm from hers.

"See, you can breathe," she says.

When I am calm, Rosa goes to get the police.

CHAPTER FIVE

I've never been good with cops. I attribute this to Professor Frances Xavier Schiller's criminal procedure class. Most of his case summaries, which were given in the form of distracted rants, contained some version of the sentence "Cop goes berserk."

Schiller taught us the usual cop gambits and mind-control techniques. He showed us how cops appeal to the Judeo-Christian desire to confess guilt. Schiller was most disturbed by what he saw as a systemic problem with uniformed witnesses. "Cops lie" was another of his catch phrases, and he used it often. Schiller worried, I suppose, that if he didn't destroy our respect for cops, we would not be ready to tear them apart on the witness stand. I thought Schiller was a bit paranoid, but he left an impression. So I don't trust cops.

Rosa introduces me to Detectives Booker Reed and Elizabeth Endel. She takes care to inform me that they are "from Robbery Homicide."

It is Reed, the white one, who goes after me right away. His voice feels like the twist of a dagger.

"What is a hot-shot corporate lawyer like you doing in County anyway?"

"County?" I ask.

"County USC," says Reed.

"That would explain how filthy everything is," I say.

Some of Schiller's spunk is in my voice, but the attempt to talk makes my head spin drunkenly. Maybe the concussion. As I try to move my leg, the pressure forces pain up my spine. I suppress a cry. I look to Rosa, trying to convince her without words that I need that shot of morphine. Right now.

Behind Rosa, a vision of Professor Schiller appears. Schiller died last year. But there he is, just behind Rosa. He has on the same clothes he wore to the lecture hall back in law school, an ill-fitting tweed jacket that fails to conceal the belly lapping generously over a cheap belt. Schiller's eyes roll up and to the left, gazing at nothing in particular while the thick glasses slide down his nose.

I close my eyes and shake my head. When I open my eyes, I try to focus on the detectives. Booker Reed's gray Italian suit drapes easily over his heavily muscled upper body. *He isn't really here*, I say to myself.

The pain seems to be everywhere. They can't expect people to endure pain like this. My consciousness seems to swim inside a dull liquid. Another shot would make Schiller go away, I think.

Did one of the cops ask me a question?

"It's something with his insurance," says Rosa helpfully. "They claimed there was a change of employment status or something."

"What?" I say.

"Don't worry, Sam. I'll follow up," Dr. Rosa adds.

"Nurse," Reed says.

"Dr. Mendoza," she corrects.

"Dr. Mendoza, we need to talk to Mr. Straight."

"By all means."

"Detective Endel and I," he says, pointing at the woman who has labored in the door behind him, "we're investigating the assault on your partner."

I look at Endel. Her wool-blend suit does not fit her well, and it bulges disproportionately at unflattering and random points. Yet she comfortably inhabits both her clothes and her body. She looks relaxed—as if the job is an interruption to a more important set of tasks she is working on at home.

"Have you caught anyone?" I ask.

"Well, actually, you're our first witness," Reed says. "Your partner Joel Green hasn't been able to talk, as you know."

"As I know?" I ask.

"Booker," Endel says in a motherly tone, "take it easy."

Endel lets out a bit of a smile. "Of course, forensics is working the physical evidence found at the scene. Before we start in on the other witnesses, we felt we should talk to you. After all, you were the only person there. Other than your partner."

"And the crazy people stabbing us."

"Is it people now?" asks Reed. His physiognomy confirms his asshole status. Reed is short—five feet six, I figure. His spine is so straight it looks like it was aligned with a plumb line. His eyes lack focus, as if a significant portion of his brainpower is permanently devoted to maintaining his posture and adapting his face into the most handsome expression he can muster in the given situation. *At least he isn't smart,* I think.

"I only saw one."

Smart or not, Detective Reed decides it is time to put me in my place.

"Mr. Straight," says Reed sternly, giving me his best angle, "we're dealing with gang drive-bys in South Central from East LA and vice versa. The Korean community is emptying all the gun stores in town. In the middle of all this, the department has assigned two senior detectives to look into why a couple rich corporate lawyers—who are behind on their child support, by the way—have had some sort of an altercation in their swank Bunker Hill offices. Now, we're gonna do the best we can, but you need to drop the lawyer attitude right now."

When I came to LA, I thought it was a place where all kinds of people live and work together. It sort of felt like that for a while, especially the time when we were all on drugs. Then came Rodney King, and it became clear we could not all just get along. And now there's O. J. Now everything is racial. I suppose it always was. I suppose I'm no better than anyone else.

"Tell us about the incident," Endel says in her best motherly tone.

"This wasn't an incident," I say. "Some lunatic tried to kill Joel, and he tried to kill me too."

"Never let your client talk," intones Professor Schiller. He is still here. There's something wrong about this. Schiller can see it. Why can't I?

"Mr. Straight," says Detective Endel, "you can call me Bettie. If we're going to figure out what happened to your partner, we're going to need to talk to you."

Professor Schiller screams, "Ha! Cops always *need* to talk to you. They just glide right by whether you want to or not. She's just playing the good guy. You have the right to remain silent, dummy. And if you dare call her Bettie, I'm changing your grade to a D."

I am silent—for a moment. Schiller is right, I suppose. Best not to be on a first-name basis with these two. But I tell them the story. The bare upper body, the cruel muscles, the dark leather mask, and the relentless knife. Detective Endel takes a few notes. None of it surprises them. They seem bored by it all.

"So you didn't see his face at all?"

"Lips. You know, healthy, young. Can't tell you the color of the eyes, or the shape of the nose. Just enough openings for him to see and breathe. Like some sort of S&M mask. The body was young, the dude works out; that's about all I can say. Did you find the knife?"

"Yeah, we found it alright. Tell us about Oddyssey. Spelled with two *d*'s, right?" says Endel.

I think about how Joel had been trying to tell me there is something wrong with Oddyssey. Now, through the murk of the morphine, I try to decide what can be told to Reed and Endel about our client Oddyssey without causing the ghost of Professor Schiller to freak out.

Professor Schiller's ghost has some advice for me. "Oddyssey may be odd, let's even assume it is quite criminally odd," says Schiller's ghost. "But it is still a client. You, my friend, can't say anything."

Schiller has finally gotten through to a part of me. After you've been a lawyer for a while, you learn to protect a client in circumstances where you wouldn't protect yourself.

Looking at Endel, I start with something safe. "Oddyssey is a client. I can't tell you much of anything because of privilege. I think all I can really tell you is that those lawsuits you read about are going to be dismissed. As you can see, I've been out of the office, so I don't know what's been happening since we got stabbed."

Schiller nods with approval. The feeble sarcasm has pleased him. I take heart that I can get through this with my dignity as a lawyer intact.

"You had a short stab wound just below your ribs," Endel says. "The knife could have punctured a lung, but it fell an inch short. I keep wondering how that happened."

"Well, the guy had a knife, obviously," I start. "And obviously it hurt. Other than that, I don't remember. I remember I was running after him—"

"Him," says Reed. "Are you sure the attacker was male? Cause you said it both ways to the ambulance driver."

"He had his shirt off for some reason. He said something. So I heard his voice."

"Like what?" says Endel.

"What do you think? Something like 'die, you stupid fucker.' There might have been another one, though, another person. Cause I got hit from behind at some point, I think. I was trying to go after the one who had stabbed me. He was the only one I saw. After that, I don't remember."

"So it's more than one again?" asks Reed.

"What makes you think the attacker was young?" asks Endel.

"What really seemed young to me were his hands."

The ghost of Professor Schiller splits in two, and two apoplectic leprechauns chant at me in unison: "Never let the client talk. Never let the client talk."

"I'm not a client. I'm just trying to find out who tried to kill my friend," I say to the Schiller ghosts. I realize I am also talking out loud.

"Huh?" asks Endel.

"Who do you think would want to knife you and your friend?" asks Reed.

I'm really tired. Schiller has merged back into a single person but continues his running commentary. "This empty hat is looking for a motive now. Who had a motive? Who cares? Motive isn't a required element of the crime."

"Hold on," I say to Schiller's spirit.

I turn back to Reed. Schiller's presumptions might be right. Reed might be arrogant, even stupid. But the conversation is going the wrong way. There is no doubt he hates lawyers and would like nothing better than to hook one up. "Hey, I'm sorry," I say.

Reed looks like he appreciates being back in control. He pulls out a note card, and almost seems to read off it, remaining in his straight-backed, camera-ready pose. "We're gonna need the clothes you were wearing, and samples of your blood."

"Once again," says Professor Schiller, "the muscle-bound one needs something. Say no."

"My blood type is AB negative. It should be easy to sort my blood from everything else on the carpet. Did the attacker bleed?"

"Do you know how to say the word NO?" shouts Professor Schiller. But his apparition is growing faint now. Maybe if I stop paying attention to him, I will feel better.

"We're not sure yet," says Endel.

Reed glares at Endel. The good guy has been a little too good.

"Rosa, can you see that they get my clothes?"

"How about these?" Reed brings out a plastic bag containing the cloth gloves I was wearing that night. There are red spots on the gloves. "Can we have these?"

"I guess so."

"We'll see if they fit," Reed says.

"Is that what you're trying to do, to get me? Like you're getting O.J.?" I sound like Schiller, I think.

Endel asks in a warm voice, "Did you touch the knife, Sam?"

"I might have. I saw it in the doorway where he dropped it."

"I told him to wear the gloves for his psoriasis," says Rosa. Then to Reed and Endel: "Let's try not to let this get out of hand. He needs some rest. It's time for him to have more morphine."

Before the detectives can answer, there is a loud firing report outside the window. It comes from below. We must be at least four stories up. It is unquestionably the fire of some sort of weapon.

Rosa moves to the window. I remember she served as an Army surgeon in Iraq. She still has the instinct that makes her go towards the danger. "Some sort of disturbance out there on the plaza," she says.

Endel and Reed go to the window and look from behind her.

"We'll have to continue this later," says Reed.

"The gangs?" says Rosa.

"They've been coming up from South Central more and more," says Reed.

"They're coming from East LA too," says Endel.

"Yeah, you're right. Maybe it's the Koreans, Bettie," says Reed. Then to me: "Don't go anywhere without calling us." He leaves his card on the night table.

"He isn't behind," I say. "And I don't have any kids."

"What?" says Reed.

"Joel isn't behind in his child support. He would rather starve than be behind in his child support. So if Ellie told you that, she was lying."

"The Bar Association told us that, Sam," says my friend Endel.

"Well, then they lied too." Sometimes I let my emotions speak, and they tell the truth when I am trying to tell a lie. It is a small remnant of humanity that law school and twenty years of practice have failed to remove. My humanity never does my clients any good.

Reed turns to Endel and raises his eyebrows. The eyebrows say it all: I realize my whole story sounds completely phony to these two.

Dr. Rosa finally rescues me. "I need to get tubes out of him, he needs a shot, and you two need a real crime to investigate. Maybe you could figure out who keeps shooting at the building." When they have left, I see that Professor Schiller's spirit is also gone, and I am grateful for that. I hear more gunshots.

"What's going on out there?" I ask.

"It might not mean anything," Rosa says. "The building's a big target. People have been known to shoot at it after a few six-packs. You gonna be okay if I get out of the line of fire for a while?"

"Yeah, I can't believe you came all the way over here to County to take care of me."

I have been gagging on the tube in my nose, which leads to a bag full of black, greasy material that is some kind of new waste product I am apparently discharging. Rosa pulls the tube out of my nose with a steady, strong yank. I gag at the plastic gliding through my esophagus. I feel new oxygen in my lungs. Then the room seems to turn, and my perspective floats free, as it does when you fall down while drunk. "I'll get you that shot, Sam. I guess you've earned it."

A nurse with large hips and bleached blond hair comes in, armed with a big syringe of morphine. "Happy trails, Roy," she says. "You're gonna like this." Then she puts the needle in the IV, and I feel the surge of warmth come up the top of my wrist, enter my arm, and spread, wonderfully, everywhere.

"Roy?" I ask.

"Don't start to like it too much, cowboy," says Rosa.

Rosa lifts the sheet and my gown, reaches between my legs, and gently pulls out the catheter. She doesn't ask. She's been my doctor for almost twenty years.

"You know, Sam, I thought I told them to fix that too. I guess they forgot."

"Thanks, I needed that."

CHAPTER SIX

"Your wife will be by in a while," says the man in the green coat, waking me.

Sentimental gratitude for this man rushes out of nowhere. Maybe it's the morphine he just gave me. He has told me his name a couple of times, but the pain wipes it away.

"You better write down your name. I'm going to write your boss a letter to say how great you've been."

"No worries, man. He'll think I'm loafing if I'm moving slow enough for someone to know my name."

Before I can again tell him how he has saved my life truly and well, he walks out of the room.

I try to sit up but keep slumping down. The sheets slip completely off the corners of the mattress. The rubber lining rubs uncomfortably against my back.

The morphine feels good, but it brings fright again as it seems increasingly hard to breathe.

Xanthe makes her entrance. My wife's face, usually a smooth, professional tan, has a wet, reddish glaze. Her white silk shirt is open and clinging, like the women on the cover of *Cosmopolitan*. The wet spots are tears, I suppose, but the orderlies are probably gaping. Her hair is in a new, clean bob that makes her look boyish. The slightly longer, feminine bit of blond hair on her forehead is uncharacteristically shiny. She has undoubtedly flipped that bit of hair back a hundred times since this morning.

I met her at the victory party Alberta threw after the verdict from the insurance company. Xanthe said she worked in the "Valley." So I knew she was a denizen of those second-tier strip clubs in Van Nuys where Alberta worked after she left LAX.

The night I met Alberta really was her last night at LAX, but not her last as a stripper. After that, she moved to the Valley. The Valley is good for very few people, but it was good for Alberta. She met her husband there. The one who would soon get good insurance.

"Oh my God, you were under for five hours," Xanthe says. "I thought I lost you." She affects a distraught manner, which strikes me as funny.

"Well, I'm back now."

"I hear Rosa Mendoza was here," Xanthe says.

Does she think there is something between Rosa and me? Rosa is an accomplished medical doctor. She is stunning, and not incidentally so— even on those rare occasions she dresses in paper and plastic. Why would she want anything to do with me? I decide not to pick up what might be the start of a discourse on fidelity. Or my lack thereof.

"Did you and Joel have an argument?" asks Xanthe, bringing me back to the present.

"No, of course not. Why do you ask?"

"Well, I guess a couple lawyers in the firm passed by Joel's office that day and thought you two were arguing," she says. "That's what the police told me, anyway." Xanthe's tone has changed. I guess the best word for the way it sounds now is "careful."

I'm shaking my head, but not sure it is moving. What is wrong with the way Xanthe is talking? I hear the John Hiatt song Alberta was playing that night I met Xanthe. Alberta really liked John Hiatt.

"I met an angel or two before, but never asked one to be my wife," Mr. Hiatt sang.

I mistook Xanthe for a real angel that night, and my soul got lost in precisely the moment when we were dancing, and she danced her pelvis into mine. Xanthe came home with me and never really left. When my first wife got back from her business trip, we both concluded that Xanthe was what I really wanted. Later I would learn I had no idea what I really wanted. Sometimes people have to get married twice to figure that out.

"I can't believe how icky the floors are here," she says. "I guess there was some problem with your insurance. They said to call the firm."

I remember the floors at the club where I met Alberta, with their glaze of beer and bodily fluid. *Why do I keep thinking about Alberta?*

Xanthe climbs into the bed and attempts to curl up next to me.

"You poor baby. I'm going to stay with you tonight."

"I don't think they will let you do that," I say.

Though Xanthe weighs a perfect 125, the weight of her arms pulls down on my chest like a pallet of bricks. I put my arm around her and try to hold her in the way that husbands are supposed to do. My body has carried off the mendacity of marital body language many times and is resigned to doing it once more. Her tears constitute a demand for a formal show of affection.

The morphine is finally helping. My eyes shut a few times, and I think there might be patches of sleep happening. But breathing requires extra conscious effort. The aching soreness in my diaphragm calls out with each breath.

If I sleep, will I remember to breathe? How will my subconscious remember the extra effort I need? To sleep will be to die. I do not want to die. And so, I should not sleep. I snap my head to keep my eyes from closing.

Xanthe's scant weight has grown heavy. It feels like she is crushing me. Xanthe moves even harder, heavier against me.

It's her fault I can't breathe. I am never going to get to sleep with her here, and I so want to sleep. If not for her, I might be sleeping right now. *What right does she have to be with me? This woman has not made love to me in three months.* It makes no sense that she would care whether I live or die. And she is taking up all the space in the bed.

"Xanthe, you should go home."

"I don't want to leave you this way." She pulls closer still. I am all out of patience. The morphine has suppressed my normal impulse to deceive.

"For God's sake, Xan, you're crushing me. I can't breathe. You have got to get out of this bed right now."

Xanthe pulls back. "What do you mean?"

Then she sits up on the side of the bed. She stares up for a second, glances at the door, which is nearly closed, and then just loses it. Sobbing. Her face turns bright red, and the water drips around the thin, lambent skin of her hands, which she holds to her face.

Her wedding ring catches my eye. My mind drifts to the day I bought it, and to my Visa, Mastercard, and Discover card bills, where the amount I paid that day, and a good deal more of Xanthe's charges, haunts me each month. When I met her she was still sort of a stripper. I loved her for the pure physical joy she had in her body, and the joy she had in sharing it with me. Some of my best memories in life are of the nights we spent drinking champagne from each other's skin.

Maybe we never really had a chance. Xanthe wanted to be more than just a plaything, and I didn't have time for anything else. The practice of law is based on the billing of hours, and lawyers like me, who have only modest gifts, must make up for that by billing lots and lots of hours.

Lonely, Xanthe finished college on my credit card. Political science. Xanthe is still stunning, but now it is clear she has opinions, the immature kind that political science professors pass out. She has taken on the aura of an educated, sophisticated woman. Anyone would want her now. Somebody probably does. A couple months ago, she started being the one who was too tired at night.

Maybe that's my fault too; I'm not as worn down as Joel, my weight is the same as in college, but I'm not so sure I'm all that good looking anymore. Still got my hair, though, and it's still blond. Not gray.

The morphine makes me brave enough to just ask the question. "Xanthe, why do you care?"

Xanthe is taken aback. Her experience with me has not prepared her for an honest, direct approach, and she stumbles, not knowing how to reply. "I, uh, I uh, I just . . . just don't want you . . . to go."

And I know for sure.

No matter how happy the marriage, every spouse waiting for a partner to come through surgery that has taken three hours too long thinks of what life might be like if the surgeon comes out with a somber face to announce bad news. And even in those happy marriages, if any there are, the partner left in the waiting room thinks about how wonderful it would be to never see a particular in-law ever again, and to clear the credit cards, and pay off the house. In a bad marriage, and I have been through two of them now, the mutual contempt builds minute by minute, and freedom is the first thought that crosses the mind when one's partner takes five minutes too long to return from the video rental store.

Xanthe has been thinking about life without me for hours. She has been planning the post-funeral cruise and deciding which girlfriends to bring along. Now, confronting the living me, she has broken down in tears.

Her tears are the same as all the other tears Xanthe has cried in her life. They are for her. She cries for her lost chance at losing me—and gaining a few million in the bank.

I stay quiet while her sobbing subsides. "Xanthe, you should just go. You can rest better at home." I give her another dishonest hug.

It is enough for tonight to know the truth. There will be time later to deal with it.

CHAPTER SEVEN

My spine curls over, forcing me to stare at the curdling plastic of the intravenous bag on the pole I'm leaning on to hold me up. No one in the dirty hallway seems to think there is anything unusual about my halting attempts to walk. Other patients make their way around in similar agony. Each is totally consumed by concentration on balance. I recognize in their faces the choruses of new pains singing within them as we suffer together the ridiculousness of adults learning to walk.

I need to talk to Joel as soon as he regains consciousness. If he has a secret about Oddyssey, he will need to tell someone he can trust, to see how to play it. Joel would not rat out a client, especially one like Kid Cauer, who has become almost a son to him.

The other hallway, four doors down, I remind myself. An empty folding chair stands outside the door of the room. Maybe they were offering him protection, but it is gone now. I focus on that chair, and move, inch-by-inch, pausing every few feet to catch my breath and make the floor stop swaying. I stare only at the chair—blocking out everything else. I write poems to the chair. *If I could just get there. I swear. I'd never wear. Underwear.* Repeating it over and over, I eventually take enough tiny steps to reach the room where Joel is lying. Joel needs to see me. He shouldn't be alone in a room in County, dying, with no company but endless repeats of *Family Feud* playing on the game channel, Richard Dawson getting older, then younger, then older again.

Because he's lying on his side, curled into a fetal position, the tape holding the ventilator in place and the bandages on his head are almost all I can see.

When I get to the side of the bed, I see that his eyes are open and visible through the wads of tape. They stare blankly at the wall. I put my head down in front of his eyes. I wave my hand across his face. Nothing. I softly exclaim, "Joel, it's me. Sam. I'm here for you, brother."

Still no reaction.

The monitors beep. I have no idea what any of the numbers or lines mean. Except for the pulse. *Good,* I think. Seventy-two is normal. At least his heart is beating. That's all that really matters right now. The rest will come.

His mouth is hanging open, and drool comes from it, as the air from the ventilator escapes his mouth and nose, coagulating in the stubble of his beard.

I move to the bottom of the bed and open the metal case in which the chart is contained. There is a small page on top, only half as big as the other papers in the chart, that's so thin you can see through it to the other papers below. "Do Not Resuscitate Order." *Why is it in quotes? Don't they mean it? Wait, they can't mean that.*

Blood rushes to my head. After "I/we" and before "fully understand, acknowledge and consent" is the printed name of *ELLEN GREEN* in clear and thickly lined capitals. Whoever wrote that name had really pressed down on the pen.

Fucking Ellie. So she just wants to go ahead and finish the job.

Moving is suddenly easier. My lack of balance, the way everything in my body hurts, none of it seems to matter now. I disconnect the intravenous tube and go into the hallway. There is a set of two pay phones at the end. I make my way to them, moving quickly now, dialing in my memorized phone card, and then Ellie's number.

When she answers, I light right into her.

"Why are you trying to kill him? That man loves you, Ellie. And he's your meal ticket. You were just Yooper white trash."

"Calm down, Sam."

"Calm down? Any minute now his heart could stop."

"Sam, Sam, he's already gone. Did you look at the monitors?"

"His heart is beating. He's still breathing."

"A machine is breathing for him. Did you know I had to authorize that? I am the one keeping him alive."

"Till you can kill him."

"I could have turned it off already. Maybe I should have. He has virtually no brain waves, Sam. For now, I told them to leave him on the ventilator. But no heroic measures. He wouldn't want that, Sam. If he goes, we need to let him go. You too."

"We're in County, for God's sake. There are no accurate measurements of anything here."

"He's being moved to Cedars tomorrow, Sam. I won't turn anything off before he gets there."

"What the hell are we doing here, anyway?"

"The insurance was cancelled. I called Richard Total. He's the only one who can seem to get anything done at Cohen. He had the insurance turned back on for me."

"For you?"

"Sam, if Joel's heart stops, it will be a blessing. Otherwise this could drag on for months and we will have to starve him to death. That's what they're telling me."

"Who's telling you? Richard? Do you realize that getting rid of a partner will make Richard's share of the revenue go up? Do you realize he wants to increase his share before the money comes in from Oddyssey? That's money that should be Joel's. Don't you understand that's what Richard's up to?"

"Richard's right, Sam. You know, I think that's what you and Joel really hate about him. That he's always right. Richard told me if Joel dies, the firm's insurance will pay double. As it is, they might only pay once if he dies a couple months from now instead of right after an incident in the firm."

"So you're selling him out for double indemnity?" They've got to stop showing that movie on television.

Ellie ignores me. "Here's another thing Richard's right about, Sam: He says you and Joel were going to be terminated as partners. That's why the insurance was cancelled."

"We're being kicked out of the partnership? No one told me. They can't do that without a vote of the partners."

"According to Richard, it's been in the works for months. I'm not surprised, the way you guys have been drinking. Do you think people don't notice?"

"Did it ever occur to you that maybe Richard Total and the rest of those snakes had something to do with getting us stabbed? Isn't it convenient that they don't need to pay for this now that our insurance was so conveniently cancelled?"

"Now you're just getting paranoid, Sam."

"And when did Richard go to medical school? You realize you are relying on the medical judgment of a Total Asshole."

"At least he's totally sober, Sam. By the way, I always wanted to tell you that you're an alcoholic. There, I said it. Somebody needed to. You and Joel are both alcoholics. Nothing you two do makes sense anymore. I'm sorry about what happened to Joel. But I'm the one who needs to look out for the family now, not you, and not Joel."

"Is that really the way you're going to make a decision here? You're going to sell his life for insurance money? Do you have any idea of how much I hate insurance companies?"

"This isn't about you, Sam."

I have a bad feeling, a flash of insight. Whenever we get these sorts of insights, we lawyers attribute it to our natural talent, the instinct that makes us great judges of character, intuitive seers of the future. When the insights are wrong, we disregard their fallibility. Right now, the insight is making me want to hit Ellie.

"Ellie, have you even been here? Did you even visit him? Or are you just taking Richard Total's word for what is going on? Is he the one who actually signed that order?" I hear the phone click.

I look down the hall. The chair outside Joel's room is still empty. I move quickly into the room and grab the metal folder hanging by a chain at the foot of the bed. I rip out the DNR order. Ellie's "signature" looks exactly like the overly neat, printed handwriting Richard uses whenever he makes changes on other people's briefs. Richard is so proud of his corrections he makes them with an impressive neatness that brings his tight-assed personality onto the paper. The purpose of the changes is usually to let you know he ranks with the client and you don't. Most of the time the brief is pretty much the same after the changes.

Sometimes when I'm shopping, and I'm about to buy something I can't afford, my bowels will suddenly seem to drop out, and I need to head to the bathroom. And that's what's happening now. I go out into the hallway and find the small toilet room reserved for guests wandering the hallways. I tear the DNR order into tiny little pieces and flush it down with the bile and waste created by my morphine drip.

Just then, there is beeping behind me in Joel's room. "He's coding," I hear someone shout from down the hall as people begin to rush towards the room. I step into the room across the hall and watch a red-haired doctor stroll into Joel's room behind a slow-moving nurse. He still has freckles. He looks like a kid.

A minute seems to go by. *Do something; I think he's dying.*

"I thought there was a DNR order."

"Can't find it anywhere."

"Keep looking."

"It's not here. Revoked maybe. You have to try, Doctor."

"Alright then, get me the paddles."

Another interminable minute. Finally, I shout out, "Do something, damn you."

"Go see who that is," and then, finally, "Clear."

It sounds like they try a few more times. Their tone changes each time, and then they quiet, and let out a happy laugh. "There he is," says the red-haired doctor. I notice the Irish accent. I hear the monitors beeping pleasantly. Time to head back to my room.

The Irish accent: "That kid Kobe is such a ball hog. He never passes the ball."

Reaching my room, I focus on the bed, intending to get there. The adrenaline from my rushing shuffle down the hallway fades. I feel as if I am out on the ocean waiting for a wave, rising and falling in the swell. A wave comes up behind me. Instead of pushing me gently towards the shore, it slams me down into a hard coral surface. Except it is the linoleum floor that slams into my face. From somewhere inside, my body tells me to cry. My insides want to get out. The childhood instinct heads me to the bathroom and forces me on my knees until I throw up every last remnant in my stomach. It is a dry heave, in the end just a pitiful puddle of saliva.

Feeling responsible for my own bodily fluids, I clean up the floor. I clean the remnants out of my beard, wash my face, and brush my teeth. Exhausted, I fall into bed. After three tries with the phone near my bed, I successfully reach an outside local line, and call the direct line of Valerie Huxtable, the first-year associate who is supposed to help me with the new lawsuit against Oddyssey. She is not in. Not a surprise. The rumors are that she leaves early to work out. Every night. I leave her a message.

Ellie is full of shit. What? Some crazy person comes into the office and starts stabbing us and suddenly everyone is so damn sure we're alcoholics? We still have jobs, we still bill hundreds of hours a month to clients, and most of them still pay the bills. My drinking is just a natural part of life, the only way someone could get through all the shit that always seems to be flying my way and still stay sane.

Reed and Endel haven't seemed close to solving anything, but they sure didn't seem to like me. With all of the unrest in the city, it would help them to at least make an arrest. No one would cry if a lawyer spent a few days in jail for something he didn't do.

Richard Total would find that convenient too. It would help him find a way to make the Oddyssey offering go through without paying either Joel or me a share of the profit. The money is so good that people are fighting on every level of the deal. Some of them even have knives. But Richard probably doesn't need to resort to murder. He murders people in court.

Joel is alive tonight. I have paid him back at last for saving my life that time back in Michigan. But it's not enough to clear the books because I've put them out of balance again. I should have gotten Joel out of Cohen & Cranston last year, before all of this stupid Oddyssey stuff started to happen, before he fell in love with this Kid's youth. As an English major, I've always learned the law of economics the hard way. A law firm is a ruthless entity, perfectly willing to screw its component parts and anyone else that stands in the way of its love of money. Everyone in this town eventually learns to love the money that everyone else pretends to have.

No, this is still all my fault, and I still need to fix it.

Joel is still a good man at heart. He wants to pull his weight, pay his child support, move on to a happier second marriage someday. The second marriage won't be any better than the first. But you can't tell people that stuff.

I need to get him to whatever safety can be found in this sea of shit. We'll go back and restart our old firm. Green and Straight. We'll be good lawyers again. It's what a real brother should do. He'll be going to Cedars tomorrow. I'm going to find that fucking Kid.

PART TWO: THE KID

CHAPTER EIGHT

Valerie Huxtable sits upright in the chair next to my hospital bed. The skirt on her pin-striped suit is longer than usual today, and it stretches tightly over the sleek, thick muscles of her thighs.

"Did you bring my coffee?"

"Grande latte, one percent milk."

I'm guilty of this new thing about fancy coffee. Seems to have started in Seattle.

"The clothes?"

"Just like you asked, Sam."

An extra-soft "sss" in the way she says my name makes me focus on how her teeth extend outward a little farther than they would if her parents had been anxious enough to get her braces. Braces would have made her look like every other one of the perfectly formed actresses on television these days. Instead, one of her front teeth is recessed, tucked ever so slightly behind the other front tooth, and it makes her *s*'s sound just a little soft. The effect charms me.

Valerie gets up to fetch the white shirt, red tie, and clean boxy suit I keep in my office in case one of the New York partners shows up unannounced. Muscles ripple up into her skirt as she retrieves the suit from the back of the door. Girls didn't get that big and strong when I was in school. Power exudes from every inch of her body.

Her body reminds me I am alive. The warmth of the coffee reawakens the feeling of humanness that is the will to live.

Since joining the firm nearly a year ago, Valerie has ignored me. Of course, that's nothing amazing. The associate rumor mill has an innate sense of my lack of pull in the partnership. The young lawyers know the real power rests with the partners who drink each night with the general counsels of the big corporations. I have no corporate clients of my own. That's why Joel and I have been demoted to non-equity partners—not much better than associates. It was supposed to be a private demotion, but everybody knows. One gossipy partner tells one gossipy associate, and all the news is out. Thus, I don't wonder why Valerie has always looked past or through me as if I were the repetition of a pattern in the wallpaper.

But now she seems to look me in the eye, like a girlfriend would. Maybe it's that she gets to work on Oddyssey, which is presumably cool since it's in the *Times* every day, albeit as the result of the depiction of the CEO's penis. Maybe she's worried that the other partners haven't been asking for her since she failed the bar exam last month. Valerie was at the bottom of her class at Harvard, and a bunch of the partners have started calling her the "affirmative action girl" since the bar results came out. A few of them just call her "action girl" with that knowing, winking look that implies they've had some of the action.

"Shoes," I say, trying to clear my eyes. Valerie pulls my shoes out of her oversize purse. Her bright white teeth gleam when she smiles. I'm starting to forget my pain.

"Okay. Stow the shoes in your purse," I say. "Put the clothes in a hamper bag. I think there's one in the bathroom. I've been told to go for a walk around the floor about once every two hours. We're going to go on that walk together. We're going to smile at everybody."

"Are you sure?" Valerie asks. She understands we're talking about more than a walk around the floor.

She returns with the suit in a plastic bag from the bathroom. As she bends over to give it to me, the unbuttoned part of her light-colored silk blouse opens into the deep shadows between her dark breasts. It is impossible to look anywhere else. I try to get up. Everything goes dark for a moment. I sit back down.

"Let me help you, Sam." She pulls a brush out of her purse. She cups my jaw in her strong hand and brushes my hair into place with the other. Then, she hands me the brush: "See if you can untangle that beard."

I make an attempt, then give her back the brush. I stand again, and everything is okay this time. The girlfriend experience is apparently energizing my body. I nod to the door and follow her out. Her shoulders are pinned back by young muscles, but they swing forward along the axis of her graceful spine as each leg advances in a walk that bounces her big gluteus muscles. *Just stop it. You've got work to do.*

We walk together past the nurse's station. I try to smile at people while hanging on the pole with the intravenous bag attached for stability. It feels like I'm grinning insanely. "You're looking a lot better, Mr. Straight," the male nurse on duty says. I smile because I can't remember his name.

Just before the elevator there is a men's room. "Tell them I had to go," I say, taking the purse, briefcase and hamper bag inside and locking the door.

When I take off the gown, no blood shows through the bandages on my chest and stomach. An encouraging sign. The pants barely fit over the bandage on my leg. I peel back the tape on the back of my hand and carefully remove the intravenous needle. There is a boost of confidence and healing at being free of that thing. I get dressed in the suit.

Out of the bathroom, I hand Valerie her purse, and carry the briefcase in my right arm. I hook my left arm under hers and lean into her. "Let's go."

Before Friday, the closest I had been to County was the view of it from the window in my office five miles away. Built during the Great Depression to care for the poor, it is lofted onto a hill off the San Bernardino Freeway, forbidding and tall. Most of the buildings built back then are abandoned or torn down. Like them, County is dirty and old, and it feels more like a storage facility or a prison than a hospital. The refuge of the uninsured.

We go down the elevator, and then out into the general visitors' lobby area. Forty or so people mill about, an anxious line of them trying to get some information from the staff working indifferently behind a large glass barrier. Young men in loose T-shirts, tattoos, and baggy shorts idle through the area high-fiving each other on their latest badges of courage. Just a few stitches, and they'll be back out there. We look unusual in our business suits, but not suspicious. A uniformed guard sits at a desk but does not look up at us.

The imploring eyes of a young Hispanic woman gaze out at me from a poster on the wall. "He said he'd never hit you again," says the poster. "That was last time," it adds on the next line.

Stepping outside, we are blinded by the pale white of the bright smog. Good old Hippocrates is embedded over the door through which we pass. "Primum non nocere," I say to him as I go past. Lawyers don't pretend to that kind of thing. A lawyer's ethics require the doing of harm. Or, at the very least, helping others avoid responsibility for the harm they do.

We walk quickly down the dirty white steps, through a black wrought iron gate. Looking back at the tower, I see the images of three women in white stone in the art deco facade, their faces dripping black beards of soot. Who are these sooty spirits that someone once immortalized in stone, but later generations chose not to care for?

I also see window panels replaced by various colors of paper or cardboard. Shot out by the kind of gunfire we were hearing yesterday.

We head down one of the many ramps curving down the hill. As we reach Zonal Avenue, we are frozen in place by the sound of police sirens. Three LAPD Crown Victorias roar by us on the tiny street, sirens flashing.

There are flashes of darkness in my vision. I need a lot more practice in walking, need to think more clearly, more in the moment. Hands shaking.

"What do we do now?" I ask.

"Let's get to my car," Valerie says.

"Shouldn't we be going the other way?"

"Yeah, but my car's down there."

Another black-and-white streams past us, sirens full blast. It turns the first corner going left, tires slipping noisily. The cop driving looks directly at us but does not slow down.

My heart slows: they are not looking for us.

Valerie pulls me to the left, and we follow the patrol car. We walk past a heavy wall topped by thick rolls of barbed wire.

"Is this some kind of prison?" I ask.

"It's a juvenile justice center," Valerie answers.

"How do you know that? The firm's never had a case here."

"I have," says Valerie.

Around a corner, a crowd of Hispanic teenagers, mostly males, masses in front of a squat brown building. A girl dressed only in a white T-shirt and white athletic shorts stands out, repeatedly lifting a sign saying "Justeicia" in clumsy letters.

The crowd chants a slogan: "Stop killing our sons! Stop killing our brothers!" They are using English for the phalanx of ten to fifteen cameramen standing straight as can be, their cameras poised on full-size tripods, pointing at us with the solemnity of flamethrowers. Several of the demonstrators hold Mexican flags.

Valerie and I slip to the back of the crowd. Six or seven LAPD vehicles have formed a line on the sidewalk between the crowd and the building, seemingly to protect a large taco wagon on the curb proclaiming *Ernesto's Tacos—3 for $2.*

Behind the makeshift barricade created by the bulk of the taco truck, I recognize the Hispanic member of the LA City Council standing in front of a rain-worn sign proclaiming his responsibility for this area of town.

A tall man with a shiny bald head shakes his arm so hard that he seems about to throw his hand at someone. He yells at the councilman: "The system will not give us justice."

"You have to give the system a chance," the councilman calls back through the megaphone. "We are going to find the people responsible for killing this boy and bring them to justice."

"Your justice murdered them," calls back the man with the shaking arm.

Something flies at the councilman. It looks like a hot dog. A thick yellow stain blossoms on his silk shirt. Two LAPD officers step between the councilman and the crowd and try to draw him back into the building. But he shakes them off.

"The press is here. We can have a press conference right here and now," he says to the aide shadowing his left arm. Then he shouts into the megaphone: "It's time to stop the killing."

"He's trying to make the afternoon news programs," Valerie says, then, "This way." Valerie points out her car, a new Lexus. Why was I worried about affirmative action girl? Maybe she doesn't even need this job.

A concussive blast of hot air erupts past us. A hundred various screams and shouts blend together—an individual yet cumulative sound of terror. The taco truck rises up and tips over towards the crowd, which scatters before it crashes on its side. A sharp bump on my shoulder knocks me into Valerie, and we fall to the street together.

The crowd suddenly seems to be gone. Three people lie on the ground with a stillness that suggests they have entered a world apart from all of those who are running away.

Valerie and I stagger to our feet and look to the juvenile justice center. The police, still in formation, now on one knee, calmly survey the situation with guns drawn. The cameramen have gone to the ground, but their cameras turned randomly in the explosion, and one of them seems to be aimed directly at us.

"This is not a good time for us to be on camera," I say to Valerie.

"Let's get to the car," Valerie says, pulling me to her Lexus.

The perfectly fitted doors of the Lexus shut softly, cutting off the smoky smell and a good deal of the revolving siren noise.

"What the hell was that?" I say.

"A Hispanic teenager arrested on drug charges last night was found hanging in his cell this morning. People are angry. They think it's a setup," Valerie says.

She weaves through the fleeing people and the arriving fire trucks. Sirens wail from every direction. "We have to go now, or we'll get caught in this."

The inside of Valerie's new car has the civilized smell of fresh, expensive leather. She sends it smoothly out to the 10 freeway. The V6 nimbly catches the strangely open road, heading west. Downtown's ghostly buildings loom above us. We pass them, and they fade behind us into the smog.

Valerie says, "Are we really going to see the Kid?"

"We have an appointment at his gym," I reply.

"Let me take you home, and I'll do the interview. I'll write you one of those fabulously detailed memos. Like they do in New York."

The morphine made the exploding taco truck a mere surreal sideshow, but it's wearing off now. Things like that are always happening in LA. Still, there is no denying the incident has shaken me up, or that I was unsteady to begin with.

If I were just verifying another useless SEC statement, going home would be logical. But it is time to find out who stabbed Joel. I figure the answers start with the Kid.

"I have to do this," I say. She merges to the 2. North to the Valley.

I think I know the answer, but I ask anyway. "Are there any cigarettes in here?" Valerie looks at me like I am a space alien and keeps driving.

CHAPTER NINE

Valerie stares at the storefront. We have just pulled into a rare open meter spot on Van Nuys, in front of the address Joel gave me. Above the display windows of the storefront, a purple sign says *JESUS' GYM* in large white letters. Below, in smaller letters, *Workouts for Body and Soul.* On the window, an artist has painted Jesus all in white, triumphantly holding a barbell over his head with one hand and four fingers, index finger lifted to the sky, his robe falling off to reveal bursting pectoral muscles and washboard abs.

From the SEC filings, I know that Joel and the accountants have toured Oddyssey.com's two large brick-and-mortar locations: a converted warehouse along the 91 freeway in Compton, and the call center in Norwalk. This third location, listed in the filings as an office, apparently uses the "Jesus" cover label to enhance the Kid's clean-living image. It fits seamlessly here in the Valley.

I swing my legs out of the passenger seat of Valerie's Lexus. My head starts spinning again. The empty whiteness of the smog-covered Valley sky gives way to a starry blackness.

Valerie is on my side of the car. From above me, outside the darkness in my head, I hear her say, "You really don't look well."

"My gut tells me that if we don't keep this appointment with the Kid, we may never talk to him in person." Actually, I'm not sure we have an appointment. I'm trusting that Joel set it up while I was smoking in the stairwell.

I used to think that the older lawyers who used phrases like "my gut tells me" were just covering the fact they were too lazy to do the research or the legwork.

Just inside the doors, we find ourselves in a small front room with scuffed white walls. The only furnishing is a metal desk and a few rickety-looking plastic chairs. There is no sign for Oddyssey, only a single crucifix on the plain wall. A teenage girl with very long black hair and a ring through her eyebrow sits behind the desk on a metal folding chair, reading a book with *BIBLE* printed prominently on the cover. She seems disturbed to see us.

"You aren't members," she says.

"What makes you think so?" Valerie says quickly. All that exercise makes these kids confident in a physical way before they really know what they are doing in a mental way.

"You're wearing suits?" the teenager says.

"Joel Green set up our meeting with Mr. Cauer for 10:30. We're his lawyers, from Cohen & Cranston," I say.

"I doubt anybody told you 10:30," she says.

I give her my best plaintive look. I'm not above flirting a little to get what I want. It weighs on my conscience less than just annoying people to get what I want, which is the other, most prevalent lawyer tactic.

Lately, I've been noticing that young women aren't flirting back. Like now. The girl stares back at my face and says nothing, makes no movement.

"Perhaps you could investigate?" Valerie says with more energy, the charming *s* sounds echoing.

The girl keeps staring at me, though. Then she says, "What happened to you?"

"I got stabbed."

"Really?" answers the girl.

"Could you check on our appointment?" Valerie says.

The eyebrow-ring girl puts her Bible down with some attitude. When she stands, we see she is extremely thin, carrying only about eighty-five pounds on her frame, which is five foot six or so. Her black spandex pants hug her legs tightly, but her upper body is enveloped in a loose, hanging shirt.

A vast swell of music resounds brutishly as she opens and walks through the only door behind her. It sounds like the pulsing background in one of those teenager movies where a meteorite threatens to destroy the world.

The door clicks closed. The music pulses on behind the door.

My body weighs me down into one of the cheap plastic chairs. Wherever Oddyssey is spending its money, it hasn't reached this reception area.

The morphine is really wearing off now, and I realize I need a drink, need the pain to be somewhere I can look at it as if I'm someone else. It's all I can do to just sit here, but after ten minutes, Valerie starts pacing. At twenty, she calls her secretary to check if she has any messages. After thirty minutes, Valerie asks, "Is this professional?"

I try not to be hypnotized by the double-*s* sound.

"If you want professional, you're gonna work for some of those boring banks and oil companies," I tell Valerie.

"I guess you're right." She defers again, as if I were one of those real partners.

"If it makes you feel any better, when you get back you can write, 'Waiting to meet with Mr. Cauer after arriving on time for a scheduled appointment' down on your time sheet."

Valerie picks up the Bible our spandex receptionist left on the little desk. "Look at this," she says. She turns the book around and I see that instead of Bible verses, the book consists of multicolored pages of a computer instruction manual, complete with sample screens. It seems well above the beginning level.

"Put it back," I say. She puts it down, carefully, just as she found it.

The door opens, and our hostess returns. Behind her walks a girl of about twenty, with neatly bobbed, brunette hair. Her heavy, crusty makeup fails to conceal some obvious acne bumps. She is dressed in neat business attire, complete with a closed-neck shirt, and a small, black, female-style necktie.

"I'm Trisha Carlson, Mr. Cauer's chief of staff," she says. "We didn't expect you. Mr. Cauer is in the middle of a staff meeting, but he said you could watch the end and talk to him while he's winding down."

As an afterthought, Trisha adds, "Oh, and this is Beverly, Mr. Cauer's girlfriend." I look again at Beverly's tiny figure. She can't be sixteen. Probably the Kid's next lawsuit.

We follow young Ms. Carlson's business-like clip and Beverly's dazed slink through the door into a vast dim room. We go around the side of the room, like worshippers late for church.

All around us, the room pulses with the harsh rhythm of rap music. Lights flash. In the measureless semi-darkness, a voice emerges.

Following the voice to its source, I see the Kid on a stage in the back of the room, lit by an intense spotlight. The Kid wears tight black pants revealing painful-looking striations in the thigh bulges. Mounds of pectoral muscles push through the straps of a loose, white tank top. Multicolored tattoos, mostly crucifixes and fishes, cover his considerable biceps. His hair has changed since the *MaryLee Lacy Show*. Then, it had been bleached white, with multiple spikes gelled into place, tipped with a pale electric blue, as if natural gas flames were coming out of his head. Now his head is shaved clean. He is Mr. Clean's younger brother.

The Kid is surrounded by at least eight stations of free weights, with benches and racks, some lifted onto mini platforms. A multi-speaker sound system—some speakers seem over twelve feet high—looms over him and the free-weight factory. A long desk in front of the speakers holds several phone banks with red lights flashing.

A lot of people appear to be on the line. As my eyes grow accustomed to the darkened auditorium, I make out ten or so figures, the sweat dropping off their shirtless, shining upper bodies and flashing in the reflected light of the spotlight that follows the Kid. The bodies are mostly white, and the hair is also strangely uniform: long dark dreadlocks, decorated with brightly colored beads. As we draw closer, I realize that some of these, like the Kid, are not men. The finely tuned bodies encase little-boy faces.

The Kid calls out the repetitions loudly as he moves from station to station, each set up with a different free-weight exercise: bench presses, overhead presses, single dumbbells, leg presses. He does three sets of twelve repetitions at each station—a very high number given the weight he is lifting. The dreadlocked boys follow him in scary unison. I lean against a wall. This is going to take a while.

Periodically, he calls out challenges: "That was 310. What did you do?" The chorus responds with a wave of unintelligible noise.

At the last station, the Kid finishes, then turns to face those who have been following him. "One Lord," the Kid shouts, thrusting his finger in the air as if he has just won the Super Bowl, and leaping off the stage with the flailing arms and churning legs of a long jumper. The Kid sticks his landing and raises his arms.

"One Lord," shout back the dreadlocked boys.

"And he's our Lord," screams the Kid. Apparently, the Kid is wearing one of those cordless mikes because his voice is the whole building, coming from everywhere.

"And it's Our World," booms the Kid's voice.

"Our World," reply the acolytes.

The Kid turns his back and strides back to the stage. A short, elderly woman tentatively approaches him, and tries to cover him with a large towel. As if he were James Brown. The Kid brushes her away, nearly knocking her down. The old woman is so unlike anything I have seen so far that I ask Trisha Carlson who she is.

"The Kid's mom," says Trisha matter-of-factly. Squinting to see in the light just outside the Kid's spotlight, I notice that Trisha might have been reading off one of those Dr. Laura T-shirts that says, "I am my Kid's mom." The T-shirt stretches tightly over Mom's old-world figure. She is no fitness buff. I look back at Trisha. "No, really," she says, "she is the Kid's mom."

The Kid hurdles back onto the stage and into the spotlight.

"China, report," he commands.

"We added thirty operatives last week," says a voice over the loudspeaker, apparently coming from an amplified speakerphone. "We've been able to get all of our cellulars connected to the servers. The cellular works really well here—better than in LA. We're gonna need keyboards—"

"You get me the reps, you get me operatives, I'll get you the hardware, Jimmy. You gave me thirty; well, I want forty next week."

"You watch, Kid. We'll get fifty."

And so it goes, with reports from Hong Kong, New York, Chicago, Atlanta, and London. The Kid loudly abuses and prods each of the minions who deliver the reports. Every phrase from his mouth brings cheers from the dreadlocked heads below the stage. The enthusiasm grows louder as the goals sound more preposterous. I wonder if these voices on the phone are really where they say they are, or whether they are all in the phone bank in Norwalk, and whether this whole scene is being staged for my benefit.

When the reports are done, the Kid walks over to the phones, and speaks more somberly, more seriously, taking long breaths after each sentence.

"I know you've read allegations about my past in the papers this week . . . Before I was reborn in the blood of the lamb, I could not tell the devil when he stood before me . . . Sometimes the devil is a woman in a low-cut dress, and sometimes the woman takes the dress off . . ."

The dreadlock beads clack as the Kid's acolytes issue appreciative laughter.

"Sometimes we can resist the ways of women, but sometimes, when the spirit is weak, and the woman is just too fine . . . well, when that happens . . . giving in is wrong, but, well . . . not so hard to understand."

The sweating boys sneer in unison.

"But now, the Lord has come to me," the Kid continues. He pauses, eyes closed, and holds up his hand as if calling for a timeout while he searches within himself for the next words.

"Yes, the Lord has come to me . . . and now I know . . . now I know that he wanted me to make this mistake so that I would not again allow my soul and our business to be destroyed by a woman . . .

"I was told, I was told. You must build your business on a foundation of stone," he continues, "and gather about you loyal men of God . . . I repaid the damage, and the Lord has forgiven me . . . And you, my brothers, you . . . are my foundation of stone."

I think of how Joel calls me his "brother."

Any hypocrisy goes unnoticed by the sweating stones, who cheer loudly.

"I know that each of you have done wrong, and have been forgiven and reborn with me . . . My brothers, we are taking this business public, and we are going to explode through the market and bring together so much money for God's purposes. We will no longer be beholden to lenders or lawyers, to venture capitalists or the other vermin who have swarmed over us like locusts. We built this business with our strength, and our sweat, and when we get that stock money, it will be our money, and we will send them away for good."

The Kid perches on the edge of the stage and in a soft, resolute voice, interrupted by breathing like that of a runner finishing a race, intones into a microphone: "We . . . will cover the world. Our Oddyssey . . . will bring our world together."

The beaded heads close in around the Kid. He seems to want to talk to them confidentially. "Be cautious; be quiet, my brothers. You can't tell them. They're not ready to know what we're going to do."

Not pausing to wonder if he has gone too far, the Kid clenches his fists, extending them in front of him, his elbows bending at right angles, with the fists pointed up. Sensing something louder is coming, his acolytes step back. "We will take Oddyssey to the world. With God's help we will give the world the answers that it is seeking. God knows all. But God does not just know all, he can do all, and we don't just give the world his answers. We give the world. . . "

And now the voices come back, from the room, and from all over the world, really, if you believe the phone bank, saying with one voice, "His Action."

Just like the slogan: "Not Just Answers: Action."

"So, this is all God's plan," says Valerie.

"That explains it," I say.

CHAPTER TEN

The disciples break away from him, running back to the weight-lifting stage. Without slowing, they bounce off mattress-like pads lining the stage onto soft mats below it. The Kid leaps up to the stage, then makes a running jump from the stage into the pile. Everybody rumbles.

The lights come up, and the dreadlocks charge out of the room, away from us, cheering at the top of their lungs. My tired jaw has gone slack.

Valerie alertly turns to Trisha Carlson. "When are we going to get to speak to him?"

"You can catch him in the steam room," she says. "It's behind the stage."

"In the steam room?" I repeat.

"That's usually the only time that he slows down enough to speak to me." Trisha whips her bobbed hair as she strides to the rooms behind the stage. Beverly drafts along. So do we.

A remnant of my sexual-harassment training stirs. "Look, Valerie," I say, "you don't need to do this."

"Don't want to miss this, Sam," Valerie says. She seems game. Maybe the other partners have underestimated her.

"How does it feel to be a woman swimming in this sea of testosterone?" Valerie asks Trisha.

"The Kid does get carried away," Trisha says. "But the view is good, and there's still a place for a woman to get paid around here."

Paid for what? I wonder when we come into the backstage room. Of course, I have that question about the entire company.

We are surrounded by steam flowing from three shower trees—like the ones in boys' high school locker rooms. Three or four naked muscle boys hover in the water coming from each tree, throwing soap and shouting at each other. They don't seem to notice us as we make our way through. They whip their long, beaded hair in the water, sending streams of it at each other.

Trisha opens a sweating glass door and disappears into a cloud of steam. Beverly follows, and then Valerie and I go along in our wool suits. Into the inner sanctum of Jesus' Gym.

When our eyes grow accustomed to the steam, we see the Kid, perched up on a high bench above our sight line. His legs are spread apart, but his torso is covered by a towel. He seems relaxed, confident, as if sitting on a throne, reading the *Wall Street Journal*. Without a shirt, his upper body is breathtaking, and the steam makes it glow like this is a Mr. Universe pageant.

"What did you think of our staff meeting?" says the Kid.

I think that the entire show was conducted for my benefit. To demonstrate once again to another C&C partner that Oddyssey is very, very real, and very, very profitable. I say, "When you talked about reps, I take it you weren't referring to weight-lifting repetitions."

"They're our representatives all over the world," says the Kid. His voice is confident, like he's used to being in charge. "I have suffered the disenfranchised to come unto me."

He pauses. I just look at him.

"You know, the people that can't get real jobs. Bicycle messengers, Xerox operators, paper sorters. We steer them away from the hamburger-flipping jobs, and into places where they have access to power. We give these kids a computer and a cellular phone, sometimes a scanner, and they're in our business."

"What's with the dreadlocks?" I ask.

"It gives them a sense of identity. Like uniforms in the military. Makes them feel they are part of something bigger. They can fold them away behind a cap to make themselves look a little more conventional."

"And the muscles?"

"Weightlifting builds confidence," says the Kid. "Look what it did for me. Hey, Sam, after I heard you were in County, we didn't think you were coming."

"I probably wouldn't have. But I'm wondering if you have any ideas about who would want to kill Joel," I say.

Ignoring the question, he says, "Who's she?" Meaning Valerie.

"She's our associate, Valerie Huxtable."

"Joel was told that it could be you and only you." The Kid gives Valerie the kind of up-and-down treatment a Chatsworth pornographer would give an eager teenager looking for extra money. "Though now that I see her, I'm thinking I should make an exception."

"The way I'm feeling . . . I needed someone to help me take notes."

"No notes," chirps Trisha.

I give her a look. "Are you a lawyer?" I ask.

"I've studied the law," she replies, as if that makes her my equal.

Beverly sidles silently into place on the Kid's left. He wraps his arm around her. The queen has taken her throne.

"Who would want to kill Joel?" I try again.

"I have no idea," says the Kid. "Have you thought about your other cases? The unhappy clients. The people whose cases you lost. The ones who thought your bills were too high."

"Yesterday the *LA Times* said you used to hang out with Jacky Real.

Is he still around?" Valerie asks. This is something new, something I didn't know. They don't give you a paper at County. Valerie has actually prepared.

Real is a Westside Mafia wannabe. Despite the Hispanic-sounding name (he was born in Mexico), he likes to give people the impression he is Italian, and very connected with the kind of people who break legs when they don't get paid properly. When I first started practice, when I was a lot more naïve, I worked for Real trying to collect some of his debts in court. He had a California lender's license, so I thought he was legitimate. But it turned out that much of the money he loaned was counterfeit. Anyone with a lender's license can evade usury laws, but his interest rates were scary, even by payday-lender standards. Real and I had our falling-out when he tried paying me with some of his fake cash. Like a lot of other cowards, however, I didn't report him. I thought that was the ethical way, in the way of lawyers' ethics.

"He was my initial investor," the Kid says. "But you knew that."

I nod. I didn't know it.

"I'm not proud of it. Joel made me pay him off. You knew that too."

"Wanted to hear it from you."

"Now you have."

Jacky Real was this Kid's "godfather"? This is the kind of thing Reed and Endel should be asking about. Jacky Real might actually be the kind of guy who could order the kind of hit on Joel that happened the other night. Now it turns out it was Joel who pushed Real out of the Kid's circle. Why didn't Joel tell me this had happened? He knew my history with Real.

"Real might be looking for more than the vig you paid him," I say. "With this offering, he probably thinks that might be available. Especially with Joel out of the way."

"Real is not a problem," says the Kid firmly.

Trisha Carlson pipes up: "Real has not been around for months."

"That won't keep people from asking about him," I say. I figure that's all they're going to tell me about Real. How he has nothing to do with Oddyssey. But I have the lead I've been looking for.

"Can we talk about the complaint?" I ask.

Trisha asserts herself again: "That piece-of-garbage lawsuit is just extortion."

I'm getting a little irritated at having to give my legal advice in competition with a twenty-year-old know-it-all. "Litigation is legal extortion," I say. "You pay to make it go away. You run a business in California. You should know that."

I feel a pool of wetness forming over my stomach. I look down and see that my shirt is pink, mixing blood and sweat. I'm getting dizzy.

"Why did you and Laurilee break up?" Valerie asks.

Valerie is sweating almost as much as I am. She has a piece of paper in her hand, an outline for the defense of the sexual harassment case. An outline is the sort of tight-ass approach that Richard Total and the robots from the New York office use. For me, the stupid lawsuit with the penis drawing as Exhibit A is just another way to get to the bottom of what happened to Joel. The rest of the outline can wait.

"I haven't talked to Laurilee for years," says the Kid. "My mother will tell you she's making all of this up."

"What about the document request?" Valerie asks. Again, very Richard-like of her. *Oh God, Richard hasn't gotten to her, has he? And when did this document request happen?* I haven't heard of it.

"We don't have any documents," Trisha says. She takes off her suit jacket and places it neatly on the bench. The nipples of her full breasts are visible through her white shirt, which has become wet in the steam. I feel like someone sent a memo saying that I was easily distracted by partially clothed women. Or maybe Joel told them my wife used to be a stripper.

"Well, you have records on computer, don't you?" asks Valerie.

"Yeah, but they aren't here," replies Trisha. "And besides, we are paperless. All we have are some computer images, not documents. They could be anywhere or, with the push of a button, nowhere."

"Computer images are documents," I interject. "Destroying anything could make you liable no matter what." I am becoming a spectator to the debate between Valerie's Richard Total outline and the faux teenage lawyer.

"We can search your offices for you," says Valerie.

Trisha and the Kid laugh.

"We're totally virtual—everything is on computers," says the Kid.

"Except for the checkbook," says Trisha.

The Kid stares at her silently. "That's private," says the Kid.

"We'll need to look at that," I say.

"How is every check we write relevant to this silly piece of extortion?" asks Trisha, picking up on the Kid's disapproval of her disclosure.

"A diligent and thorough search needs to be done," says Valerie, reading off her paper. I think about Compton. And Norwalk. But I'm too tired to say anything.

"We did that," says Trisha. "Like I said, we don't have any documents."

"You'll have to state that under penalty of perjury," says Valerie.

"No problem," says Trisha. Clients lie so easily once the lawyer explains why a lie might be convenient. But lies won't get me to the bottom of who tried to kill Joel. I have a feeling it is futile, but I gather up my remaining energy.

"Look, we need to know the truth so we can defend this case," I say.

"Ah, the truth," says the Kid, as if I've said something peculiar or stupid.

"Take Ms. Huxtable outside," I say to Trisha.

"Why?" protests Valerie.

"Just go," I say.

But Valerie doesn't move, and before I can insist, the Kid puts down his *Wall Street Journal,* and throws away his towel. He disentangles himself from Beverly's bones, and climbs up to stand on the bench, legs apart, arms akimbo, a great wide smile on his face.

There is no hair anywhere on his body. Despite the Kid's obvious pride, the organ does not appear to be as large as portrayed by the sketch artist who drew Exhibit A to Laurilee Geller's sexual harassment complaint. Of course, in Laurilee's memory the penis was probably larger. But then I see—unlike the penis in Exhibit A—this one is . . . well . . . the Kid has apparently changed religions. Is there anything people won't do for money?

"Hair grows back," says Valerie, failing to appreciate the defining difference from Exhibit A.

"Reasonable doubt, though, wouldn't you say, Mr. Straight?" the Kid says.

"It's a civil case, so all they need is a preponderance of evidence. And there's a record of things that happen in a hospital," I say.

"We've taken care of that," says Trisha Carlson.

"It's an interesting factual issue for trial," Valerie adds. Her Harvard education has taught her to sound knowing.

"This case is never going to get to trial," says a squirrely know-it-all voice coming from behind me. Someone new has come into the steam room. I turn and see the fully-dressed, dumpy figure of the LA office's only twelve-year associate: Eddie Guarnieri.

CHAPTER ELEVEN

The C&C partners look at Eddie Guarnieri as a useful drudge. There is no denying he's smart, and if you try to deny it in his presence, he will remind you he is a member of Mensa. Despite his Italian-sounding name, Eddie loves telling people he is "technically Hispanic." He will tell you he was entitled to admission preferences at Harvard but eschewed them because he is so smart he didn't need them. If you say you don't understand, Eddie will explain the word eschewed to you. Then he will tell you how well he did at Harvard. His brains are not all talk. There are partners who get most of their wins by stealing ideas from Eddie. Richard Total is one, and Richard is no dummy.

Despite his intelligence, Eddie's career is way behind. He's been passed over for partnership twice. Most of the partners would be happy telling him to leave, but Richard Total continues to find him useful. Richard keeps promising Eddie he will make him a partner—next time. Next time is now scheduled for next year. Richard can tell a lie better than most, and so Eddie hangs on.

Eddie's problem is not his aptitude for legal issues. It's not even his obnoxious obsession with himself. After all, narcissism can be an asset in the legal profession. Eddie's problem is the way he looks.

Part of it is the overweight aspect. Eddie will tell you he despises exercise, finding it a bit simple minded, like banging your head against a wall. What is the attraction of repeatedly throwing the same-size ball into the same-size circular rim? What indeed is the attraction of running around to do so? It's all just a pointless pain in the ass, he will tell you.

It is most especially in the ass that Eddie does not carry his extra weight well. His chest and upper body are peculiarly narrow and flat, and the folds of fat fall straight down. At the point of his belly, however, his body seems to balloon, and the irregular bulges of his buttocks sag behind him. He tries to reduce the effect of these bulges by wearing extremely baggy Brooks Brothers' suits. He cinches the belt a little above his belly button, but this tents the loose pants in a way that accentuates rather than conceals his peculiar body shape, at least to people who aren't looking at Eddie's mirror.

I often hear the New York partners say Eddie just isn't presentable in the way you expect a partner to be. The way they say it always makes me feel like maybe Joel and I aren't very presentable either.

Now here is Eddie's bulging ass sweating under his tent-like pants right in front of me in the sauna, an evil angel sent by Richard Total to torment me.

"Richard said that if I saw you, I should tell you to call him," Eddie says.

"Why didn't he call me?"

"We couldn't reach you."

"Somehow he managed to find Joel's wife."

The Kid takes his turn condescending to me: "Sorry, big guy, the internet does not wait for people to get well. You gotta get on the board and get your money out. Our whole idea could be yesterday by next month. We have to have the money now. Pretty cool guy, that Richard. You and Joel are down only forty-eight hours, and Richard was completely up to speed. Did he tell you how we're going to defend against little Laurilee?"

"Not yet," I say.

"Cross-complain," exults the Kid. He continues as Beverly wraps a towel around him. "Against everybody. It's brilliant. We're going to sue the websites that display the complaint. According to Eddie here, they've violated four federal laws on the distribution of child pornography. That penis in Exhibit A is only sixteen years old. Of course, your draft answer was great. Deny everything. Good strategy. Total says it drives the other side crazy. But Richard also says that the cross-complaint he wrote will throw everything into a tizzy while the media gears up their constitutional-law specialists. And it'll deter other people from suing. Besides, we just need to get through the IPO. Then we pay Laurilee off out of the money from the IPO. That money will make any settlement look small. She'll be cheap. It doesn't take much to appease her."

"It all seems pretty unethical," I venture.

The Kid laughs and looks at skinny Beverly. He whispers in her ear. Then he adds, "There's also the evidence problem," knowingly looking down below his waist.

Eddie takes the floor again: "So you see, there won't be a trial, Valerie."

Valerie's Harvard pride doesn't take the last word from Eddie's Harvard-haute analysis. "I'm not sure this gets him off," she says to Eddie.

"If I have any trouble getting off, I'll let you know," says the Kid.

The room spins. The disorientation is much more than just physical. I have entered an alternate, evil universe in which Richard Total and Kid Cauer are completely in control, and I am a lifeless meteorite spinning off into space.

Beverly lifts off her baggy shirt, revealing small breast points, which push up and through her wet bra. She has the most remarkable tattoo of a snake wrapping twice around her body, ending with its head, jaws unhinged and flared wide around her petite left breast, its teeth obscured by the feeble, transparent cloth of her bra. The devil himself, come to feast.

My knees buckle, and I kneel down. It is cooler near the wet tile floor. "I'm going to need some air," I say.

Valerie says to Trisha Carlson, "Help me get him out of here."

Valerie's strong hands pull my biceps, helping me to my feet. But it is Eddie's all-knowing voice I hear: "Right now, Mr. Cauer, you and yours have to get moving. There's a process server out front."

The interview is plainly over. Now fully clothed, the Kid's acolytes fill the sauna, the beads on their dreadlocks clacking, surrounding the Kid and Beverly. They move, as a mass, out the door.

With the help of Valerie and Trisha, I stagger out of the sauna. My brain cells immediately appreciate the oxygen.

"Come with me," Eddie says. Valerie and Trisha follow him, pulling me along by the elbows.

I say to Trisha, "You know what I keep wondering? Where are all the parents? Where are Beverly's parents? Where are the parents of all these guys in the beads? Where are your parents?"

"I'm twenty, now," Trisha says defensively. "The Kid—well, all of us—we're emancipated. We've got a law firm that specializes in it." How many lawyers do these teenagers have? C&C is just the tip of the iceberg.

We emerge into the painful smoggy light of Van Nuys. A tall man in a neat business suit stands there talking to Eddie, who has walked ahead of us. As we walk up, the tall man focuses on me. Apparently he has been getting nowhere with Eddie.

"Is Caleb Cauer here? I have some important papers to deliver personally."

"We are attorneys for Mr. Cauer," I say, taking the papers. "Who are you?"

"I'm a licensed process server."

"Mr. Straight has no authority to accept service of process," Eddie puts in quickly. I forgot: Total Assholes like to play service-of-process games. "We'll contact the client and discuss it," Eddie adds.

"I can wait. We have good information that Mr. Cauer is here. Would you be with the firm of Cohen & Cranston?" This guy is no messenger. The service of process on Oddyssey cases has gone upmarket. They are hiring investigators now. This guy, who might even be a lawyer, is trying the professional approach. If it doesn't work, a devious approach will quickly follow.

"All you need to know is that we are attorneys who will discuss this with the client," says Eddie.

"Yes, I'm from Cohen & Cranston," I say, trying to show I don't play service-of-process games.

"You're a partner, aren't you?" asks the process server.

"I'm Sam Straight."

"You've been served, Mr. Straight. You'll see the firm is a defendant, and so, my friend, are you." The neatly suited man walks away. I hate that "my friend" thing.

I open the envelope. It is a federal summons, directed to Cohen & Cranston and what seems to be a list of my partners. I scan the complaint, hearing the traffic in my ear but feeling it's miles away while I dwell in a little world on a piece of paper where my career is evaporating. The complaint alleges that Oddyssey is nothing more than a front; it's purported "business" is just a cover for what is in essence another LA Ponzi scheme. These attorneys are sharks, of course, the kind that file a complaint every time a stock turns down. I guess they don't believe in the audited financials, in the scores of reps around the world.

There is an additional cause of action. It accuses the firm of Cohen & Cranston, specifically through its partner Joel Green, of aiding and abetting the securities fraud. All of the partners, including Richard Total and me, are personally named as negligently failing to stop the Kid from his perfidy.

The firm has twenty days to answer this. I want to go home.

"Here, Eddie, you better give this to Richard and his coterie. I imagine you'll find him at the Beverly Wilshire. Perhaps the concierge will take it up for you."

"Yes, thanks to you it will be hard for the firm to argue that it hasn't been served now," says Eddie. I feel like punching him, but his pathetic physical presentation puts me off. The urge passes. Overwhelming fatigue returns.

"What does this mean?" asks Trisha as Valerie and I walk away.

Valerie turns to her. "I've got to get him home," she says, taking my arm and leading me north along the street to where her Lexus is parked.

Trisha runs after us. She has a jacket on now, but I'm still thinking about the wetness of her blouse plastered against her chest. The male brain is a stupid thing. She seems strangely unsure of herself, almost as if the last hour has been an act. She hands me a business card. "Please call me at this number as soon as you can," she says.

We head along Ventura to Valerie's Lexus. At the north corner, a white van pulls up. From around a corner, the Kid emerges, surrounded by four of his weight-lifting giants. Apparently, they all came out the back entrance. Dressed in baggy shorts and loose T-shirts, they remind me of . . . bicycle messengers. They all jump in, and the van door closes behind them as the van turns on to Ventura and heads north.

The neatly dressed process server has been watching. He doesn't look disappointed, even though he never got the chance to attack the phalanx. He gets into a nondescript Toyota Camry and calmly drives after the van. Something tells me he will get his man.

Valerie helps me to the passenger seat, and I sink into the new smell of the leather.

The ante has been upped. There will be no limit to what the uptight partners in New York will do to cover their asses on this one.

"At least we don't have to look at his cock anymore," Valerie says.

CHAPTER TWELVE

alerie's Lexus is trapped in the Bruce T. Hinman Memorial Interchange, the concrete bowel where the 101 laces together in arteriosclerotic misery with the 134 and the 170. A poor soul died here trying to help someone, and the best that could be done for him was to bring his name to the attention of millions of motorists each day in precisely the moment when they most want to be somewhere else.

"Did you know Richard had taken over the client?" I ask.

Valerie pauses too long for a yes-or-no answer.

"Come on, Valerie."

"The executive committee sent out an email. I thought you knew."

"It would have been nice if they told me. I'm Joel's best friend."

She changes the subject: "So, the firm is now a defendant?" she says.

"And all its partners. Take me home, Valerie."

She drives on quietly. I realize she has not asked directions. "You know where I live, don't you?"

"Sam, it's nothing sinister. I looked in the firm directory."

We don't say much for a while, I contemplate whether she is on my side, or whether she has already thrown in with the Total Assholes. I decide to give her the benefit of the doubt. I'm missing the girlfriend experience.

"What was that about a document request?" I ask.

"There was no document request."

"Was it your idea to ask about it, or Richard's?" I ask.

"It just came to me," she says.

"Well, now we know," I say.

"Yeah, obviously they'll lie about anything."

"Making it much more likely. . . " I can't quite say the next few words, which will take me farther than I want to go. This client is Joel's last hope for enough money to bail him out from his soon-to-be nasty divorce from Ellie.

"That Oddyssey *is* a complete fraud," Valerie finishes my sentence.

"Let's not get ahead of ourselves," I say. But she is right. And the partners are wrong about this girl. There are some things the bar exam doesn't measure.

"Don't forget to put something about that checkbook in your notes," I tell her. "Carlson was trying to tip us off."

"Do you know anything about Jacky Real?" Valerie asks.

"I'm afraid I do. He's a bad guy. Not as bad as he thinks he is, but bad nevertheless. I had no idea he was involved in Oddyssey."

"Joel didn't tell you?" she asks.

"No."

Valerie cruises north on the 2. We begin to soar towards the mountains, lifting free from the bonds of the traffic. She exits onto Foothill Boulevard, and then finds her way into the mountains above a canyon. She parks halfway onto the dirt on the side of the narrow, irregular asphalt road. A new full-size vehicle like Valerie's would never fit into the ramshackle carport that is my house's face to the world.

As we step inside, Valerie grabs a railing, disoriented as she looks down at the three levels below her.

"It's like you. Everything below the surface."

"First stop, the bar," I say.

We walk down the first flight of stairs to the kitchen.

As we come into the kitchen, we see a note scotch-taped on the cutting-board island in the middle of the room, where dishes and glasses have been piled with incongruous, neat care. In Xanthe's handwriting: *They served a search warrant. Thanks for letting me know, Xan.*

I feel anger at her criticism—how could I know?—but also sympathy for Xanthe dealing with that. She must have been terrified.

"Xan?" I call out.

No answer. In my mind, it has always seemed as though Xanthe came with the house.

We walk into the kitchen. Food is scattered, broken dishes, a few random pots and pans everywhere.

"What happened here?" Valerie says.

"Either the police went berserk, or Xanthe went berserk because I didn't warn her about the police."

"Beautiful kitchen, Sam, but this is some mess."

In the corner of the kitchen, a large jar of Santa Barbara olives lies split open. The olives have rolled out in every direction across the white, marbled linoleum, but four of them sit in a bit of juice collected in a shell of glass at the epicenter. I step over the wreckage and cup the olives in my hands. Still moist. No obvious bits of glass. "How about a martini?" I say.

I do not feel anxious for Valerie to go.

"Sure, Sam, whatever you're having." Two charming *s*'s. I push a hidden button beneath the countertop, and a circular cupboard opens in the corner. Cool mist from the refrigerated space crawls over the olive mess on the floor. As the air inside the freezer clears, frozen bottles of Stoli and Bombay stand revealed. They look like an oasis to me.

"Nice," Valerie noted. "I guess you can afford this type of thing as a partner."

"I'm just your average guy with a large second mortgage."

I get glasses from the cutting-board island and ice from the refrigerator. I want the comfort of the white liquid with foamy ice chips made by a shaker, but I can't assemble the fortitude to properly organize that ritual. So I dump the rescued olives into two glasses with some ice and pour the frozen Bombay. As soon as the glasses are ready, I take a long swig from one, closing my eyes. When I open them, I can already feel the way the gin brings me clarity of thought, an opening through the assembled pains in my head.

"At least they didn't disturb the frozen hard liquor."

"I don't get them investigating you. You were attacked too."

"I was there. They don't know of anyone else who was there. I'm the logical person to roust."

I give Valerie her drink. She sips a little, and winces. She is close to me and moves her other hand to lightly touch my shirt where the rusty-brown color from the blood has crusted over. Her touch feels passive, tender, no longer the aggressive grip of the young lawyer.

"Should you?" she says, looking down at my glass, nearly empty now. "You're still bleeding."

"Yes," I say, as if pronouncing a sentence. I am worried about how close we are. I move away and refill my glass with frozen gin.

"Let's see what they did with the rest of the place," I say, and we descend to the next level.

Each level of the house expands on the footprint of the preceding level. This allows us to look from the entryway all the way to the edge of each succeeding level: kitchen, entertainment room, bedroom, and outdoor terrace. And from the edge of each of the lower floors, we can look up to the entryway.

The third level has the television, the stereo, the more formal bar, the bookshelves and audiovisual library. I look at the shelves of books, tapes, and CDs. Some of the rows look as though they've been disturbed. I am upset that anyone would touch these things—I've been collecting them since high school—but after running my fingers over the lines of books on the shelves, I lead us down to the next level, which has the bedroom and main bathroom.

The mattress is slightly off-center—as if someone has looked under it. Everything in the room seems to be just about an inch off. I feel violated at the thought that every aspect of my life has been inspected in this way. I don't say anything.

Valerie senses my despair. She moves close and puts a hand on my shoulder. Her touch is motherly, comforting. This time, I don't move away from her. For whatever selfish reason, I just can't overcome my deep need for a human being's touch. I reach over and touch her bare shoulder, leaning to hold myself steady. Her black skin is cool, soft, yet I can feel the strength of the bulge in her shoulder muscle.

Valerie takes my hand and arm off her but wraps her own strong arm around my waist and anchors and lifts my arm around her shoulder. I feel the lift, and realize she is both taller and stronger than me. She takes my drink from my hand and walks me into the bathroom. She puts the drink on the sink, and turns on the showerheads, which begin to fill the room with a cleansing steam. She unbuttons my shirt, and gently pulls it off where it has begun to stick to my bandages.

"Let's take these off," she says, peeling away my bandages. I wince as they separate from my skin. She undoes the belt and drops my pants to the floor. She looks behind me.

"The bandage on your leg is soaked through with blood too. Let me try to get it off." She kneels behind me, and I lean against the sink. I drain the glass of gin, swallowing as the bandage comes off.

"You need to do the rest," she says, flexing her eyebrows in the direction of my boxer underwear. "Get the wounds as clean as you can. We'll put on clean bandages."

"There's some under the sink."

She picks up the pants from the floor and folds them. I guess she doesn't need much modesty from me, so I dispense with the boxers and climb in the hot shower.

"Hey, Sam, look at this," says Valerie.

I stick my head out from the shower curtain, and she shows me the business card from Trisha Carlson, which she has retrieved from my pants. She turns it around so I can see the handwriting on the back. In small, neatly printed letters, it reads, *If you want to know what Oddyssey really does—ask your partner.*

"Apparently, Oddyssey is not as happy a place as it seems," Valerie says. I hand the card back to her.

"Apparently they want to point the finger at Joel," I say.

"Sam, you're going to have to let me follow up on this. You have to take a break."

I decide to trust her. "But you have to call me, not Richard, when you get through."

"I will, but we have to get you to bed."

"And the checkbook. Remember the checkbook. If somehow you can get that, you have the key to everything."

"How am I going to get it?"

"I don't know. But you're the associate here. Find a way. That's how you get to make partner."

Valerie's eyelids appear to drop. She moves to leave the room with Trisha Carlson's business card.

"Get me some more gin before you leave," I say.

She returns in a few minutes and puts the glass down on the surface of the tub just outside the shower curtain. "There you go," she says.

"In the drawer," I tell her. "Cigarettes."

Valerie finds the cigarettes. "I shouldn't do this," she notes as she puts the pack and the Bic lighter down on the edge of the bath surface. Then she heads out the door.

There's a little part of the soap dish where you can park a cigarette, and I park it now after a couple of deep inhales. At last my head can clear. I didn't realize how much I missed the clean smoke, the brace of the nicotine. I don't usually bother trying to stand up in the shower. At this point, I couldn't if I wanted to. I sit flat on the floor between the two opposing sprays and let the water roll over me while steam fills the room, sticking my head out of the spray every so often for a sip of the gin.

I stare at my hands. While the hot water comforts the rest of me, it makes my hands ache with pain that penetrates even the lovely, building gin haze. The tension of the last few weeks has activated my psoriasis, wearing away big chunks of my fingers. Blood oozes out of my fingertips. I need my creams and my cloth gloves.

I stay in the shower until the cigarette burns down and the gin is gone.

I come out into the room covered from the waist down in a long bath towel. Valerie has folded the blanket neatly back. Bandages and tape are placed tidily on the bed. She sips her own glass of gin, although it looks like she has also found some tonic.

She throws me a pair of boxer shorts. "Put these on," she says. I go back into the bathroom and do what she says.

"Let me wrap you up." She beckons me to come towards the bed, and she sits in front of me while she places new bandages and tape on each of my wounds.

"I didn't realize Eddie was so involved," she says. "But I guess we shouldn't be surprised by anything. The Kid is just a force. I guess he swept up Eddie in the latest wave." She needs to talk business during the intimate administering care she is giving me.

"Eddie does what Richard says, Valerie—no more, no less."

The girl has put in a solid day's work. She is looking for me to let her off the hook.

"Valerie, I couldn't have done anything today without you. Look, you should go home. The police will undoubtedly be back. Based on what they've done to my house, I'd say they were in a bad mood. You're gonna have to bill some hours tomorrow, and you need some sleep."

"Okay. But you need sleep too."

"I'm feeling fine," I say. I do feel better. "Maybe another gin. . ."

"Stay there; I'll get it for you." After she starts up the stairs, Valerie turns and says, "I reset the answering machine, and put it on the night table. You might want to listen."

I hit the button on the machine. Xanthe's voice.

"Sweetie, if you're getting this message, you know the police came to the house. It was so frightening. I—I just wanted to call you, but after what you said in the hospital the other day, well, I just don't know what . . . I . . . I just don't understand what's going on with you."

Sounds of crying.

"I was just so upset. I'm sorry. I just started throwing things. I don't want to, but I think I better get away for a while. I'm going to take a trip." A flight is announced, drowning out Xanthe's attempt to begin the next sentence. She is in the airport. "Maybe when I get back, well, maybe we can talk." The tape ends. It feels like an abrupt hang-up.

The next message plays. It is time-stamped only a few minutes after the first message. "Hello, Sam, Richard Total. That was quite a stunt you pulled today visiting the Kid. I didn't think you would get out of the hospital so soon. Look, we appreciate what you've done, but we're going to need to take you off the Oddyssey case. I'm in LA. I'm here at the Beverly Wilshire. I need to hear from you."

And then another airport announcement. There is no mistaking that it is the same volume and tone as the previous one.

I look up at Valerie, who is coming down the stairs.

"You knew this too?" I say.

"What do you mean?"

"I mean Total. And my wife."

Through the short pause, I wonder. *Am I so far down that I'm just giving in to the temptation to pound myself fully into the ground?*

Valerie says, "Are you sure? Really? No. No, Sam, I would tell you. I just don't think it's what you're thinking. I don't think your wife is his cup of tea. His MO is girls at work. Young girls."

Xanthe is thirty-four, but I guess that's old to Valerie. And she thinks it's too old for Total. Valerie comes down the stairs and hands me the new glass of gin. One sip tells me she's watered it down with at least half tonic, but I don't complain. I'm starting to like getting looked after.

With my free arm, I reach over and gently balance myself against the notch above Valerie's hip bone. I was losing my balance, but still, I can't believe I'm being this forward. I feel the gin. I just let my hand stay there on her hip for a moment. Her eyes widen.

I put my other hand on her shoulder. I feel her shoulder cap tighten into a rock. She grips the wrist of the arm on her shoulder with the opposite hand.

"Sam," she starts.

"You don't need to say anything," I say, letting my arms drop off. "I understand." And I do. She has only been trying to be nice in a nineties sort of way. In reality, I look like a Ziploc bag of gray ashes in her young eyes. She looks upward to the balcony.

"Go home. I'll talk to you in the morning."

I watch her go up the stairs.

She looks at me from the balcony before turning to go. "You know what? You're different than the others," she says.

"Yeah, yeah."

"And one more thing. If you're really interested in younger women. . . "

"Yeah?"

"You have to stop smoking."

PART THREE: JACKY AND RICHARD

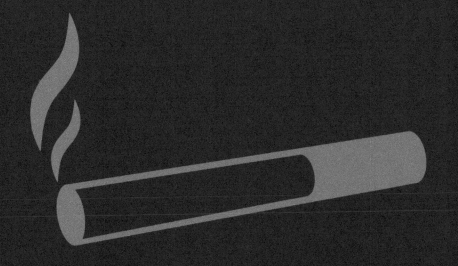

CHAPTER THIRTEEN

My head hurts, but not as much as the pockets of pain where the knife went in and out.

I try to get up. I think it's highly unlikely I will be going anywhere today.

My mattress is low, so I ease myself onto the floor as a first step. I crawl a little of the way, and then pull myself up by leaning on the television console. I am sort of walking now. Incrementally, I get to the bathroom.

There is a little refrigerator here in the bathroom because sometimes it's just too much trouble to go upstairs for something. Opening the door, I see a half gallon of grapefruit juice. I feel I must drink this pink liquid. In the little freezer portion of the refrigerator is a bottle of viscous Bombay Sapphire. My body is telling me I need that too.

Valerie has left a glass down here. *Thoughtful girl.* I pour some of the thick, gluey fluid into a glass. As the frost starts to form, I pour a little down my throat and feel the warmth in my chest. I put in some grapefruit juice and drink the whole glass.

That first glass is making me feel better. Maybe I will get something done today. Drinking in the morning is never a good sign, of course, but this morning I need something to kill the pain, and alcohol is the only thing available. I pour another glass. No grapefruit juice. I look at the clock. It's one in the afternoon. *So much for drinking in the morning.*

And a Kool. As a cloud builds in the room, I can focus. The Kid is obviously some kind of phony. The lawsuits and short sellers might even be right to say that Oddyssey is just a front. But a front for what? And if it's all a fraud, where are they getting all the money to keep up the facade? They threw so many naked bodies at us at Jesus' Gym on Van Nuys that we couldn't get anywhere near the real story.

The thing that really bothers me about the Kid is the way he doesn't seem to care one way or the other about Joel. Joel was responsible for putting the Kid in touch with the Wall Street types who were ready to issue any stock you could describe using the word *internet*. Joel adored the Kid and was working his tail off to make the current public offering a success. Why would the Kid want to take Joel down? Why doesn't he give a shit that someone else has taken him down?

And why would anyone want to take me down? Or was I, as usual, just a bystander, just the guy who happened to be there when he should have been smoking a cigarette in the stairwell?

Richard Total, of course, would like nothing better than to get rid of both Joel and me. He and the New York partners who manage the firm have grown fond of terminating what they view as "unproductive partners." They think of it as a "healthy" thing, like "pruning the deadwood" from a tree. At the very least, it serves as a warning to keep the others working.

Eddie's role? Are he and Valerie getting swept up in this? Are they instruments of Richard or the Kid? Or just bystanders like me, playing their bit parts?

Jacky Real, on the other hand, is a different species. Jacky might really be a killer. He at least likes to give people that impression. Although many say he embellishes his mob status, some of his enemies really die. The Jacky connection makes me worry that Oddyssey's real business might be loan sharking or counterfeiting, which are Jacky's specialties. That would certainly be more likely to make money than running searches for people on the internet.

Once upon a time I had held Jacky Real's counterfeit dollars in my hand. I knew they were really good fakes, but fakes nevertheless.

I was desperate for clients back then. Jacky came up to me after law and motion calendar hearings in one of the civil departments in the Hill Street Courthouse. His lawyer and his lawyer's San Fernando Valley toupee had been humiliated that morning by good old Judge Madrigian. I was next up, and won my motion in a similar case without saying anything but "Good morning, Your Honor" because my papers were the way Madrigian liked them—every local rule followed, every magic form-book phrase invoked, all the citations Bluebook, spelling perfect, punctuation right out of Strunk and White, delivered to him personally in chambers in case the filing clerks lost them. All the clerks hated Madrigian, so his papers were always getting lost. He was always blaming it on the lawyers, always imposing sanctions.

Jacky let his lawyer go and waited for me.

"I thought my problem was the judge," he said to me in the hallway. "But I actually think it might be my lawyer."

"Madrigian seems psychotic, but he's just an older guy who took the time to learn the rules and so he hates sloppiness," I said. "Those of us who went to school in the seventies tend to view rules as optional. But it's a good idea to make an exception for Madrigian."

Jacky invited me to Carmine's that night, and I started doing some easy collection cases for him. Carmine's was Jacky's favorite Italian place on Ventura Blvd. We had martinis. He always paid for dinner, and we always had something with Carmine's fabulous red sauce accompanied by Sonoma red wines that never ended. Jacky was not a snob. He picked wines with animals in their names: frogs, horses, bears, etc. I remember them as wines that never gave you a hangover. Jacky seemed to know a deep secret about everybody in town and could tell you hilarious stories about their surprising sexual preferences.

I knew the rumors about Jacky's counterfeiting, but I ignored them because the work was good. It was easy, steady work that helped pay the overhead in the little office Joel and I ran. For about six months, Jacky paid me by check and on time. I collected more than a million for him from the losers who owed him money. What was this I had heard about him being a loan shark? His interest rates were high, but only 20 or 30 percent more than most credit cards. He seemed very reasonable about reaching settlements. One of the defendants claimed that Jacky had given him some phony cash, but that guy was a deadbeat and a liar, and I didn't give any credence to it.

Then my bill for legal services started to mount up. I didn't like to bring up billing with clients, but when it got over $100,000 I had to mention it to him.

"Look, Jacky, we have a small office. I need to pay my staff."

"Sam, Sam, why would you worry? I'm a little short right now and I'm waiting for you to collect some more. Don't you have some other clients who can pay your bills this month?"

"I do have other clients, but most of them are contingent fees. And I have a few who are behind. Like you."

"Why don't you just sue them?"

"Jacky, I don't sue clients."

"Shouldn't of told me that, Counselor."

Next time we met at Carmine's it seemed like everything was okay. I had recovered enough new money for him to pay my bills. He told me to wire it to his bank, and he would give me cash for my fees. I trusted him and sent the wire. I don't know why, but coming from the Midwest I trusted a lot of people in those days. After the wine that night, he pushed over a big brown paper bag. I remember it was a grocery bag, from Ralphs. It was full of cash, twenties and fifties.

"This should take care of it," he said.

I gave one of the bills to a friend of mine at the US Attorney's Office. When he came back to me, he wanted to know where I got it. I told him I couldn't tell. He said he would keep it. He also told me the FBI would be watching me to see if I had any more.

I decided to see Jacky at his office because I didn't want him to dissuade me with a lot of alcohol and not-so-funny stories about who in City Hall was light in the loafers, or with Carmine's fabulous red sauce. I had something serious to say.

Jacky's office was a penthouse suite in Westwood. It was filled to the brim with a lot of art that looked like it had been stolen from Europe during World War II. I said hello to the old man who always seemed to be on the couch in the waiting room. I brought the bag from Ralphs and put it on his desk.

"What's this?" he said.

"This is me giving you back your grocery bag so I don't get arrested next time I buy groceries."

"It's good stuff, Counselor. No one ever gets arrested for it. Just mix it up with your other money."

"I counted it. It's twice what you owe me."

"It's a bonus. You do good work. Besides, I made you wait. You earned some vig on this one. You're going to learn to like how it feels to have more than you deserve. It's a good feeling. A feeling like you have a real place in the world, a safe place, above the deadbeats and losers. After a while, it feels like you deserve it."

"Jacky, you hired me because I am a real lawyer. Because I have real hair and real legal arguments. You can't pay a real lawyer with fake money."

"So sue me."

I rose up in anger out of my chair.

"Early, can you take Mr. Straight out?"

Turning around, I braced for Jacky's hit man. I had been expecting something bulky and brutal, but Early was the skinny seventy-year-old man I had seen sitting on the couch in the lobby. He was straightened up, and I saw that his wiry brown arms were hard with muscle. His small eyes had been burned gray by the desert sun. He looked sad. He pulled back his suit coat, and I saw a large revolver stuck in his belt—one of those belts with a Western pattern in the leather and a big silver buckle with turquoise stones. He seemed like he might be a nice old man when he was with his grandchildren, but he did not seem of a mind to hesitate to do whatever Jacky asked of him.

I walked out the door with Early.

"I guess I should say thanks for not hurting me."

"It was your choice. You were smart enough to understand. You don't have to be a monster to kill. All it really takes is knowing how to use a weapon and being willing to use it."

Early and I had a nice chat about his grandchildren in the elevator.

Jacky and I have not talked since that day in his office when I returned the grocery bag of fake lettuce. There was a rumor about Jacky and the Kid, but Joel told me there was nothing to it. Based on my meeting with the Kid, I no longer believe that.

The evening comes on, and there is a beauty in the way the sunlight dances in the smog. The sun is going down, but I feel a rising resolve to do something about this mess. My best friend is on the verge of death. The police think I might be the problem with an internet company whose CEO is a Bible-spouting teenage sex maniac. Nobody has even thought of looking up Jacky, a guy who practically takes out ads to make people think he is a bad dude. I decide not to be just another nineties wimp. I decide to go see Jacky and get to the bottom of this. I know exactly where to find him.

CHAPTER FOURTEEN

This 1984 Nissan Pickup truck I drive to Westwood is about what I had when I married Xanthe, and it will be about what I have when I get through the divorce from Xanthe.

Driving and drinking, but just enough to roll through the pain. Moving around Los Angeles isn't really driving anyway. You just become a tiny molecule entering the bloodstream of a giant, ugly, unhealthy beast. The beast has a very sluggish bloodstream, so all you do is keep a short distance from the other molecules, especially trying not to get close to any of the ones that seem like viruses. This is especially true when going down the 405 to Westwood. Carmine's is just across the street from Jacky's office, just a little out of the bustle, on a side street heading towards the UCLA campus.

Jacky is at his booth in the corner. He has only a few wisps of hair remaining on the back of his head as he faces the kindly old gentleman sitting with him. Early's eyes level at me the instant I enter the back room. Jacky's head disappears. Watchful old Early.

Jacky's head pops up. He moves very slowly and unsteadily out of his booth. He has aged frightfully. I happen to know he is still in his fifties, but he looks older than Early, who is still the wiry tough guy.

"Counselor. Excuse the ducking. Early kicked me under the table. You wouldn't believe how many misguided people have decided to go after me these days." His eyes are bloodshot, and don't seem to focus on me. They dart around the room as if they are trying to find a reference point for his balance. Early stands and frisks me, very gently, but very efficiently. He pulls the pen out of my inner pocket and shows it to Jacky.

"I thought we should talk," I say.

"By all means, have a seat," says Jacky, and he sits down with a relief that makes clear it was a great deal of effort for him to get up and look around. The waiter has come over. They are very attentive here.

"Two martinis. The counselor here likes our usual way," says Jacky to the waiter, and then, back to me: "You really look like you could use it."

I decide not to comment on his appearance. It doesn't seem wise. But he does it for me.

"I know. Two fucking heart attacks. Diabetes, the usual. But I'm not giving up these," he says, taking a deep sip of a martini. "And I'm not giving up Carmine's red sauce. Bring us a couple bowls of the linguini with the sausages, Daryl."

I can taste the red sauce already. It's been days since I've had a good meal, so I don't protest. I nod to Early.

"Early, I don't remember you eating dinner with Jacky in the old days."

"None of my friends will be seen with me anymore," Jacky says. "Damn US attorneys. Always coming up with some bullshit. And it's so damn easy for them. Anything anybody says on the telephone can be called wire fraud if you look at it with a suspicious mind. You know what it's like. People think you're somebody when you ain't anybody at all."

"I always thought you were somebody, Jacky."

"Yes, Counselor, I remember. So naïve, so trusting. How's that working out for you?"

"I guess you heard." I look down and see that brown ooze has begun to come through my shirt. Time is running out. I decide to come to the point: "You have anything to do with what happened to Joel and me?"

"Counselor, do I look like I could run around stabbing people in the middle of the night?"

I looked from Jacky to Early. Even Early doesn't look like he would run around stabbing people in the middle of the night. That kind of unnecessary expenditure of energy is beneath his stature. He would screw on a silencer and shoot someone cleanly and quietly and dispose of the weapon permanently.

"No one ever said you were an up-close-and-personal kind of guy," I say, acknowledging how Jacky prefers his alleged godfather status.

"How's that martini?"

"Still the best. I really appreciate the sidecar. No one does that anymore."

"That's the thing about Carmine's. It never changes. They'd rather go out of business. And they might," he says, looking at the empty tables.

I consider all the plaster Roman columns and think about the fall of Rome.

"What are you doing with Oddyssey, Jacky?"

"That Kid's a good kid. Clean, no drugs. Can't I help out a nice young man in my old age?"

"It's a company my partner is trying to take public. The last thing they need is to be tied up with you."

"I can be discreet. See, you didn't even know. And he's your partner."

"So you had Joel stabbed because he told you to stay away."

"You are more naïve than I thought, Counselor. Who do you think pays for that silly operation? All the phones and the weight lifting? How do you think they keep going when they don't make any money?"

"You're saying you're still in?"

"That's just what I always liked about you, Counselor. You believe in people. You believe they are good. Your belief is so strong you can make judges and juries believe your client is good. I want you to come back and work for me. I've got plenty of work. I'm going to need someone to make a jury believe in me next month, make them believe that I'm just a good guy. Like you." Jacky is facing another wire fraud trial.

I might need work if I have to get our old firm started again. Maybe I can make him pay what he owes me—in real money this time. That would sure help us get started.

He seems to know what I'm thinking. "I can pay you a retainer right now. Early, can you pay the man? Do you have a shopping bag or so for him?"

Early is almost out of his seat to get the shopping bag.

"Answer the question, Jacky."

"Not only good, but persistent too. Devoted to your friend, dogged in your pursuit of the truth. It's all very beautiful, very admirable, very fucking nice. Look, Counselor, I'm sorry to be the one to tell you the world isn't so nice. Of course, if it was, guys like you would have nothing to do. As it is, you can make a good living explaining guys like me to saps like you who still want to believe in the goodness of people."

"I don't want your money, Jacky. Or whatever it is."

"Ah, Joel. Your friend, your partner. He isn't half the lawyer you are. You should know that because you've been carrying him around all these years. But he does know the way the world works. He does know how to be realistic. He does know what needs to be done. The Kid was out of money and somebody needed to do something."

"What are you saying?"

"I'm saying Joel didn't take me out of this deal, Counselor. He brought me in. I'm in, and I'm staying in. If I don't stay in, then nobody is going to get paid because there isn't going to be any fucking public offering."

"So it was you." I wish I wasn't so nice. I wish I had a gun.

"No, it wasn't me, Counselor. Joel is a cipher, a useless piece of crap if you don't know what that means, but Joel brought me to the deal, and I have honor, my friend. That's why I have friends. I've always liked you. As a courtesy to you, I wouldn't touch him."

"You're lying."

"Okay, Counselor. I'm lying. You would know, of course. You attorneys really get me. There's always truth and lies with you. Truth and lies aren't really important to the rest of us. We know there isn't much difference between the two. You ought to try looking at it that way. It also might do you good to let go of that loser."

The waiter brings the linguine. My appetite is gone, though, and I get up.

"Counselor. You look like a starving child in those charity ads. You need to eat." He waves at the waiter to come close to him, and he whispers something. Then he looks back at me. And there it is, growing in the middle of the pockmarks and the red eyes and the bursting blood vessels on the bulbous nose: a grand and growing laugh. It grows until his great belly shakes.

I turn to leave.

"Be careful, Counselor." Jacky's voice sounds almost paternal through his laughter. "There's somebody who wants to cut down on the number of payees in this deal. And to me you look like the one to take out next."

"I don't want anything from this deal, Jacky. And neither does Joel."

"I'm not so sure you speak for him anymore, Counselor."

Outside, as I wait for the valet to bring up my truck, Daryl the waiter approaches and gives me a box filled with warm linguine.

"He said not to be mad," Daryl says. "He really likes you." I notice that Daryl has a nice manner. Like he has been through the striving and the myths of this town and has learned that most of us are always going to wait on other people. So at least we should get a tip for doing it.

"Sorry, I don't have anything for you," I say.

"Jacky takes care of me," he says with compassion.

I look down the street and see a couple of young men waiting outside a dirty white van. One of them seems to be holding a camera. When they see me looking their way, they turn quickly and get in the big sliding door of the van—hair clacking.

CHAPTER FIFTEEN

The house is dark. Still no sign of Xanthe. I pour myself a couple inches of frozen Bombay in the kitchen and take it downstairs. I sit on the floor, turn on the television, and light me a Kool.

An elegantly dressed woman of Chinese descent articulates the end of the 11 p.m. news. Her hair is so spectacular, and so strangely curly, that I cannot focus on her face.

"This just in: Reputed mobster Jacky Real and his assistant, Early Watkins, were brutally murdered outside Carmine's restaurant in Westwood late tonight. Police are not saying how the murder occurred, but they were alerted to the bodies in the parking lot by a waiter who had gone out for a smoking break. Carmine's, a famous watering hole for Hollywood agents in the forties, has been reported to be close to bankruptcy in recent days."

There is some rough footage of Carmine's in better days. There hasn't been time yet to get a Breaking News reporter to the scene.

"This may be the end of Carmine's," says the man sitting next to the curly-haired woman. His hair is also a thing of beauty, folding over in a crisp blond wave, breaking in a tunnel you could surf through. "The linguini with clam sauce was always something there. I'm sure we'll be hearing more on that story, Annie."

"I'm sure we will, Ron. How did the Lakers do tonight, Ricky?"

Ricky, the sports reporter, has been leaning against the news table. He has wide, hopeful eyes that tell me the Lakers have won before he says a word. I turn off the television.

Somebody got the drop on Early? It would have to be more than one guy. I think of the dreadlocks by the van down the street. Could Oddyssey and its weight-lifting teenagers really be a deadlier force than Jacky? And what about Joel? He doesn't have a piece of the deal to my knowledge, but he has knowledge. Will somebody try taking him out again? What about me?

———

The phone rings next to my bed. I let it go to voicemail and listen.

"Sam, this is Rosa. My recollection is you think cell phones are silly, so I'm assuming you don't have one yet. I'm just going to leave the message here and hope you get it. I understand why you had to leave the hospital, but you should have told me first, honey. . ."

I decide to pick up. Dr. Rosa has known me for two decades. She has been through all the different ways my body has coped with the defeats of life in LA. She knows my history with Joel. Joel even went to her for a while. But he stopped when she suggested a prostate exam. That's what he says. Dr. Rosa says she told him to stop drinking.

"Rosa. It's me."

"Oh, Sam."

"Tell me about Joel."

"Well, he nearly died, but they saved him. His wife, Ellen I think is her name, had a do not resuscitate, but they brought him back anyway.

They couldn't find the paperwork. I'm thinking you had something to do with that?"

"Maybe I did."

"I took out the breathing tube a couple days ago. It's funny, but he still is acting like he can't talk. He's going to be okay, Sam."

"Watch out for him, will you?"

"I'll do my best, but they already told me a couple times that he's not my patient. And, Sam?"

"Dr. Rosa?"

"You know I'm doing this for you, don't you?"

"Have the police interviewed him?"

"Not yet. We've kept the cops away for now because of the breathing tube. They'll be back tomorrow. Same two geniuses."

"Keep checking on him, if you can. These people, whoever they are, aren't just trying to scare people anymore. They killed two pretty tough guys tonight. And they may be coming after Joel."

"Those Mafia guys in Westwood had something to do with Oddyssey?"

"According to them, Joel brought them into the deal."

"Why would a legitimate deal need guys like that?"

"It's starting to look not so legitimate, Rosa."

"Well, then, it's time for you to go to the cops."

"Going to the cops at this point would probably tie me up, maybe result in charges. There's a waiter who can place me with those guys right before they died. You saw what passes for case analysis at the LAPD. They think I had something to do with Joel as it is."

"Listen, Sam, they ran some blood work on you while you were here, and the liver numbers were really scary. You still look pretty good—good genes, I guess—but Jesus Christ, how much are you drinking?"

"Just enough. You know me."

"Well, look, if people are trying to kill you, you're going to need your wits about you. I can get you some help. I can get you in a place where it will be tough to find you. A place with security."

"I need to figure this thing out, Rosa. After that we can talk. You're wrong about me, though. It's just been a bit tough lately."

"I'd say. I'd further say that is what they all say."

"Will you watch out for Joel?"

"It's you I'm worried about. It seems Joel has already made his deal with the devil."

"Jacky Real did tell me that, but he also told me he can't tell the truth from a lie."

"You know what I think? You've been carrying Joel too long. From what I can tell, it's not doing him any good. And I'm especially worried that you're starting to drink like he does."

"Did you ever think he could do something . . . well, you know, something criminal?"

"He's been desperate for a while, Sam. You know that. Desperate people are capable of anything. The whole time I've known you, you've been obsessed with him, protecting him, supporting him, worrying about him. Both of your wives have tried to tell you he's a loser. I've tried to tell you. You can't help him anymore. You've got to save yourself."

"Rosa, I owe him my life."

"Well, from what I saw at County, you just paid him back."

"Please watch out for him. He's like a brother to me."

"Like I say, I'll do it for you, Sam, but really, it's time for you to take care of yourself."

We hang up.

I realize I haven't eaten anything for a while. I go upstairs. The Styrofoam takeaway box from Carmine's is there with the last linguini Jacky will ever buy me. The thought of eating it is ghoulish, and I toss it: "Rest in peace, Early," I say.

I still need to eat something, so I open a bottle of red wine and take out some cheese and crackers and fruit. Eating makes me feel better, but I feel that something is terribly wrong.

I bring the end of the bottle out on the balcony, and finish it looking up at the meaningless, gray Los Angeles sky. I remember a Michigan sky that was filled with stars the night that Joel saved my life. It was at least twenty years ago.

CHAPTER SIXTEEN

We stumble against each other on the way out the door of the bar. The beer has given me the courage to ask Wendy to ride home with me on the roof of Joel Green's Volkswagen Squareback. It feels like the only possible decision one can make in a moment like this. Joel is, I tell her, an excellent driver. She says she thinks so too.

As the roof begins to move beneath us, the immediate feeling is of rising, as if the roof is carrying us like a magic carpet from the parking lot of this cheap Upper Peninsula bar into the lights of the dark Michigan sky. Our hands tightly grip the luggage rack. Our toes wedge under the front bar for stability.

The wind dries our eyes as the car begins to speed through the woods on the dark two-lane road. The metal rails of the rack feel light, hollow inside. My right hand rubs slightly against Wendy's left hand on the back rail; I think of the wonder of holding her hand.

I stare at her long, straight brown hair as it flaps across her face like palm leaves in a hurricane. We pick up even more speed, and her hair strings out behind her in the wind. The car lurches around a corner, and we can see the long line of tall pines ahead. Instead of rising into the sky, we are being sucked into what feels like a river of air. Pine branches blur in the corners of our eyes. Our weight makes the luggage rack groan against the loose screw at the right rear corner just behind us.

"Pretty cool, huh," I say.

"I can't believe you guys do this," she says. There is wonder in her voice. It feels like adrenaline to me.

"Every night," I say.

Our shoulders brush. *This must be when*, I think. I lean over and Wendy looks surprised, but I keep leaning and our lips touch. Then Joel lurches the car to the left, and her head turns away. We say nothing. I look out at the rushing trees on my left side.

Joel brings the VW to a smooth stop, our feet jamming against the front of the rack, which groans another protest. For the briefest moment we surge forward, and then we settle back. Safe landing. I used to wonder whether I'd keep flying forward, but Joel is good at this.

Below us, Joel and Ellie leap out of the front seat. Wendy untangles her long legs from the luggage rack. I watch them unfold, smooth beneath loose khaki shorts. She jumps down feet first from the roof of the car without looking in my direction.

Ellie and Wendy hug and laugh. Ellie's head barely makes it up to Wendy's chin. Ellie is small and plump, with short, curly blond hair that makes her seem more like a boy to me. I don't like Ellie because she treats Joel like shit and seems to be encouraging Wendy to do the same to me. It doesn't appear to faze him, but it bothers me alright.

"We will see you guys tomorrow," Ellie says with a grand finality, as if she is saying something brilliant instead of something that breaks the part of my heart that never wants to be apart from Wendy ever again. She and Wendy lock arms, and go running into their cabin, giggling about an inside joke.

I look at Joel. With impressive nonchalance, his powerful arm sweeps forward broadly, and then up to his mouth to remove his Kool. I wonder why he smokes menthols, but it's just one more thing about which he is supremely indifferent. He really doesn't care what people think of him. There is something about this nonchalance that makes men and women both want to be near him. He blows out an impressive cloud of smoke. "I think we need to go to the beach," he says, and jumps back in the car.

"Did I really drink a whole pitcher?" I say.

"Two."

"That would explain the way I'm starting to feel." Using a complete sentence makes me feel brilliant.

We are on the beach now, and what I felt in the car is getting worse. I'm in some sort of danger. My brain feels detached from my eyes and rolls in the opposite direction from where I look. My feet lurch under me. I look out at the sky over the lake. There are no cabins at this lake, no lights at all, and in this dark northern sky I see more stars than I have ever seen in my life. The lake water rolls only a bit, its long, flat surface reflecting the light of the stars.

No woman will ever want you, says the voice in my head.

Joel lights another Kool as he looks out over the lake. He seems calm and contented.

"You know what, I just don't care anymore," I say.

"Take it easy," Joel says.

"You realize I've never been laid?"

"You realize you're sixteen?" Joel says.

Joel takes another puff and rolls up the pack under his sleeve like they do in the movies. His cleanly shaven face is soft and as shiny as the water on the lake, rounded like Marlon Brando's. He's nineteen, but his hairline already recedes, and the last line of hair curls over on his forehead in the style of a Roman emperor. Whether there will be one more or one less woman tonight is a matter of no concern to him. I imagine he has had so many women he has lost count.

I kick off my Converses. The laces have been untied for a while. No socks. I take off my shirt. And my pants. I leave on my underwear.

"Sam?" Joel says. I don't answer. I run into the water. It was hard to stand up on the beach, but now, in the water, my body has balance and grace. My elbows lift high to each side of my head as I stroke cleanly out to the center of the lake. The alcohol feels like fuel in my blood, firing my arms like pistons in a combustion engine. My kick, which has never been strong in my high school races, discharges powerfully, the strokes long and deep in the dark liquid. The weight of the water seems light at first, my legs thunking hard behind me in a surging rhythm, whipping it into the air. My head lifts, and I suck in the night air. I see my old swim coach crooking his arms to show me how to get leverage. *I don't need to breathe*, I think, so I stop breathing, and focus only on the churning of my arms below me.

I lose all sense of direction and the shoreline of the lake. I stop caring about moving and hang on the surface, looking down. Even in the darkness, I see something swimming upward from the bottom of the lake. It's Wendy, I am sure of it. I don't question why she is here. She laughs and motions me to follow her down into the depths of the lake. Everything gets darker.

Somewhere in my chest I feel a burning, and realize I need to breathe. I look up, but I cannot figure out which way is up. It is so dark I cannot see Wendy anymore. I can't see anything anymore. The water is still. I am still. I stare at my right arm, studying its stillness with interest. It is better that way, just hanging uselessly in the water.

Strong hands slam into my armpits from behind. The water is moving again. My chest hurts, but I have forgotten how to breathe.

My hand rises from the water. The whole weight of a man pins it to a wood surface. There is a surge of water as Joel rises out of the lake beside me. I am lifted up out of the water as he pulls me from above, landing me awkwardly on my hip bone. Splinters from the surface of the boat deck pierce the skin on my side. Joel's mouth around mine. Disgust and gasping. The beer belches back out of me, putrid, burning.

Joel brought out the pontoon boat to rescue me, and we lie on its long, flat deck, gazing up at the sky, beached and drying. I smell the smoke of Joel's next Kool. The breathing comes easy now.

"Looks like you're going to be okay. I need to burn off some alcohol too," Joel says, and dives in. He heads straight out into the night lake, but then turns his graceful butterfly stroke towards the side, rising up and plunging down with the form that took him to the Florida state finals in the 100 IM last year. He swims with the grace of a porpoise in a neat circle around the boat.

The stars turn liquid, and flash across the sky in waves.

He finishes his circle around the pontoon and vaults up onto the surface of the boat.

"What is that?"

"Northern Lights," Joel says.

"Never seen them," I say. "Thought I was just drunk."

"Well, you are drunk, no question, but that's probably just making the lights a little more amazing."

"Jesus, you have bad breath," I say.

"No beautiful women with fresh breath were available to revive you tonight," he says.

"That's what they say in jail," I say.

"I've come to believe that women are a bit lacking in usefulness in moments of crisis anyway," Joel says.

We watch the lights dance across the sky for what seems like a long time. No words seem appropriate.

"You scare me," he says after a pause. "But I always wanted a brother. Never had one, but now I think you are it. So stop trying to kill yourself, Sam. It's getting exhausting."

The smoke floats over his broad, wet shoulders. I decide to smoke Kools from now on.

CHAPTER SEVENTEEN

From the moment Joel saved my life on the lake that night, I have tried to be like him. Where he went, I went. I went to law school because he did. He never had the aptitude for the material and didn't make law review. I helped him through it.

While I had shown a willingness to part from women who dragged me down, he stuck with Ellie, who spent every dime he made and teased every inch of his self-respect out of him until his powerful body was surrounded by fat.

I continued to model myself after Joel, but it was the Joel smoking his Kool on that pontoon boat, not the Joel I saw deteriorate before me for the next twenty years as I compensated for his inadequacy as a lawyer.

I bring in the end of the wine from the balcony and notice that the message light is still blinking on the phone.

There is another message. In fact, there are two fresh messages from Holly, the latest young paralegal to fall under the spell of Richard Total. These buttoned-down ingénues usually end up sleeping with him. They eventually go to law school to escape him. Total counts the development of these paralegals into freshly minted new women lawyers as one of his great qualities.

Holly's last message seems insistent: "Mr. Total insists that you come by the office at ten tomorrow." There is also some crap about the executive committee and a reference to some obscure provision in the partnership agreement to the effect that failure to provide assistance to the executive committee on request is now a ground for "separation" from the partnership.

Holly is obviously reading from something. I have never heard of the provisions of the partnership agreement she is discussing. Richard is going to terminate me; that's clear. Why not just have a letter delivered? I guess he wants the pleasure of humiliating me in person. That's the way things are at C&C these days. That's Richard.

I turn on the financial news channel to make myself feel like it's a normal day.

And there I see Richard and the Kid.

They are in the setting of a classic LA lawyer's news conference: multiple microphones at the table in the firm's interior conference room, surrounded by neatly stacked legal books, the force of law and law firm behind them.

The Kid is dressed in a suit that fits sleekly over his broad, muscular shoulders. His pectoral muscles burst beautifully from the front of it, creating a valley for his red tie of truth. For once he is silent, looking admiringly at Richard. Richard does the talking.

"A law enforcement contact to our firm just last night alerted the firm's management of a possible past relationship between two of our law firm's partners and Jacky Real, the reputed racketeer who died last night in Westwood. As the result of our internal investigation, which proceeded promptly under my direction, we have learned that two partners of the firm, Sam Straight and Joel Green, did indeed have a previous relationship with Mr. Real. I want to emphasize that this relationship was not previously disclosed to the firm by Mr. Straight and Mr. Green, who have only been partners at the firm for the last three years. We believe that it was this relationship with Mr. Real that led to the attack on our firm's offices and on Mr. Straight and Mr. Green last week. While we are sympathetic to their injuries, it now appears that both gentlemen will recover, and so we have taken prompt action to suspend them from the firm's legal work as the investigation proceeds."

The Kid picks up on his cue: "Well, I just want to say how impressed I am with Richard and Cohen & Cranston and at how they reacted so properly and quickly to the situation. I have every confidence in them, and their guidance as we go forward to market next week. In a way, our lawyers have shown just what Oddyssey is: Not just answers, action." The total energy of the Kid's muscles musters behind his repetition of the slogan.

The camera switches back to Richard: "We now have every confidence that next week's offering will proceed as scheduled, and that the baseless securities lawsuits that have been filed will be dismissed promptly. Otherwise we will move to dismiss them and seek sanctions under Rule 11 of the Federal Rules of Civil Procedure."

The camera cuts away to a fusty financial reporter, who states, "The markets have generally been satisfied with the resolution of the investigation made by Oddyssey's law firm. Although the price of the new offering has been adjusted from $24 to $20, the offering is still set for the same opening bell. Oddyssey's share price has actually gone up to $22 today, from the low of $16. It opened down six points this morning after speculation ran rampant on the news of Jacky Real's murder. But it looks like the Kid and his new lawyer have really brought order back to the situation."

In one short press conference, Richard has shown a remarkable panoply of the dark arts that have made him the darling of the firm's major clients. First, there was the careful iteration of small truths in support of a larger lie: that there was no connection between Jacky and

Oddyssey. He took responsibility for an "investigation," thus focusing the audience on the apparent integrity of a well-dressed, well-spoken lawyer, and taking the focus off the client's utter lack of integrity. He created the false impression that information was new to him because it had been stated by the authorities last night. There was the accusation of incidental wrongs leveled against innocent third parties, who just happened to be Joel and me, shifting the focus from the client's own wrongdoing. All of it was pulled off with the overwhelming confidence that jurors often mistake for candor and followed with the flourish of a threat against those who were foolish enough to disbelieve. I feel nauseous.

The Kid is a criminal. He needs Lucifer for his lawyer.

I go upstairs to the Sub-Zero refrigerator that Xanthe installed with my credit card and get the two beers I keep there to clear my head. I still drink Miller High Life in the clear bottles. The old men in that Michigan bar we drank in kept saying those bottles were bad for the beer, and I was stupid to drink that sissy beer, but Miller High Life is the beer Joel and I drank anyway. You cannot underestimate the wonder of a cold beer sweating in a cool dark room on a muggy summer afternoon when you are sixteen years old, or the comfort it gives to the wounded inadequacy of the teenage soul.

The Miller is good. It seems to reactivate the clearest thinking parts of my brain. Most of my best thinking is done in the shower at night with a beer on the ledge and the Kool resting in the soap dish. I take the next Miller into the shower, sit down, and let the water rush over me as I think, watching the sweat form on the beer bottle. The glass of the bottle settles the uneasiness of the psoriasis on my hand.

When I come out of the shower, things seem more certain to me.

I am not ready to part ways with Joel.

I just can't believe Joel would be so stupid as to get involved with Jacky. I told him many times of Jacky's perfidy, and why I had to walk away from the $100,000 or so that Jacky owed us. Maybe Joel went behind my back, but it was only for some short-term financing. He can't really be in on the whole enterprise, the sleaziness that lies at the heart of Oddyssey. Sure, Jacky Real claimed that Joel is at the heart of the cancer in Oddyssey, but the fact that Jacky was killed an hour later makes him a less than authoritative source.

I've been married twice, so I'm used to thinking of myself as a unit with another human, but with my marriages that feeling only really lasted a month or so. After that I looked at every door wondering if I could just go through it alone, and not bring the woman with me. Most days the answer was yes, and when it was yes every day, the only question became when and how I would be leaving. It's been like that with Xanthe. For a while. I'm getting to the point where I blame myself rather than the women who try to get to know me.

Joel is different. I think of him as a part of me. When he started drinking too much, so did I. I don't want to be something that he is not. Even after we joined the firm, I've always thought of us by the name of our little law firm: Green and Straight.

I need to rescue both of us. We will be Green and Straight again. We'll get a little office in Tujunga, or someplace where we hardly need to pay any rent at all. We'll take contingency fees and start helping real people. Xanthe can have half of whatever I make doing that.

The Millers make it all feel like a plan that will work.

But I am not going to walk away. I'm going to put that Kid in jail where he belongs. The cops will bring me in eventually. When they do, I want to know enough to bring down Oddyssey for good.

Knowing that I will not be cutting Joel out of my life, I feel better about whatever Total wants to do to us.

CHAPTER EIGHTEEN

In Los Angeles, when you call a cab, the switchboard you reach doesn't always take you seriously, and this day would be no different. After about half an hour, I pour myself an inch of frozen Stoli. And call again.

This time, he does arrive. I can tell immediately that the driver is from the most feared of the cab-driving species: the talker. Swarthy, sweaty, and earnest.

"I am Ali," he says. I don't introduce myself.

He drives down the hill towards downtown, but he keeps looking back at me. He closes the windows. The hair on the back of his head is short and straight, black mixed with a little gray, flowing like a boundless lawn into the longer, more curly hairs of his back, which sprout up through his ribbed tank-top T-shirt. Ali is bouncing in his seat. Bouncing while driving is apparently hard work, and the smell of his sweat seems to emanate from the upholstery of the backseat, indeed from every surface in the vehicle.

Thinking I will regret this, I venture, "You okay?"

"I am good always," he says.

I congratulate myself for failing to open conversation. I open my briefcase and pretend to read. I am hoping to close my eyes when he says, "You like read."

"Sometimes. I don't like a lot of what I read."

"After a few minutes I get tired as I do not understand most of the words. I must stop."

"I'm a lawyer. Sometimes I have to keep reading."

"Oh, that is a good job, easy job. In my country, I wanted to be lawyer, but here I do not, what do you say, qualify. I drive cab. I like taxi better than lawyer. Taxi is job God want for me in America. If a man just does the job as God want, it is easy for him. For you, lawyer is easy job, I think?"

"Most days I don't find it easy. Today it is not easy."

"Then, my friend, you are not to be lawyer. God make job for each person. If he make people hungry, he make persons to feed them. If he make people lost, he make others find them, and others lead where they should go. Perhaps I take you where you should go, and if so, it is God who says so."

He realizes I have nothing to say to that. He says, "Maybe you drive cab too. With me."

"I might like that," I say. "But I don't think my wife would appreciate it. Or my ex-wife."

Ali ignores this. Apparently, the opinion of mere women does not matter enough to be a point of inquiry in the conversation. But I have not stopped him, only given him time to inhale.

"Only God decide such things. Only God say your meaning. Man cannot decide what man should do. For God choose you lawyer mean you read better than another. It is written. The seed from a sacred man's pen is the holy word of God, that this must be so. As lawyer, you must apply the rules to the people, so you must be more than others. Only God makes choice. God chooses the rulers. No one will ever choose someone to be better than he is. So God make choice. A ruler needs people and people must have ruler, but only for God to make choice."

"In this country, the people choose the rulers."

For Ali, this must represent another irrelevant point, because he does not address it. He cannot be derailed by the silliness of mere American culture.

"Ah, so you believe. The rulers and the lawyers, they are only second level. The higher level is the prophets. It is the prophets who bring the rules themselves from God. The prophets are like your Jesus. It is for God to make the rules, and it is for prophets to tell us the rules. It is for rulers and lawyers—they are only enforcing the rules."

"I don't believe in God, Ali."

"You will see, my friend, it is the only way. You will see. It is already written."

Religious people never say anything just once. It's like those guys on television in the expensive suits, with the gold posts in their collars. They pay for a half an hour of airtime, and by God, they're going to fill it no matter how many times they need to say "In Jesus' name we proclaim. . ."

I am not surprised by Ali's religious cant. Nor am I surprised by the way the Kid is using religion. LA has always rivaled the Middle East for breeding misuses of existing religions, as well as new and unprecedented religious faiths.

We are near our destination at the Library Tower. Whether I believe in him or not, I am ready to thank God for making this cab ride end. As we come around the corner, I see C&C's name marked on the wall of the first floor of the tower, just above the fading name of a now-dissolved law firm. Even through the numbness from the Stoli I had going out the door, a feeling grows that there is something wrong. Looking to the front of the cab, I realize there is no meter. There is no identification card or license. How did I miss that? How did I let this happen?

We are only a block away from the front door, so I decide not to ask him the source of his infinite knowledge. I figure it is the religious tract of another of LA's tiny screwball religions. If I ask, there will be a daily delegation at my door trying to explain it to me and to make me buy a thousand copies for my friends. I ask a smaller question.

"Are you a prophet?"

"I have small prophecy for you, my friend. I am prophet only in small way. I, I tell you this. Your friend is meant to die. His time . . . it is coming. You must accept it is now his time. Or you will fall with him."

We are in front of the Library Tower. I open the cab door the second he stops talking. With my feet on the ground outside, I lean back and ask, "Who are you?"

"I am just Ali. But I bring a message from Kid. Let me drive you home, Mr. Straight. Leave Kid alone."

"You tell the Kid, tell him I'm going to stop him. And tell him to stay the fuck away from Joel."

I slam the door and don't look back. I get just inside the door of the tower and think to get his license plate. But Ali and his cab are gone.

Maybe Ali is right. That damn Kid is everywhere.

Of course, I'm not in the habit of doing the prudent thing.

CHAPTER NINETEEN

When I get off the elevator, Sandra, the permanently aspiring actress who doubles as our receptionist, motions me with an elegant wave, bending her hand from the wrist. Sandra has long, dark-black hair, with the kind of healthy shine I'd only seen on television—before I moved to LA.

Sandra tried for hair commercials when she first came to LA, from Connecticut, I think. She developed a regimen to ensure her hair is always perfectly laid out, always tumbling in those smooth layers over her shoulders. When Sandra was in her thirties, she looked pretty much like Liz Taylor in her forties. Now, in her forties, Sandra looks like Liz Taylor in her thirties. You can hardly blame her for moving to LA. But after all this time, there are still no acting jobs for Sandra. I guess Liz Taylor ended the market for women who look like Liz Taylor. So Sandra has been waiting in this waiting room for the big break that now looks as though it will never come.

If her life is to be her only movie, it is a pleasant movie to watch. Watching that movie has a way of captivating those who wait in the office of Cohen & Cranston. Or those like me, who just pass through.

"Hey, sweetie," she says in a hushed tone, as if about to dish some Hollywood gossip she thinks might be in poor taste. "I was worried when I saw the blood. They're looking for you in a way that makes me think they're going to do something bad to you."

"Richard?"

"And his little hench-people. Bigwigs from the executive committee seem to be crawling everywhere. I'm so sorry. Should I let him know you're here?"

"Do we have to call right away?"

"Let's go hang up your coat," Sandra says. I don't have a coat, of course. No one in LA wears a coat this time of the year. Or virtually any time of the year. But C&C has a walk-in coatroom. The place was laid out by partners from New York.

Once inside the coatroom, Sandra closes the door, and reaches up to get a circular Brooks Brothers hatbox off the shelf above the hangars. It actually has a hat in it—brought by an old New York partner who left it here. It is the perfect place for Sandra to keep her emergency kit. Lifting out the old hat exposes a couple small fifths of generic vodka, and about twenty prescription bottles with the labels torn off.

"Richard will smell the alcohol. You know him. I'm afraid I can smell it a little myself, hon. You're trying to kill the pain, aren't you? Here, take these," she says, handing me some Altoids from a small tin among the prescription bottles, and one of those airline toothbrush-toothpaste kits. She sends me to the bathroom, where I brush my teeth and pop in the Altoids.

"Vicodin?" I suggest, after returning to her desk.

"Sounds like what you need. But don't take more than one at a time." She gives me one of the unmarked bottles, and I take a couple pills.

"You're a good girl, Sandra."

"You're a good man, Sam." Sandra gives me a hug. "I've always said that to Joel. To anyone, really."

Sandra returns to her desk and puts on her headset. She keeps the earpiece loose, and I can hear her latest caller shouting from five feet away. She smiles at me. No amount of abuse or profanity from Richard is going to cause her to lose her cool, or her impeccable manners. Her eyes dance, and she says, "I will send in Mr. Straight directly." Sandra is always at her cutest when she says something in this formal, stilted tone. Occasionally, she will put in a bit of an English accent. More than one lawyer in the New York office thinks she actually is from England, and it's sort of a game with her to keep them going. Richard is one of those she is playing along.

Then to me: "He said you should. . . " and she pauses, thinking of the right way to phrase what she has just heard. Her eyes become pools of warm concern:

"Wait for Valerie to take you back. Be careful, Sam."

CHAPTER TWENTY

Valerie comes up close to me and takes my arm as I walk into the hallway. She is shorter today, wearing flats and a fully buttoned blouse instead of the usual inviting open collar. Her loose skirt comes below her knees. All of it is completely sensible, and completely ineffective in disguising the perfection of her body.

"You don't look much better, Sam."

"I feel pretty awful," I say. "But it's time to deal with all of this."

"Things are getting weirder around here," Valerie says.

"What did you find out from Trisha Carlson?"

"She seems to have disappeared. Kinda like the Kid did. She doesn't answer her phone. I've tried every Oddyssey number I can find. No one seems to know where she is."

"Are they saying anything about Joel?"

"They were on television this morning. Did you see it?"

"Ah, the performance."

"That's the latest. Pretty sickening, but the firm wants the offer to go through. We are circling around the Kid."

Valerie is giving me the girlfriend look, so I decide to ask her for something. "When you leave today, can you go down to Cedars and check on Joel? Make sure there is some kind of protection for him?"

"Sure, Sam." There were those entrancing *s*'s again.

"Stay for a while and see what's going on."

"I will, Sam. It's good that someone cares about him. You seem like the only one around here who cares about anybody other than yourself." Valerie reaches over and gives me a hug. I didn't realize how much I've needed that kind of touch, and my guard goes down.

As she moves away, I say, "Listen, Valerie, I'm thinking of starting my own firm again. I know we've just started to work together, but . . . would you be interested?"

Once again, I have presumed too much. She steps back to look at me, appraising how that might turn out. I'm sure the way I look is not helping.

"I'll think about it," she says. "I worry about Joel . . . but we'll see. Let's talk when this Oddyssey thing is over."

"Call me. Let me know what's going on."

"You don't have a cell."

"Leave a message at my home. It's in the directory, I assume." I smile.

She returns the smile and goes back to her office. I go into the bathroom to get ready for my meeting with Richard. I comb back my hair. On the whole, I don't look too bad. I like the effect of Sandra's Vicodin. I take another.

Richard is centrally placed in the largest corner office in the very back of the floor. I march through the stares of silent associates who pretend not to see me through their glass cages. When you look their way, their eyes go back to their desks. The executive committee is in town, and everyone wants to be seen billing time.

Richard is talking loudly on one of those big rectangular cell phones.

People are actually starting to carry these things around. As if that is somehow a way to live your life. But why is Richard using a cell phone when he has a perfectly good phone on his desk?

I walk in and sit in a chair so old it could be from a medieval torture chamber. That might be the ambiance Richard and his interior decorator were going for.

Then I see it. One of those tiny, disgusting little white dogs that faux celebrities seem to always have around. It comes over and rubs my legs. Then it looks up and barks. This is the infamous Twelve-Bee-Six, named after Richard's favorite federal rule of civil procedure.

Still, Richard doesn't turn around. He keeps jabbering to some sort of travel agent. He is making vacation plans.

"Yes, first class; didn't I just say that? Are you aware that my time is worth more than $500 an hour? This phone call is costing me more than the ticket. Why am I talking to someone who can't keep a thought in her head for two straight minutes? Is there anyone there with an IQ over eighty-five?"

Richard is famous for these rants, which always seem to occur at the precise moment when associates have been summoned to his office for a meeting. Many of the rants are repeated with awe by the admiring little assholes who emulate him.

Richard's skin is a bit different than I remember it. It has always been the sickly yellow associated with those liquid tan products. It still looks a little yellow today, but there are parts that look healthily, legitimately tanned. Maybe Richard is getting serious about his vacations, which would be a new development for him.

Total hits a buzzer. Holly appears. Richard likes summoning people with machines.

Holly wheels a cart with a large metal basket on top. In it are three crisp new boxes with the name of a well-known document-storage company on the side. The tops of the boxes are open, and they are stuffed with neatly packed client files from the file room: pleadings, correspondence, client documents, separated by red welds. Everything is marked with case names and billing file numbers. I recognize the names of some of my pro bono clients on newly retyped labels.

Holly seems to have lost weight since I last saw her. It's hard to gain weight working for Total. At this point, she's beginning to look like a prisoner. There is plenty of new wear and tear in her young face.

Holly brings the steel mesh cart to a stop and places a neatly typed document of several pages squarely in the middle of Total's desk. Holly makes sure that the document is equidistant from all corners, well aware that you don't just give something to Richard Total. Documents are *placed* before him.

Total flashes his hands quickly about three inches from her eyes, without pausing his lecture to the hapless airline phone operator. As her eyes fix on him, he lifts a soggy tea bag from his saucer and dangles it in front of his eyes, while moving his gaze from the teabag to Holly, lifting his eyebrow.

Holly holds up a note card with some writing on it for Richard to read. Richard reads it. Turning to Holly, he says, half into the phone and half to Holly, "I'm giving my power of attorney in this phone call to my paralegal Holly King. You insisted on talking to me; now you have talked to me. And I'm telling you to talk to Holly, which you should have done in the first place."

Then he hands the phone to Holly, who whispers into it, "I'm just going to put you on hold for a second." Then Holly draws another brick of a phone from her bag, and hands it to Richard. *How many of these things does this guy have?*

"He's on hold," she says. Richard immediately punches a button on the brick. "Delbert," he said.

Delbert Cranston, the chairman of the executive committee, is a hoary personage of sixty-eight years whose credibility has enabled the rise of Richard and his profit-hungry brethren. They are really in control these days, but they try to make Cranston feel he still runs the firm. Richard listens; I can only hear the rumblings of Cranston's legendary courtroom baritone coming from the brick. Richard replies to the brick in a knowing tone: "Oh, we've reserved our rights regarding future discoveries. . . "

Richard laughs at Cranston's reply. Richard has a great laugh, an infectious sound that appears to discover something wonderfully humorous in the complicated legal situations where hardly anyone looks for humor. It is, I suppose, part of his allure, one of the reasons he has more clients and more little assholes following him around than any of us in the LA office.

I am concerned that the joke at hand may be on me.

Richard turns to Holly and opens his mouth wide. He sticks his index finger into his mouth in a theatrical way a couple of times. Then he points to the dog that is still at my feet. Apparently the dog needs some food too.

I have to hand it to Richard. Nothing can deter the onslaught of imperatives that emanates from his mind to the rest of us, the subservients.

Richard wants me to be sure I know he and Cranston are equals. He gestures to me by rolling his palm forward as if to say, "I wish this old gasbag would get on with it." Finally, he says to the phone, "I understand. I'll give him the message and get back to you." He hands the brick to Holly.

"Where's Eddie?"

"He's waiting outside," says Holly.

"Get him in here."

Before Holly can move, Eddie Guarnieri slumps into the room and fits himself awkwardly into the chair next to me. He must have been just outside the door, listening to every word, and waiting for his cue. Eddie is now the witness that is always necessary in these types of things. As usual, Eddie's huge, blocky ass fails to fit properly into the chair.

Richard looks down at the neatly typed document Holly placed on his desk. I know this to be an outline. An outline for a meeting with me.

Richard never does anything without an extensive outline containing verbatim statements that he plans to make. Typically, Richard's outlines also contain the expected responses of the others in the meeting. After each possible response, there are directions to another section in the outline where Richard's next rejoinder is stated, again verbatim. For all legally required statements, the outline contains footnotes with citations to legal research materials. Even the simplest meeting becomes complicated when thought out in this way, hence the reason why Richard's acolytes, the "Total Assholes," can be observed in long, often all-night "outline sessions," endlessly trying to guess possible responses and comebacks. The outline process is legendary, as are the new little assholes that are torn when Richard believes that an important meeting pathway has not been properly covered by the outline.

My only chance against the outline is to take the initiative during Richard's first sip of tea.

"Oddyssey was Joel's account. I'm pretty sure he would have wanted me to take over until he is back on his feet."

Richard is nonplussed. The outline method has been very successful for him. Putting down his tea, he slowly pages through his outline. His expression relaxes as he finds his response. He swallows his tea and reads, "Oddyssey.com is a firm account. The firm has the ultimate responsibility to the client, and the firm needed to make the best choice for the client with respect to critical, rapidly occurring developments that threatened the client's best interests. Your drinking and drug use would have placed the client at serious risk if you had been consulted in those situations."

Richard gives me an opening as he pages back to the first page of the outline, but the only question I can come up with is the same one I've been asking everyone: "Given that you are the partner in charge now, maybe you can tell me exactly what it is that Oddyssey.com actually *does* to make all that money."

"Are you saying you don't know?" Richard has responded to this inquiry with a question, as a Richard outline often recommends.

Eddie snorts. His derision and the Socratic method are pissing me off. I have a question that's not on the outline, but I decide to hold it. The Vicodin helps.

Paging on in the outline, Richard tries for a compassionate tone. "Actually, Sam, I have the sad chore of telling you that you are not a partner anymore. After a vote of the executive committee, we have reached the conclusion that you must be removed from the partnership, effective today. We have filed notice with the courts in your cases that you are not associated with the partnership. Certain of your clients have elected to be represented by you personally, and we have prepared substitutions of attorney. They are included in your files, which, as you can see, we have assembled. The remaining clients will remain with the firm, and their matters will be reassigned."

Richard nods to Eddie, who promptly un-slumps and leaves the room.

"What about Joel?" I say.

Richard is determined to make the complete statement as recommended by the outline: "The grounds for your removal on this emergency basis are your inability to perform services, your failure to advise the firm of your past association with an organized crime figure, and your alcohol and drug use. We reserve the right to rely upon other grounds that may arise in the course of the investigation now underway."

The magic words have now been said.

I had to fire a bunch of people once. Clients used to have lawyers do that before it became a separate profession of its own. When you fire someone, you have to say it once clearly, right at the beginning, in legally certain terms. After that, you can empathize, but the key is not to say anything to give the terminated person any hope for further time at the job. You can't let them think that there is any recourse other than walking out the door, hopefully after signing a release that gives up their right to sue over the inhumane action you are taking. So I know the method, and recognize it in what Richard is now doing to me.

"What about Joel?" I repeat.

"This meeting is not about Joel Green," says Richard. "I suppose we will need to address Joel at some point, but that is none of your concern."

"None of my concern?" I try.

"After all, you're the one with the relationship to Jacky Real. . . "

"I had nothing to do with Jacky Real. . . " But then I stop myself. I was about to blame Jacky Real on Joel, as Jacky himself had told me. Even without an outline, however, I know that I don't want to blame Joel. And by saying that I heard anything from Jacky, I would just be proving

Richard's point. I am a convenient scapegoat, and I set myself up by going to see Jacky last night. I decide to change the subject.

"Everybody in this firm drinks. You drink, Richard. And you have no proof of drug use," I say.

Total stares over my head at the doorway behind me. Then he lifts an eyebrow, suggesting I should look too. I turn around. Eddie has escorted Sandra into the doorway. He is holding the hatbox. She looks pale. She turns and walks away, without saying a word. Holly follows to see to the needs of Total and his dog.

Total again tries for a conciliatory tone: "Don't worry, we won't fire her. We may need her."

"Richard, I've been meaning to ask you. Is it really necessary for you to be so mean to people like Sandra?"

"Sam, my friend, I've been meaning to ask you: Have you considered the ramifications of being nice all the time? I look around this office, and I see the results of the lack of discipline around here. You don't have a single associate billing more that 2,000 hours. No one's ever been fired. Why aren't you firing the low billers? There's nothing like the sting of a bit of discipline to snap performance back to acceptable levels."

"I make money for this place. I made more money than any junior partner has ever made for the firm when I brought in the Great Homeowners' settlement."

Richard goes back to reading. "A review of your accounts shows that the firm has lost money having you as a partner for every calendar year since the settlement of the Great Homeowners' insurance matter."

The "calendar year" analysis is a convenient way to slice off the Great Homeowners' settlement from the analysis. That settlement generated a fee big enough to make four years into good years.

"Your collections have never exceeded $700,000 in any full calendar year since then," Richard continues.

"And neither have my distributions. You're telling me the senior partners aren't making money on me?"

"This is Cohen & Cranston, not Green and Straight." Eddie chortles at this. Richard cannot avoid emitting a hint of his infectious, conspiratorial laughter before continuing. "You do realize that collections need to be at least three times your draw for the firm to make any money on you. In a real law firm like C&C, we view ongoing profitability as a baseline of performance."

Holly returns with a new, and piping-hot, cup of tea. She also has a plate with an egg-white omelet, toast, and a neatly cut banana. She carefully places these offerings at acceptable geometric angles before Richard. From the bag of cell phone bricks she apparently always has slung from her shoulder, she removes an opened can of expensive dog food, which she scoops into a bowl on the floor near Richard's desk. The annoying little dog rushes over and eats hungrily. Richard does not pause to marvel at these developments before returning to his outline.

"A review of your open matters shows that many are costly cases to pursue and there is neither a hope that the client will potentially have the ability to pay the bill, nor is there a reasonable probability of a successful outcome which will result in the bill being paid."

Now. I pop the question I've been holding to disrupt the outline. "I'm appreciating all this legalese, Richard, but what I really want to know is why you dropped my wife off at LAX last night."

"Your wife?" Holly stares at Richard. She is suddenly ashen. Richard looks at her as he says, "I wasn't aware you were married, Sam."

Richard has it—most successful lawyers do: the ability to disconnect the brain completely from the rest of the body, the twitches, the nervous looks, the things that tell the truth when the brain lies. But the tell is that he doesn't look me in the eye. Instead, he moves to pick up his toast. His finger recoils, and he looks over at Holly: "The toast isn't crisp."

"I got it from Raymond's," says Holly, confused.

"Well, whoever is making toast at Raymond's today did not get the message that the toast should be crisp."

Holly shrinks back, troubled. She knows: Richard likes everything "crisp." I have been present on many occasions when he demanded that a client's testimony be rewritten to be more "crisp," which was code for "more favorable to the position as described by Richard Total." Richard has fired many an associate on the grounds that "his writing isn't crisp." Many an associate has tried to figure out what crisp writing could mean. I always advise them that crisp writing is writing that imitates Richard's writing. "Listen to him. Write down what he says. Then write like that. If you can't, just type up what he said," I advise. "You will find that works surprisingly well."

Richard briefly pauses in case Holly wishes to make an attempt to defend the hapless minimum-wage earner at Raymond's who is the source of the soggy toast. Of course, Holly knows better.

"Get me some crisp toast," says Richard. Holly rushes out of the room.

"How do you explain that you were both at the airport last night?" I say.

"This is a city of at least six million people, Sam. Do you think it's possible for two unrelated people to be at the airport at the same time?" Richard goes back to the outline. I imagine he must need it at this point. "Eddie's been doing an audit of your 'clients.'" Richard likes making air quotes with his fingers and hands. "Eddie, what is the total amount of Sam's clients' unpaid bills?"

"$674,322."

"But those can't be real bills. I've never sent out bills like that to these clients."

Richard turns crisply to me. "And therein lies the problem, my friend. We had to have Eddie go back into the files and reconstruct your time by looking at the letters and briefs you wrote. We probably missed some."

"Sounds like a lot of work," I point out. Eddie nods in agreement, appreciative I would notice his effort, though it was in an evil cause.

"It's work you should have done."

"You know, so what if I didn't charge for all my time? I thought the firm had a rich tradition of pro bono work."

"The firm does work 'pro bono publico.'" For some reason he places a cloying emphasis on the hard *u* in *public*, which makes his sentence into a sort of iambic pentameter. Richard is now giving his outline the

Shakespearean treatment. "That work is much different from what you're doing. The firm is helping people in genuine need, not the lame and shiftless friends of Sam Straight." He turns to the crisp new boxes.

"Are we totally beyond any notion of doing the right thing?" I ask.

"You know the problem with you, Sam?" Richard is going off script. The Vicodin tells me to bide my time. "It's not just that you're not a good lawyer. I'm not sure you were meant to be a lawyer at all." Richard always says the word *lawyer* with a bit of a hard *i* sound mixed in. It almost sounds like "liar," but not quite.

"What are you talking about?" I say.

"No wonder you're an alcoholic, Sam. You're completely hung up over this doing-the-right-thing nonsense. A lawyer only does the right thing when his client wants him to, which is only when there is no more attractive option. Only the client gets to choose between good and evil. It is not your job, my friend."

You can only be Richard's "friend" if he has no use for you. "My friend" was his designation of you as a worthless form of life.

I never had a chance here. I remember how badly I'm going to need some money, especially if I'm going to try to restart our old firm. "If you're going to drop me, I want my capital account and I want it now." Since joining C&C, 10 percent of my yearly compensation has been funneled to my "capital account." We've always been told to view this as money in bank, available to us on leaving. But there is a potential catch some of the exiting partners have been complaining about.

"You need to sign the releases first."

I see now the trap I have been in since the beginning of the outline. Unless I give Richard the release, C&C will keep my capital account. Once someone has been "outlined" in the Total way, you can answer all of your own questions yourself.

"Section 7.9 of the partnership agreement?"

Richard nodded.

"The capital account is my money, and if I don't get it by the end of the week, I'm going to—"

"File a lawsuit? You and I both know you won't do that. There are two releases in your package. One is by you, and the other is by the firm."

"What kind of claim could the firm possibly have against me?"

"The firm has a claim. . . " Richard looks back through the outline, and starts reading again: ". . . for $674,322, the loss to the firm caused by your failure to bill properly. There are other claims as well, but that one alone is bigger than your capital account."

I look at Eddie. He looks down at the legal pad he has been writing on, and scribbles furiously.

"I'm not signing anything," I say.

"I believe you will sign, because we are willing to give you a $10,000 severance payment if you do."

I don't react. The shock is too great. My capital account is worth over $300,000.

"Perhaps when you run out of gin," says Richard. He's full of acerbic remarks today. Richard reaches down and pulls out of his drawer the half-empty bottle of Bombay from my office. He's been waiting for this moment. It's probably in the outline.

"Fuck you, Richard."

Richard turns to Eddie. "Make sure that Mr. Straight's words are recorded in the minutes of this meeting, Eddie."

"It's spelled *F-U-C-K*," I say to Eddie. "Both of you."

Richard puts his finger down on the intercom. "Holly, bring me a fresh phone."

Holly rushes into the room. She is reaching into her bag of bricks. I stand, sensing the need to protect her.

I put my hand on Holly's arm as she goes to pull out the phone. She is shocked. I turn to Richard and spit out, "Richard, my friend. I need you to be a little kinder to Holly here. Please and thank you would be a good start." Holly's face warms to me.

Ignoring me, Richard returns to the outline: "There's a warrant for your arrest. Give me the fresh phone, Holly." Holly is frozen, looking at me. Taking it from her, he begins to dial.

You have to hand it to Richard: an outline always has a crisp ending.

"I'm calling now," Richard says, and begins dialing his brick while looking at the outline.

The wolf may have his prey, but I am raging now. I face him full on, my fists clenching.

"And stay the fuck away from my wife."

As I pass through the hallway of glass offices, one associate after another looks up at me as if I am a ghost. A man who was a partner until just a few minutes ago is now an accused murderer, walking through their midst, getting away. They are still billing.

―――――――

At reception, Sandra looks up at me. Her face is flushed red. I walk past her, go to the elevator, and push the down button. I hear her headset clatter on her desk, and she rushes over to me.

"Don't leave without saying something, Sam. You're the only one who always says something."

"I deserved better. Joel deserved better."

"I'm sorry, Sam. This job is all I have."

The switchboard starts beeping. Sandra goes back to the desk. Multiple lines begin beeping in electronic singsong. Sandra puts on her headset. "Cranston & Cohen, may I help you?" She listens, then says, "I'm transferring you to the office manager."

I stare at her and think of how she makes this ordinary position at the desk seem so graceful even after the interrogation she went through today.

She pushes another button. She listens, then says, "I haven't seen him." To me she says, "Sam, the police just called through. They wanted me to hold you up."

The switchboard is beeping wildly now. "You better get those calls, Sandra."

She looks at me. Then at the switchboard. "Goodbye, Sam." She answers the next call with an English accent and a smile in my direction.

I step into the elevator, and plummet down. When you're in a bad marriage, you dream of the day you can say, "I left my marriage." It's when you can start counting the days that push it behind you. When you hate the law firm you're stuck in, you dream of the day you can call your friends and say, "Hey, I left the firm."

Now I can say those words, but there is little time to say them, or to think about what they might mean.

PART FOUR: PEACE AND THE RIVER

CHAPTER TWENTY-ONE

The elevator descends in something it calls EZ mode, always a thrill ride. Hoping to stop the free fall to the lobby and the arms of the LAPD, I push the button for the eleventh floor. One of the newer bankruptcy firms recently moved downtown as a display of the success it has built on others' misery. An elaborate build-out is underway.

The elevator door opens. The tired eyes of a heavy, middle-aged man covered in drywall paste look right past me as he gets on the elevator to go home. I dodge through the building waste, finding the stairwell. Same location on every floor. I make my way down the remaining eleven floors of stairs and push through the door with the red sign announcing *Alarm will sound*. No alarm sounds. Another phony sign in a phony town.

I weave behind the buildings of Fifth Street, up the stairs to the Wells

Fargo Tower at Fifth and Flower, then down the escalator past the empty floors where Perrino's sits empty. Yet another bankruptcy.

Reaching the sidewalk on Flower, I hear the sound of sirens. Might be LAPD Crown Victorias leaving the Library Tower to find me. Or just another of the nameless emergencies always happening.

I could call Ali. *I might as well call Oddyssey.*

The evening rush hour is in full force. The lanes of Flower are filled with one-way traffic. I begin to run north against it, seeking ill-defined shelter. Pain builds from the stitches pulling against the wounds in my abdomen.

Just past the Bonaventure Hotel, and just before the Security Pacific Plaza, a steep hill of jagged rocks forms the foundation of the skyscrapers overhead. A group of bike messengers gathers at the base of the hill. The smell of their marijuana drifts my way. Maybe one of them will sell me a bicycle. I have about $300 in cash, which should be enough. As I approach them, one of them cuts in front of me and knocks me down against the hill. The sharp edge of a rock cuts into the bottom of my forearm. The blood looks bright red, healthier than the brownish seepage coming from my stitches.

The bike messengers tightly surround me. A few of the faces are young, like the boys at Jesus' Gym, but most are worn, aging, unshaven. Haphazard, irregular T-shirts. They all have stringing long hair, in dreadlocks, just like the guys at the Gym. The clacking of the beads on their dreadlocks tells me they belong to the Kid. These are not kids. A darker, more grizzled side of Oddyssey has found me.

One of the messengers steps closer, his bare legs planted right in front of my face as I sit on the ground. He has an earring, from which a wispy red feather drifts. His features are large and exaggerated, especially his nose, which is shaped like a broadly tented dorsal fin. The fin divides long spacious cheeks severely pocked by angrily active acne, smooth reddish mountains capped with whitecaps of pus.

"Who are you guys?" I say.

"Just know we're from Oddyssey. And you need to come with us."

"You know who I am?"

"The Kid needs to talk with you."

"Look, is it . . . ?"

"Leonard. I'm the captain here."

"Captain Leonard. Okay. I think the Kid didn't know I'd already been fired when he sent you. I don't represent him or Oddyssey anymore."

"Well, he wants to see you."

"I'm out, man. I'm not even part of the law firm that represents Oddyssey. They fired me, which is what I think he wanted. I just want to go home."

"You can explain to him."

Leonard pauses. He seems to wonder how to put the next part. Then, in a low voice, the calm but direct voice that judges use when they tell you very nicely that you are losing and that there is nothing more you can do or say about it, he says, "We have orders, Straight."

"Whose orders?"

"Look, I know you're a lawyer. But I'm not into a bunch of arguing. This isn't a discussion."

While I've been talking with Captain Leonard Red Feather, two of his dreadlocked disciples have moved in on me from the flanks. They grasp my arms both above and below the elbow and pull me to my feet. I feel the prick of a needle in my left arm, and then a burning sensation.

"Why don't people ask me if I want a sedative?" I say. My head sags and I try to brace myself for a fall. "Maybe I would say yes," I add to see whether I can still talk, but I don't hear the words I just thought. The two dreadlocked men on either side of me still have my elbows. "After all, I have a reputation for taking drugs, you know. . . "

I look across the street and see Ali, standing by his cab, waiting in the line for the Bonaventure bellboys to load the next passenger. His eyes open and his shoulders shrug as if to say, "You should have called me. I could have helped."

CHAPTER TWENTY-TWO

Stretched out on the floorboard in the back of some kind of van, I feel my stomach going around the turns ahead of me. The drivers are in no apparent hurry, but every slight change in direction seems dire to me. Plastic ties bind my hands, cutting into my wrists. I can't see my feet, but they are also bound. My mouth is sealed by masking tape, and it's hard to breathe through my nose while lying on my chest. I push off and roll onto my back. Nausea strikes. Can't afford to vomit.

The beads in the stringy dreadlocks up front click in rhythm as the car moves through traffic. The one driving is wearing a Dodgers baseball cap, blue brown with dirt. Oddyssey messengers.

"Oddyssey kills? When did that start?" says the Dodgers cap.

"When necessary. How did you think we keep the discipline in so many groups?"

"I didn't sign up for that," Dodgers Cap says.

"You'll find it's important to do what you're told. Resentment is bad for you, brother. Bad things tend to happen to you when you start acting bitter."

"Okay, then, why didn't we just kill him back there?"

"Can't leave that kind of a mess in the middle of a city. Too much DNA."

"Good to be careful about evidence. But I'm thinking I didn't sign on for a life of crime."

"Did you notice you're not making minimum wage?" says the one in the passenger seat.

Dodgers Cap should shut up. He's not done, though: "Why even bother with him? It's just another lawyer."

"Look, it's the Kid's call. When you start your own company, you can make the decision."

"What are you, the new boss?"

They are quiet for a while after that.

"We'll both get more beads for this," says the boss, and now I recognize the voice of Captain Leonard. "And you could use some beads."

"But the LA River. That's disgusting," says Dodgers Cap.

"That's the point."

They must think I'm still under from whatever they gave me back on Flower Street. Must be developing a tolerance for this kind of stuff. There were the hospital drugs, which had their moments. And to be honest, I know my way around Sandra's coatroom.

I can see the Kid's logic. The river is as good a place as any to dump a dead body. More sewer than river, it flows through the backside of LA like the infested lower intestine of an old movie actress dying of bowel cancer. I know the river from bike rides Joel and I did before he got fat and stopped doing things like bike riding. The bike path along the river runs all the way to the ocean, diving under the roads and freeways, providing underpass shelters for the homeless people who live there because it's a place people leave them alone. Bike messengers, drug dealers, and the many others who live on the edge of survival or starvation feel at home there.

I recognize this is my last opportunity to escape. No extra locks on the rear door of the van, so I should be able to open it from the inside. I inch towards it, hoping to strike it quickly with my foot, push it open, then spill my body out onto the road. Long odds, but what choice do I have? There is rolling out on the road, even knowing that every empty space on the roads of LA is filled or to be filled shortly by a moving vehicle, and there is waiting for Oddyssey messengers to dispose of my bleeding dead body in the putrid waters of the LA River.

We pitch downward, and my body scrapes across the floor of the van to the back of the front seat. The tires grind through thick gravel. The van stops. My shoulder bangs against the hard surface of the wall behind the seats, and I grunt with pain. So much for my escape plan.

"Let's go," says Captain Leonard. Dodgers Cap kills the engine. Both front doors open, and the messengers exit. They come around to the back and open the doors. Grasping me by the legs, they pull me out of the van. I see freeway overhead. They have parked in one of the underpasses.

They drag me along a small path behind a concrete column. The path here is bordered by an aluminum chain link fence, with large, gaping tears in the links. At the end of the path, they pull me through a circular entrance into a pipe deeply embedded in a gravel pile supporting the towering freeway overhead. Darkness forms around me.

I have always lived by my mouth. But it can't do me any good here because I can't open it. I want to talk, to dissuade them, or at least to utter some last words. I deserve at least that. I start grunting, hoping that they will think I know something, that they will decide to earn extra Oddyssey points or beads or whatever and take off the tape to let me talk. But they keep drawing me deeper into the darkness. I accept that I will die.

My cheek lies on the dank, cold surface of the floor of the pipe. Dodgers Cap and Captain Leonard are arguing again. I wonder whether there was any good to my life, or whether I will be just another nameless fuckup that nobody bothers to bury. If anyone finds me, that is.

The cave smells vaguely of old beer, old piss, and new shit. I look across the surface of the floor, littered with newspapers, food wrappers, and used condoms. In the distance, about fifteen yards away, lumps of piled gray blankets come into focus as my eyes become accustomed to the dim light.

A part of a blanket moves, just slightly.

A head pokes its way out of a corner of the blanket, revealing the groggy, thin face of a young woman, mid-to-late twenties. Her blond hair is fine, straight, but dirty. She has the classic high cheekbones of a model, her nose straight, perfectly centered and proportional. Her almost uncomfortably thin arm emerges, stick-like, and I see a couple small brown spots. Her eyes are squeezed together. It seems she is struggling to open them against the resistance of a drug.

She pushes the blanket away from her body. She is thin to the point of malnourishment, though no worse than the current run of models. She is nearly perfectly formed, long and angular. She rests on all fours. Her face registers alarm.

The naked female body skitters over the floor and picks up an object, a baseball bat. She stands. Even here, even now, her body strikes me where men want what they cannot have. She swings the bat.

From behind me, Captain Leonard has seen what I see. "Whatcha doin'?" he shouts in his best command voice, using contractions to calm the anxiety of the voice.

"Go back. This's our home."

The voice is quavering, uncertain, as if from an old woman.

To me, the voice feels like hope.

A whoosh and a whack like the action of a metal bat at a kids' little league game. She keeps banging the bat on the metal pipes.

The remaining mountains of blankets move explosively. From within the blankets there emerges a large, naked, muscled mass of sun-darkened skin. It stands fully tall, a towering man. The moonlight strikes the strands of his long blond hair, making his head glow. I look, and then look away from his nakedness, having seen too much. But I see he is holding, and raising, a handgun.

"Back off," shouts Captain Leonard.

The woman rushes towards me. "Sparrow, no," says the giant. But the woman just keeps running towards me, screaming a crazy, hellish, quavering noise. She is going for the space behind me, going for Captain Leonard. As she leaps over me, I flip onto my back, hoping to see what happens next, staring at the opening of her legs vaulting by.

A shot rings out, and her head comes down, leading her body behind it. Her head lands on my chest and bleeds out onto my neck as I look down into her eyes. She says nothing. Her breath spews out on me, then drool, then more blood from her mouth. Her eyes close over. I rock back and forth until she slips off of me. Her head lands with a thud on the metal of the pipe floor.

The voice of the blond giant echoes: "What. Have. You. Done?" From the side of my eye I see the flashes as Leonard and Dodgers Cap begin to fire. The blond man is firing back, and bullets pass back and forth above me. Six, seven, eight shots are exchanged. I hear a body fall. Looking back towards the opening of the pipe cave, I see Captain Leonard's nose looking at me from the floor surface, blood flowing down either side of the nose to the bottom of his face. Everything goes silent.

Dodgers Cap is standing, fear spreading over his face as he scrambles to reload his gun. He drops the magazine with a clank.

"Don't do it, young man," says the blond giant. Dodgers Cap does not listen. He stoops, fumbles for the magazine, jams it into the wrong place with a curse word. The naked man is rushing towards him. With another try, the magazine clicks into place, and without stopping Dodger Cap raises to fire. The naked giant fires first. The Dodgers cap and adjoining head snap back. The ingenuous face bursts open. The messenger lands on his back, arms open, wondering.

The transcendent naked man holds the pistol out in front of him in a ready position as he examines the still bodies of the Oddyssey messengers. He folds his forearm back into his chest in the manner that Ali stood over Liston on that *Sports Illustrated* cover. He grimaces.

"Kid, you are a fucking greedy piece of crap. Is this what you wanted?" he says.

CHAPTER TWENTY-THREE

H e must be at least six foot five. And his blond hair must be two feet long. He comes towards me and bends down to examine the naked woman bleeding next to me.

His head bowed, his hair hangs completely over his face, and over the woman's face as well. He kisses her, saying her name, over and over. It sounds like he's saying, "Sparrow, Sparrow."

"What did you think would happen when you gave guns to children?" he asks of no one in particular.

The gunman is Caucasian, about fifty, judging from the way his hair recedes in front. He is flush and sweaty. There is youthful vibrancy beneath his facial skin; it glows red beneath the permanent tan of a lifelong surfer. The wrinkles in some faces makes them seem older, but the gunman's wrinkles fit neatly into the contours and angles of his features. One of those people who looks good old.

After a few minutes he stands, drawing in an enormous breath, still failing to acknowledge me. I grunt as he walks away. Back at the pile of blankets, he pulls out some shorts, then puts on a polo shirt and jacket. He stands into what look like dirty deck shoes. He picks up the gun, clicks on the safety, and puts the gun behind him, wedging it into the top of his shorts at the small of his back.

He walks back to the naked body he called "Sparrow," carrying one of the gray blankets. He picks up the body, places it inside the blanket, then composes it with care. There is no doubt he loves her. He carries her into the dark until they both disappear. When he reappears, I grunt again. He ignores me again, and I give up on getting his attention. I should have just played dead.

He grabs the Oddyssey messengers by the backs of their shirt collars and drags the bodies into the darkness.

The gunman comes back and stands above me. As he reaches down, his tears drip onto me. He grabs my shirt at the back of my neck and, with one powerful jerk, lifts me up and to my feet as if I were a ten-pound dumbbell. He tears the tape off my mouth. I have been plucked from hell by the hand of God the Father reaching out from the ceiling painting by Michelangelo.

He pulls out a knife and slashes the plastic ties on my legs.

"I've got to hand it to you, Mr. Lawyerman. You really know how to make a mess." The gunman stands and goes behind me to cut the plastic ties holding my hands together. I feel suspicious that he knows me.

"You're not from Oddyssey too, are you?" I ask.

"I invented Oddyssey."

"Then you can tell me what it is."

"I can tell you I regret it."

I am damn tired of riddles. Anger surges up in me. I want to yell at him about how Oddyssey has been trying to kill both my best friend and me for about a week, and I damn well need to know who the fuck they are and what the fuck has been going on. But then I get control. This guy has a gun.

"You were at Oddyssey, and then you left?" I say cautiously.

"Something like that. I'm kind of an outcast."

He puts the knife back into a sheath somewhere in his jacket. He puts a hand on my collarbone and seems to contemplate crushing my entire shoulder into dust.

"So, you know me?" I try.

"I get the news. Not always from the usual sources, but my sources are reliable regarding you, Sam Straight."

"What's your name?"

"JD."

"That's your whole name?"

"Yeah, okay, this isn't the time for whole names. We need to go. Can you walk?"

I try out my legs. There is a moment of darkness, but the blood starts flowing in my head again, and the darkness clears. *Look, whatever this is, it will have to do. If he wanted to kill me, he would have done so by now.*

CHAPTER TWENTY-FOUR

We make our way along the bike path at the crest of the great concrete banks of the LA River: the tall, blond, Herculean crazy man, and me. He has just killed two men with astonishing skill and speed. I have just escaped a squalid death. Half an hour ago, I envisioned my body oozing towards the ocean with the rest of the sewage down below. Now we are just two guys walking along as if we need some exercise. His jacket, and the poplin plaid shirt underneath it, are marked with the symbol of an effeminate fashion brand. My violent savior shops at Nordstrom.

"You're not just looking for a better place to kill me, are you?"

"I'm still thinking your life is worth something. Don't know why."

"So this is extortion?" I say, but instantly regret using the word. What some people consider extortion describes a lot of lawyer behavior generally thought perfectly legal as long as it occurs in Los Angeles. Again, I tell myself to control the anger.

"You know, at this point, I think you should just shut up and do what I tell you to do."

I shut up.

We reach the next overpass, and a new group of ratty river ragamuffins comes out from under it. Their hands and feet are going, their eyes are going, but they are trying to stand still, as if to show respect. They're tweekers. The meth-damaged faces look at JD with admiration and love. They chatter:

"JD, brother, what you bringing?"

"Has he got some more gin?"

"That or something else, man."

They seem to be guarding a neat canvas wedge, nearly invisible because it is colored and flecked to match the color of road concrete. This tent seems designed for creating a barely noticeable dwelling under a freeway overpass with these exact measurements.

"Is it a tent?" I ask.

"Something like that," JD replies. "But better." Then, to one of the tweekers, he says, "Show'm, Squirrel." The dirtiest of the meth heads says, "Sure, JD" and reaches up to touch the top of the canvas, which falls neatly in a small pile and then recedes and blends into the concrete of the crevice. I wonder whether I would have even seen the tent if I had not been specifically looking in that direction, but no one would notice it after it retracts like this.

"I invent things." JD shrugs. "I invented this for dwelling under freeway underpasses. Someday it may be useful on a larger scale. Get me a couple bikes, Squirrel," he commands. "Just toe clips. Nothing fancy."

Squirrel reaches into what looks like a pile of shiny metal trash and pulls out a metal road bike. Then he pulls out another. He and the other meth heads dust off the bikes and bring them down to the bike path for us.

"Alright, Squirrel, guys, listen. The wedge tent, and everything in it, is yours now. You're going to need to keep it hidden. The cops are going to be doing sweeps around here. There's some dead bodies down there in the pipe caves. A couple of Oddyssey guys killed Sparrow."

"What happened to them? What did you do?"

"Just don't go near. There's nothing you can do for her now. Don't know anything about it. You're not going to see me anymore for a while. It's best if you don't know anything about me."

"You got it, JD."

"Yeah, don't think about us, man."

Their words are few and monosyllabic; their voices have the strange shakiness that hesitates even within single syllables, as if they are unsure of how each word ends.

JD gets on one of the bikes. I'm still standing there.

"Get on the bike," he says.

"I don't know if I can ride a bike at this point."

"You can wait here for the LAPD then, Straight. You have your own mess, but you'll probably have to explain that mess back there too. In a minute, I'll just be a ghost with a couple of initials. You don't even really know who I am."

I get on the bike.

"Good choice, Lawyerman. We're going to the ocean. Follow me."

"Do your friends have something to drink?" I venture. The word *gin* awakened something in me.

He looks me up and down. "Oh, I forgot. You're a fucking alcoholic."

Then to Squirrel: "You got some vodka?"

"All out, JD."

"Squirrel, I just gave you a tent, a bike, a radio, a fan, and a place to keep some ice. I'm disappearing for a while. But I am going to be seeing you."

Squirrel cocks his head suddenly, as if he's just been hit by a thought. He pulls a small, plastic half-pint bottle of generic grocery store vodka from a pile of trash. As he comes over to hand it to me, I look at the sores on his lip. The bottle looks new, even if it has been opened, and everything in me is telling me I need to drink it.

The liquid makes my esophagus burn, then my stomach. The alcohol starts to seep through the stomach lining and into my blood. I give the bottle back to Squirrel.

"Go ahead. Drink some more," JD says. "I don't want you seizing up on me."

After a couple hungry sips, JD takes the bottle. My face starts to glow. I touch the little blood vessel on my nose, as if to reassure myself that it isn't that noticeable. JD puts the bottle in one of the pockets of his cargo shorts and says, "Alright, let's go. Follow me."

There is enough moonlight to see the path, which flows pretty smoothly from that point to the ocean. We ride down into the depression underneath each freeway overpass, then up again onto another straight, flat stretch. Then down again. My legs are moving, the pain deadened by the lubricant of the vodka.

I try to focus on JD's legs. Beneath the Façonnable shirt and jacket, JD's legs pound up and down relentlessly in that impossible rhythm you see in professional riders. My panting grows louder as he moves out ahead of me. He falls back each time, and glances over with disdain. Finally, he stops. He hands me a water bottle, then lets me have another swig of Squirrel's vodka.

After drinking, I feel better, and try some conversation, if only to keep the break longer. I feel like he is bike-riding me to death.

"You don't supply them, do you?" I want to be clear I am giving him the benefit of the doubt.

"I don't deal anymore, Mr. Lawyerman. I help them out with other things."

"Like the tents."

He nods.

"I'm going to assume Squirrel is not his real name."

"The tweekers tend to die a lot. But then another one comes along, and that one looks like the same animal, so I give him the same name. Like I said, real names don't matter out here."

We start riding again. Soon he is fifty yards ahead of me on the path.

I call out to him, "JD, I have to stop," but he doesn't hear me. I look at turnouts as we come to the bridges. I could just go up the next road and ride my bike away. *Really, where would I go?*

As the river opens wider in its gaping concrete canyons, the wind blows harder in our faces. At times, we are barely moving forward. Just before the beach, we reach a road where we stop and get off the bikes. Beyond is Long Beach Harbor, and the ocean. I figure we are done. I figure wrong. We keep going to the beach, then climb back on the bikes to head east down the bike path along the sand.

"How far, really?" I am too tired and disoriented to be ashamed of the cowardice in my voice.

He slows, turns, and rides back to me. "You'll see."

The stench of the river has now blended with the endlessness of the ocean. No one would call it clean, but you could imagine someone swimming in the water.

We stop in a spot strategically out of sight of any guard tower. Seven surfers float out at sea, searching for a wave. We drop the bikes in the sand, and JD walks up to a bike rack by the path. JD produces a key and brings out a battered, short surfboard from a storage locker.

"Just an old one," JD explains. He then carefully locks our bikes with a lock from the storage locker. "Someone could be looking," he says, nodding towards the houses up the beach. "Get close to me."

He uses my body as a shield as he pulls out the gun he used to shoot the messengers. He hands it to me. I think about my fingerprints while he takes off his jacket. He takes back the gun, then wraps it in his jacket. He strips off the other layers of his clothing, leaving just the cargo pants. His back is broad and muscled, his skin brown. He grabs the surfboard and the wrapped gun, and heads down to the ocean where the surfers are bobbing.

"Stay here, and don't move till I get back."

"You really think I can move?" The adrenaline has receded. The bike ride drained me of all normal energy.

He places the jacket with the gun on the board and then lies down on top of it, the bundle nestled between the ridges of his abdominal muscles. JD paddles out into the waves. He seems entirely at home on the board, floating above the water.

Now wet, JD's long hair coats his shoulders, hangs over the edge of the board, and drips into the water, popping up and flinging water into the sky as he looks from side to side. His muscular arms pull him out to the ocean with the rhythm of a professional swimmer.

My head down, I sleep the kind of sleep you catch at a traffic light during a long drive home from Vegas with a hangover. A few minutes later, I roll over, and the pain from my deepest knife wound wakes me. The Tuesday morning sun is coming up in the east now, first as a glow, and then as a glare on the water. I spot the glint of JD's hair as he sits alone on his board, about twenty yards to the east of the dim specks that are the other surfers. The jacket, and presumably its contents, are gone.

What can he possibly be doing out there? Doesn't he realize what I've been through?

JD is in his element. He keeps trying a wave, then surfing out of it at an angle, waiting for a better one. None of the other surfers seem inclined to do much surfing either. JD paddles over to one of them, says something, then slips off his board.

He pulls to shore with a strong, workmanlike crawl, hand over hand, from over his head to under his body. I think of Joel's strong stroke across the Michigan lake where we worked so long ago. JD disappears under the curl of a wave with a flourish at the end of his toes. That kind of wave usually slams me against the sand, but JD strides out of the waves, throwing the water off his hair with a whip of his head—his magnificent body, the rippled abdominals, the long, smooth swimming muscles of his arms, all framed in the glare of the new sun.

"That was a good board," JD says. "Sorry to see it go."

"Don't you need it?"

"Its life seemed over to me."

JD talks as if his mind is shut, or out on the wave.

"What did you say to them?"

"I just said they should make sure it went out to sea. They said they would." He stares out into the ocean.

"Who was she?"

Then he says, "Her real name was Amanda."

"A name you do remember."

"She was another one of those kids from Iowa or Indiana or one of those other flat and faceless places. She came here because in high school she was the prettiest girl."

"Talent?"

"Not that I know of. But pretty enough to photograph. As long as she would work nude or nearly nude. As long as she was skinny. She had an underwear commercial a couple of years ago, just before she started with the meth. She needed to be impossibly skinny all the time. The meth helped with that. It replaced food for her. But then it did the other things."

"So, you were with her?"

"To the extent anyone gets with girls like that. They have the habits of the sex acts they do for drugs. Efficient. She was cold. So, I covered her up and stayed with her."

"You loved her?"

"You believe in love?" He laughs. "I bet that causes you a lot of problems."

We walk up to the houses, passing through a wall meant to keep out the highest tides, then enter a small back street that dead-ends at the sand.

"Pretty neat disposal," I say. "You don't you think the tweekers will talk?"

"They might, but nothing they say makes sense for very long when you take away their drugs. In a few days, whatever they remember will be mixed in with the need and the things they think they see and they think they want to see. Safest place for any kind of information is inside the head of a meth addict."

"They seemed to worship you."

"They'll forget me soon. Meth erases the good with the bad."

A freshly cleaned yellow cab pulls up.

It is Ali.

"No way," I say. "He works for the Kid."

"There's a few of them who are the originals," JD said. "Some of them still respond to me. If you had gotten in his cab instead of running yesterday, you could have dodged both Oddyssey and the cops."

"So, there's a good Oddyssey and a bad Oddyssey?"

"Just get the fuck in the cab," he says and pushes me in.

Exasperated, JD settles in beside me as the cab pulls away.

"I probably would have let them kill you. But they killed Amanda."

My life has been exchanged for that of a meth addict named Amanda, who was as frail as a sparrow.

CHAPTER TWENTY-FIVE

For some reason, Ali does not like the freeways this morning. Once he gets as far north as the 405, he swerves off, and soon we are going through the worst part of South Central. We even go through the intersection of Florence and Normandie, where my hope for the city died in 1991.

The car lurches forward and seems to take my stomach with it.

"Something's wrong," I say. My hands start to shake. I stare at them, and then up at JD, who is looking out the window.

"Pull over here," says JD.

A freshly painted sign proclaims, *Sharp James' Liquor Palace.* Three bums sprawl outside it, as if they are being paid to provide some decor.

"I don't stop in places like this, my big blond friend," says Ali.

"I know this guy," says JD.

"That's very good for you, my handsome friend, but I am not feeling welcome. My God may not protect me from infidels here."

"Ali, if there is a God, I'm going to presume he wants me to keep this man from having a seizure in your cab."

"I do it for you, my strong blond pilgrim."

"Two minutes," says JD.

I look down. The shaking in my hands seems to be going into my arms. No matter how I feel, I have no intention of staying alone in a cab with Ali. I have plenty of fear for the dark side of Oddyssey.

As we approach the door, one of the bums puts out his foot and blocks the doorway with his dirty jeans.

JD draws a gun with a long barrel and points it straight down into the man's forehead. *Jesus, how many guns does this guy have?* Ali must have given him this one.

"We're just going to walk in," he says. This works like some kind of password, and the bums scurry away like cockroaches. JD puts away the gun.

Inside, the store is incredibly clean, as well lit as any new Rite Aid in Pasadena. A Plexiglas wall stretches all along the back of the small store. Beer cans lined up like ammunition fill the refrigerators covering the side walls. We walk past shelves filled with junk food and high-priced remedies in small, brightly colored packages. We are greeted by a white man with short-cropped gray hair wearing glasses that make him look like an accountant.

"Sharp James," says JD.

"JD. Why haven't I seen you lately?" James speaks in the soft voice of a concerned friend. He isn't sharp at all.

"I've been in another place, James."

"You been in the waves today. I can tell from the light in your eyes."

"Some days the waves are the only place where I feel like living."

"Don't talk that way, JD."

"Look who's talking."

"You been to your meetings?"

"No meetings on the river. One reason I like it."

"What about Peace?"

"I think maybe Peace has had enough of me."

"And so, the river?

"You know why."

"Glad you came back to the world."

"It still sucks pretty much, James. Give me some Stoli."

Sharp James keeps the hard liquor, and stacks and stacks of cigarettes, behind the Plexiglas.

"If you're going to be drinking this stuff, at least have the Grey Goose."

"Just trying to keep my companion here from having a seizure."

"From the looks of him, you better hurry. Sure it's not for you?"

"Just give me the Stoli."

"Forget the money. I don't want you on my conscience."

"James, it's not for me."

"Here, then, take the Grey Goose. Do some good with it. Maybe help some of those meth heads keep their skin on."

"Stoli is good enough for us, James." JD and I are finally on the same page about something.

James puts something like six fifths of Stoli in a bag on which Sharp James is portrayed as a black man dressed in the nature of Sly. Of the Family Stone.

We moved quickly outside and into the cab.

"Does he work for Oddyssey too?" I ask.

"Used to. Then he decided to go the honorable route."

"Liquor in South Central?"

"Better than what you do." JD opens one of the bottles of Stoli, and hands it to me. I take a long swig.

"Hang on to it for now," says JD.

I watch my hands until they stop shaking.

Ali takes us north to downtown. He leaves us on the urine-soaked concrete of the square named after the guy who could not vanquish Pancho Villa. JD takes me through a couple of alleys I am too sick to recognize.

I look up, at an iron gate. We are at one of those new high-rise condos the developers are building downtown. The hope is that there is a market containing humans who will fork over $1,000,000-plus because they think it is actually stylish to live near one of the most disgusting places in LA. Kind of a New York concept.

To add to the New York feel, there is a doorman to open up the second door. He is taller, even taller than JD, with a shining black bald pate.

"Morning, Tiger." Still with the animal names.

"JD. You look tired, man," Tiger says.

"Not as tired as this one."

"'Bout to say that. But I'm not really seeing him, am I?"

JD just nods, and we take the elevator to the top floor.

JD's unit takes up the entire top floor. Being the penthouse unit, it has twenty-foot ceilings.

The entire east wall is a glass window, from floor to ceiling. The other walls have intermittent floor-to-ceiling windows, about six feet wide, followed by six feet of wall, followed by six feet of window. The view has the effect of living on a mountain and looking out at the other mountains and the city below. To the north, the San Gabriel Mountains are shaded in the unusual colors the setting sun makes as it sifts through the late-afternoon Los Angeles smog.

"I get the sense that you don't really need to live on the river," I say. "Unless they are trying to kill you too."

"I figure they are. Especially after you and your partner got stabbed, and that gangster went down."

Most of the unit is consumed by the work of an art studio. JD must work in every medium, the results of which have accumulated across the large open floor: oil paintings, sculptures in various stages from clay plaster to bronze. The largest section of the floor is devoted to a series of indefinable combined works. The idea seems to be to create a work of art by welding old musical instruments with parts of modernist machinery, combined with painting, or whatever else might occur to the artist. A saxophone is welded with a toaster oven. An entire woodwind section is sawed apart, and then intermingled with well-polished automobile engine parts on a painting that combines a service station and a concert hall. Most of the works look unfinished to me.

In a corner, five or six large tanks are grouped together. Each of them is marked *DANGER FLAMMABLE.*

"This is amazing," I say to be friendly. Listening to myself, I hope he fails to recognize my lack of enthusiasm.

"Stopped all of it," he says. "The art, that is. When I stopped drinking. And the meth. Somehow the art needed that too. Without the alcohol and the drugs, I'm not any good. I can't see how anything ends anymore. It's just a bunch of useless shit now. Still sells, of course. People seem to like unfinished shit. Probably a lot of them don't know the difference."

A large, floor-to-ceiling painting takes up the entire wall space between two windows on the south side of the studio. It is totally unlike any of his other work. It is strikingly realistic, though soft focused in the way of an eighteenth-century Dutch portrait. It looks complete.

"Last thing I finished," he says. "It's Peace. Her real name. Hippie parents."

The painting is of a thirty-year-old woman finishing getting dressed. The background is the windows of this very apartment, looking out over the city. An extraordinary beauty glows from the exposed skin of her face and neck, forearms and ankles. The painting conveys the woman's hurried attempt to hide this beauty in plain jeans and a cheap, thrift-store T-shirt, which she is pulling unevenly over her half-exposed chest. The artist has devoted the same care to every line, whether a line of the clothes or the open, inviting face of this woman, whom the artist plainly loves.

"Is she why you quit drinking?" I ask.

"Peace thinks normal people can do what I did with my art. You know, people who quit work at five and go home and go to sleep. They spend time with their families, go to church, watch television. Sleep as if they finished things during the day. People like that never finish anything—they just tell themselves they do. Nothing like art, nothing that really matters, ever gets finished without drugs."

"This is really good," I note. It is.

"She told me to try living without finishing anything. I've been trying that out." He looks at me, pauses, as if wondering why he is telling me so much, then goes on. "But I actually like finishing shit. It makes me feel . . . worthwhile."

I think about Xanthe not understanding all the late nights, and all the briefs that I've finished after a good couple slugs of vodka. I think about some of the legal work I've done at night, drafting interrogatories asking the same question over and over, or providing the same nonanswer over and over to the repetitive questions asked by other lawyers. I don't think I could have finished any of that sober either.

"I think I know what you mean," I start, but before I can give a sympathetic example, he cuts me off.

"No, you don't," he says. "You don't have a fucking clue what I mean. Look, there's a shower in back, and a quiet, dark room without windows where you can sleep."

JD leads me into a room with only one window and shows me the switch that renders it completely dark by shading out the outside light. There are more switches, for fans, and an embedded sound system with sounds of the ocean, or quiet forest, or—the one I choose—just noise canceling: quiet.

A long hot shower cleans off the stale sewage smell of the river. JD has left a robe for me, and some fresh clothes, so I dress and walk back out to the main area of the condo. JD bustles efficiently around the kitchen.

"I think it's time you had some breakfast. How do you want your eggs?"

"I don't feel much like food. Got any of that Stoli?"

"Shut up for a minute and watch. Eat something and I'll let you wash it down."

He flips the omelet in a sauté pan, using olive oil into which he squeezes some juice of a fresh Meyer lemon. He covers slices of rosemary bread with heavy raspberry preserves and pours me some kind of green juice. The omelet tastes better than anything I've had for a while. Why wouldn't he be an amazing cook, on top of everything else? I realize I'm hungry. But the green drink looks revolting.

"I don't drink green things."

JD can see that my hands are shaking again. He opens a cupboard and one of the Stoli bottles. He pours a nice serious dose of it into the green drink and hands it back to me.

"It's still green."

"Shut up and drink, Lawyerman. I'm in the process of saving your fucking life."

I feel better after a long drink gets a little vodka into me. I eat silently for a while. I see him watching me. I start to do what lawyers do. I start questioning what seems too good to be really true, looking for the corrupt inner core that law school taught me is at the heart of all human affairs.

He seems to have more than enough money. Maybe he cashed out of Oddyssey early on somehow. I wonder why I haven't heard of JD in all the due diligence around Oddyssey. Maybe the Kid is paying him to stay silent, to disappear. But that is not the biggest question.

"Why would you run away from this?" I try. "Why would you run away from her?"

"She's one of those AA people. She keeps wanting me to turn my life over to a higher power. They say you can choose your own higher power. But they keep pushing you into choosing the same God who is in all those churches that keep asking for money to build a better church, then more money to build more churches. Then the television stations. Somehow, they never seem to make it out to the river to help the pathetic beings who really need help."

"Maybe those people can't be helped," I say. There is something about him that warns me that I'm in the presence of a higher intelligence. I feel stupid every time I say something.

"Nobody really tries," he says. "They just pray to their mythical savior and expect him to do it. But he never does. The savior never comes."

"You were my savior today."

"Don't be confused, Counselor. I'm just another part of the devil."

It occurs to me that when the devil saves you, it's time to ask yourself whether you're living your life the right way. *Where will the devil take me now?*

"Where do we go from here?"

"You're safe for tonight. But my guess is it won't take them too long to figure out I'm back from the river. Or that you're with me. We'll have to find a different place to be in a couple days."

He seems like he isn't too worried about finding another place. Like he has plenty of them. "Here," he says, and gives me a cold can of Fresca, and a cold bottle of Pellegrino. "You've had enough alcohol for tonight. If you wake up wishing for a drink, drink one of these. See how far that gets you, at least. I suppose if you get desperate, you'll find your way in here."

He seems pretty sure I'm going to get desperate, but there is a kindness about him as he says these things. As if he has been through this sort of withdrawal and knows exactly what I need. Even if it isn't exactly what the doctor ordered. My hands have stopped shaking.

———

I attempt to sleep, but lying there, enveloped in the soft, comforting king mattress covered with a clean white comforter, and listening to sounds of the ocean, I feel as jarred by comfort as I was by the filth of the tunnel by the river. After an hour, I am still awake. The idea of drinking a Fresca is revolting. Time to check on the devil. I find the cupboard with the Stoli. Four bottles left. Thank God for Sharp James. I pour a glass. It makes the knife wounds fade, and I go to explore.

In the corridor outside the sleeping room, I find a wall of books. At the far end, the shelf starts out with the *Origin of Species*. Next comes the Bible. The Bible has a leather cover jacket, and JD's initials on the spine: *J.C.D.* The Koran and various of the Upanishads come next. The Book of Judas, and the Gnostic Gospels. I've tried most of these things too. Didn't get them. Worse gibberish than the Bible itself.

JD's copies are filled with mad marginalia. Much of this is just plain rejection, as in "No," or, more often, "Fuck no," but once in a while there is an exclamation point or a "Yeah!" The bookshelf has an ominous ending: *Darkness Falls*, and *Final Exit*. I decide not to look for marginalia in those ones. It appears that JD has been having a raging debate with God about whether God exists.

Looking around the corner from the bookshelf, I see JD painting at the end of the studio farthest from the hallway. I back behind the corner. He seems oblivious to my presence. He is the focus of an intense spotlight on the canvas; I decide to remain in the shadow. His shirt is off, displaying the powerful, symmetrical bulges of what must be a well-disciplined weight program. All these Oddyssey people are obsessed with lifting weights.

Trancelike, he works in long strokes on the canvas. Seems like a lot of red. Putting down the brush, he uses a welding torch to melt things onto the bottom of the painting, spraying sparks in every direction. Some land on his bare chest and torso. He doesn't appear to feel them.

Music is playing, and JD turns it up. John Prine singing Blaze Foley's "Clay Pigeons." An extremely odd song choice. JD sings along, "I sing a song with a friend, change the shape that I'm in, and start playing again." He has a smooth baritone that seems to love the words, pushing Prine's rasping to the background. A large, blond, apparently wealthy Adonis, who can shoot or save you, pour you a drink, and make you an omelet, is singing about hiding his sorrow in the last seat of a Greyhound bus.

Then comes Marvin Gaye's gentle "What's Going On." JD puts down the torch and lets the music guide more strokes onto the canvas. Then, Johnny Rivers's "Secret Agent Man" comes on, and he is not just painting: he's dancing. He works every kind of dance step in. He can waltz and pop and lock and boogie. He is in some kind of safe place. It's a spectacle that somehow calms the terror of what happened to me out on the river today.

I go back to the kitchen and pour myself some Stoli. Just a couple sips.

CHAPTER TWENTY-SIX

Seizures aren't so bad really. A bit of terror when it first takes hold and you don't really know what it is. When it's over, though, whatever was depressing you is gone. For a while.

In the main area of the condo, the coming of the morning is confirmed by light from the east wall. The stereo system plays Bob Marley's "Redemption Song." JD sits on a stool by the wall where he was painting the previous night. There's a glass in his hand, his arms hanging at his sides. He slumps down, but his bare torso, blackened in spots by the sparks, bunches muscle upon muscle. The strange and haggard look on his face says he has been up all night.

Like everything JD, the new painting is big, covering the segment of the wall next to the section of the portrait of Peace. It is set in the River Universe. Its predominate background is an odd chemical blue, edged by the blackness of the night on the river. An insurrection of color and story. The bridge, the tunnel, the freeway all establish the spot of yesterday's killing.

My reaction is lawyerly, of course. I worry that the painting could be used to find the tunnel in which I was thrown to the ground, bound, and gagged. My body lies just outside the tunnel, as JD has painted it. The terror shows in my eyes, though the rest of my face is obscured by the tape pasted over my mouth. In my mind, it is perfectly obvious that the body in the painting is mine. Two other, more lurid bodies lie on the ground: there is Amanda, beautiful and lithe in death, and one of the Oddyssey bikers, his face in agony beneath his dreadlocks. On the right side of the painting, JD and the remaining biker are still standing, JD pointing the gun. No mistaking JD. The head of the last Oddyssey biker is spraying blood. JD has mixed exactly the color of blood as it comes freshly out of a human body. It may be my imagination, but he has found a cruel color for the gun flashing.

Bits of junk that could have come from the path on the river are welded from the bottom of the painting down to the floor: fragments of broken beer bottles, shiny hubcap parts, and those truck tire treads that peel off and lie on the freeway broken into small pieces. More realism for the all-too-real scene JD has painted. This is the most extraordinary work of art I have ever seen, and not just because it portrays a bloodbath I witnessed a day ago. Still, something is not quite finished.

He successfully distanced himself from the evidence at the scene by our long bicycle ride. He effectively destroyed the key evidence, dropping the gun in the ocean. Yet now, JD's conscience has caused him to recreate the entire scene, dramatize it, and paint himself as the centerpiece, an admitted murderer.

Looking over at his slumped form, I see that neither JD's muse nor his conscience were sober last night. Next to JD's stool is an empty bottle of the Stoli from Sharp James' Liquor Palace. Even with the alcohol, JD is still having trouble finishing things. An eye opens, and he looks at me.

"I thought you didn't drink," I venture.

"I drink on days that I kill at least two people."

"A bit sui generis, don't you think?"

"You're preaching what to me? In dime-store-lawyer Latin no less?"

After a night spent painting, welding, and drinking, perhaps for the first time in years, JD is ready to talk. His words have the taste of vodka, but they flow like river rapids:

"You know, that's the thing the people at the fucking meetings never seem to get. Those people act like there are no days you need drugs to get through. 'Just don't drink,' they keep saying. Well, that only works until you see the day you can't live through without something to numb the pain. You look at all those Arabs living in those, you know, those fucking—I don't know—godforsaken countries. They don't even know what anything less than 110 degrees even feels like, and they go around wearing a bunch of drapes. Those lives shouldn't have to be lived without drugs and alcohol. There's a lot of fucking lives that can't be lived without drugs and alcohol. Yesterday, my life just happened to be one of them. You were there, Lawyerman. As I recall, you were drinking your share."

Yesterday was bad, I guess. But JD provided just the right amount of alcohol to keep me from seizing, enough real food to fill me up, a real bed, quiet, a shower with hot water that didn't end. He'd stopped people from shooting at me. Nothing's bleeding or seeping anymore. I'm actually feeling pretty good. I can feel *me* coming back. My sympathy for other people. My drive to help the unfortunate and the weak, without questioning whether the client is really a victim, or just a complainer, or another liar. It's this naïve motivation that makes me a good lawyer, and my life an inescapable prison. This morning I want to extend it to this man who has saved my life.

I say, "Is there some more?"

"You know where it is."

I walk into the kitchen, get two clean glasses, and fill them with ice from the external ice dispenser on the Sub-Zero. There are two bottles of Stoli left in the cupboard. I take one down, and feel the satisfying click as I twist off the new top.

JD comes in behind me, takes the top, and puts it back on. He dumps the ice into the sink.

"Fuck the ice, Lawyerman."

JD opens the Sub-Zero's freezer, reaches into the very back, and pulls out a bottle of frozen Stoli. He gets a couple new clean glasses from the cupboard and pours each of us a couple inches of the syrupy liquid. Ice forms on the outside of the glass.

"My secret," he says.

It's hard to understand how someone as strong has JD has fallen apart this quickly. Something else must have happened while I was asleep. I feel somehow that whatever I drink will protect JD. Heroic drinking needs to be done.

"What is it?" I ask.

"I never thought anything I did to someone else would actually hurt me. Now I kill a couple of the Kid's thugs, and I realize that there is something that can hurt me."

I wait.

"I'm not a fucking killer, okay?"

"No," I agree. "You are not a killer, JD."

"Actually, that's exactly what I am—a fucking killer. You like vodka, huh?"

"Sure, but what's with the Stoli?"

"It's all the same after you drink it. And I don't like phony stuff."

"Phony stuff like. . . "

"It's all phony, Lawyerman. The law is phony, these paintings are phony. This apartment is phony."

"You shouldn't have had to kill anyone."

JD takes a drink of the cold syrup. "I did it to save your fucking life." Another drink. "It remains to be seen whether that was a good idea."

We finish the first glass. He pours us each another. *Oh well, my work as a hero is not yet done.*

"I'm sorry about yesterday," I say. Then, to change the subject: "So, you invented Oddyssey?"

"I invented what Oddyssey was supposed to be."

"Is that how you paid for all this?"

"Oddyssey never made me any money. It wasn't supposed to be about money."

"How did the Kid get Oddyssey? Did he take it?" I have trouble imagining anyone taking anything from JD.

"I let him have it. I thought it was something that wasn't worth anything anytime soon. I was moving on to something else. To artwork. To tents. To the river, I suppose."

"If you didn't get money from Oddyssey, where did you get all this money from?" I say.

"The stock market. Short selling. I was a drug connection in those days. Just some coke. Fuck, it was the eighties. I had a gun, of course. Never really needed it. I was on Wall Street. Just having a gun was enough to scare suits who needed coke. They liked me. They gave me tips on short sales. I had a knack for it."

JD fills up his glass and walks out of the kitchen into the main area of the condo, looking wistfully at the tall buildings of Los Angeles, as if contemplating how he could again dominate the world of short selling.

"Eventually, I even had an office, World Trade Center, eightieth floor. Man, that felt like flying, and I guess it was. One day, I looked around and saw I had more money than I could ever need, so I just stopped."

He walks over to his art.

"I decided I was an artist. And you know what? Pretty soon I was. The same people who bought my drugs bought my art. Their brains were too fucked up to tell whether it was any good or not."

"It's good, JD."

"No, it's not. I'm not saying there's nothing good about it, but all of this shit I put in, it's just for the art critics. No one can just appreciate a good painting anymore. You have to be 'building on the work of assemblage pioneers.' Throwing a bunch of junky stuff into the paintings got the attention of the phonies who talk that way."

He looks towards the painting that dominates the north wall.

"Peace," I say.

"Yeah, that one is good. It made me start thinking I could just do my art. Then she got me to stop drinking."

I stop drinking in mid-sip and look self-consciously at the nearly empty glass of cold vodka. JD drains some more of his.

"Actually, the truth is she's going to be gone," JD says. "That's the way it is with the people from the meetings. Once you take a drink again, you're a worthless piece of shit until you go to another meeting and tell everyone what a worthless piece of shit you are. But you know what, Lawyerman? The day those people stop drinking, and every day after that, they are the same worthless human beings they were the previous day when they were drunk.

"And, one day, when they're all alone, and there's nobody from one of those fucking meetings around, they realize how stupid and pointless their lives really are, only now when they go to the refrigerator and look for the bottle in the freezer that was keeping the voices quiet, it's gone, and the voice says, 'Give me Death 'cause I'd rather die if I can't drink,' and then they get the very logical idea that the next step is to go to the grocery store and get a very large, very cheap, very full bottle, and all they hear are the thousands of moralizing voices that are now in their head from the meetings telling them that's not the way out, even though for most people it's the only fucking way out.

"Then they start thinking that the only way out that's left is the way out the window or the sleep that comes when you take all the pills. So they drink because that seems more sensible. Drinking's not so bad after all, they think, and that night they have a pretty good fucking time and for once they can finally get to sleep. The next day they go back to the meetings. Only now they're just a little more worthless than they were before, and they have to say so to everyone else. They're all phonies too. Some of them are just able to stay alive for a little longer by pretending they have the answer, and today, my lawyer friend, I'm done being one of them."

JD's cat jumps up on the counter. He laughs like the devil himself. "This is Lilly. She's my sponsor. Sorry, Lil. I'm tired of telling everybody

I'm a worthless piece of shit." Then JD turns to me and says in complete seriousness, "When Peace gets here and sees us like this . . . it's those AA people . . . it's their fucking fault."

Lilly snuggles up under JD's powerful hand. He keeps talking to her. "I can get her back in the end, though, can't I, Lil? She can't help it. She wants me. She really can't live without me, can she?"

The subject must be changed. And there are some things I really want to know.

"Just what the fuck is Oddyssey?" I ask.

After another drink, JD takes a wistful tone: "I wanted to do something real, something useful. Not something evil like the drugs, not something phony like the art. Oddyssey was supposed to be about giving people, people everyone thought were completely worthless, giving people like that something to do."

"Like those out on the river?"

"That's what made me think of it. Yeah, it started with them. I saw how I could get a message from one bridge to the next through their network. And it was completely safe. No one can hack it. But there are lots of sober people, or at least functioning people, people even wanting to work, and willing to do almost anything, who can't find a goddam thing to do in the world. I figure this problem is only going to get worse. I thought Oddyssey would give those people something to do. You know those people. You shut them out of your mind, but you know they're there."

"Some days I wish I was one of those people."

"No, you don't. Even I can only live out there for a while. Eventually, you're going to want a shower and some good food that is clean and warm and to sleep without worrying whether someone will be stealing your stuff."

"Are you saying Oddyssey isn't an internet play?"

"I thought of it as an after-the-internet-takes-over play. This new internet thing, I thought, is incredibly fast, and it seems to make every other way of sending messages or money obsolete, and when it does, all of these insane, money-losing companies will take over the world. I'm not kidding. That will be a time for shorts for sure. But there is going to come a time when no electronic message will be safe, no message carried by a machine will be safe from another machine. The real value in the internet will come when the people who can sell you stuff realize that they can use it to know exactly where you are and what you want at all times. And when that happens, the only safe secrets will be the secrets passed between actual people."

His voice is different, almost manic. Could he be on speed too?

JD stops for a second. He seems unsure about whether even he understands what he is saying. It gives me time to reflect. *This guy is crazy,* I think, *if he thinks that the likes of Hewlett-Packard and IBM and all of those are going to somehow make an army of drunks and homeless people into a useful commodity.*

Thankfully, he is done: "But really, monetizing that idea was decades away."

I feel I should take the edge off where he is going: "You think only people are capable of trust? I would say only people can betray a trust. For money, of course. Especially for money. Machines have more honor."

He looks at me with resignation, even pity, as if he wonders whether it is really worth it to explain it all to me. Then he charges off again:

"The computers will be tiny. First, they will be in your pockets, in your phones, and not like those ridiculous clunky phones rich people are using now. Then they will be in your body. Nothing will be safe. There will be no private acts. They will follow you everywhere. With anyone and everyone carrying a computer, no one will be alone. They will watch you have sex. And then, that's when it will happen. That is when words written on paper in the woods will be important again. Secrets spoken between people will be the only secrets there are. Oddyssey will be important then."

"So, what you're saying then, what you're saying is that Oddyssey is just people?"

"Yeah, people will be important again."

"Why *O-D-D?*"

"The Kid added the extra *d.*" He laughs. "Brilliant, huh."

We're talking now. Two guys drinking and talking at ten o'clock in the morning. Here I am with the last man on earth who thinks that someday people will be more important than machines.

"How did you meet the Kid?"

"I met him at an AA meeting, of course. He was networking, looking for vulnerable older people to blackmail. Heard he made a bit of money sleeping with some of the women. That antidrug act of his is phony, like everything else about Oddyssey. He's never stopped taking drugs. He still thinks they're fun."

"He looks healthier than that."

"When you're young, a couple of workouts cleans you out."

"Did you ever like him?"

"Oh yeah, I saw myself in him. He's very, very smart. He was homeschooled. At first, I just thought he was brighter than average. But there was always an evil side. He's studied Rockefeller. Robber Barons 101. He knows what works, how to steal in a way ordinary cops can't follow."

"So, I get that he stole the idea. But how does he make money? Just having a worldwide concierge service, even one connected by phones and internet, doesn't sound like something that would make the kind of money he says he's making."

"At first I thought it was silly too. I didn't take him seriously. He was just a kid, after all. But then he falls in with that Jacky character, and starts talking big, pumping himself up with the weights, and more drugs of course, and driving around in a fancy car."

JD pauses. "I have to say that he seemed to get smarter after he hooked up with your law firm. There's a lot of talk about your partner Joel. If you ask me, I think he's moving money, washing money. Lots of it. And your firm—or someone in it—is helping."

"Doesn't sound like Joel." It sounds more like a resentful evil genius. "Anyway, how can you launder money with bike messengers?" I ask.

"The Kid figured out—I think it started out that the beads, the things in their hair, were some sort of alternative monetary system, a marker. The messengers don't even know what it is. They think it's some type of lucky beads, like a corporate recognition trinket or something."

"Hair beads as an alternative monetary system?"

"Yeah, that's ultimately unworkable, another phony front, but I got him thinking about something else. Banks all use databases now. So I suggested just eliminating the money and creating a database."

"How is that possible?"

"Just do what the government does, only you don't need a printer. Just set up an account of pretend units—he calls them beads—and move it around the world."

"So the beads are just for show?"

"One time . . . I'm the idiot who told him money is anything you say it is. As long as you create a belief that it exists, it exists. Apparently, there are people who believe in his money."

"And you think my firm knows?"

"The Kid is good, but he needs help to pull this off in the financial markets. He's smart, no doubt, but he isn't that smart."

"So, the concierge thing, the magical internet-search thing, the get-anything-done-anywhere illusion, the slogans, the antidrug message, they're all a front?"

"You really think you can make money doing those things?"

The door opens and Peace walks in.

CHAPTER TWENTY-SEVEN

eace is incandescent, her life force more vibrant than her portrait. As in the portrait, she has intentionally marred her beauty. She wears dirty cutoff jeans and a very short top that looks like it's made with rags from the cleaning closet. Her bare midriff displays the not-particularly-well-executed tattoo of a smiling Mr. Sun surrounding her belly button.

At first, she says nothing. A little spot under one of her cheekbones turns red. Her face moves in tiny random places. She starts to cry. JD doesn't say anything.

"What is alcohol doing in this house?" she says after a minute. "No, let me rephrase that, JD. What is it doing in your hand?"

"Look, I needed to keep this guy from having a seizure. And I told you. On the phone . . . about the river." JD's powerful voice is weak, but very, very angry.

"And you think that's an excuse?"

"Um, yeah, I think it's a pretty good excuse," JD says. He pauses, as if to think of the right thing to say, but then he gives up trying. His voice is angry instead of comforting. "You actually have no idea what I went through last night. Our lives—yours and mine—and this lawyer, you, we are in danger now."

"We agreed this would never happen."

JD mutters something, but Peace is not listening.

She goes to the door.

"This time I'm not coming back. Not because I don't want to. Because I can't."

The door slams. A camera flashes, and then there's shaking in my head, like the light has hit the switch on my seizure. I see the tops of JD's strong, weathered bare feet. Everything is white and blank.

CHAPTER TWENTY-EIGHT

My eyes open but can see only a little, as if a level of sight is shaved off the top. The world assembles from blessed erasure into unforgiving reality.

A tall, blond man stands in front of a giant canvas glistening with fresh paint showing a tall blond man just like him shooting another man through the head. The real-life blond man has his hands at his side, and he holds something in each one. It seems like he has been waiting for me.

I wonder why he is just standing there while I lie here on the floor, in obvious distress.

My own eyes shine through the darkness at the bottom of the painting. The fear in the painted eyes enters me. JD. That's his name. Something is wrong in this room.

"You know," JD says, "the people who go around saying it is never an option are the ones who have never really felt pain that doesn't go away."

"You. The camera flash. Why? What happened to me?" I say.

"You should have stayed down, Lawyerman. The seizure would have done you more good."

"I had a seizure? Help me up, man."

"Even with the drugs," he says. "Even with the good drugs, it just doesn't go away. The drugs wall it into the corner of your brain so you can step outside the wall for a little. But the pain is always there, and after a while you realize that the drugs are just as much of an illusion as God is. And then you notice you are back in the room, and there is your depressing old friend in the corner reminding you that your life is shit.

"They just have no idea. When the pain is bad enough, there is no pretending anymore. Then you just never tell anyone what you are going to do. Unless it's someone who isn't in a position to do anything anyway. Like you. The people who say you should never do it are the people who don't understand because they are the ones causing the pain that makes it the only option, and they just can't accept the fact that they are the pain that won't go away."

I try to get up, but my legs won't move. I try moving them with my arms, trying to get them under me.

"Out on the river are the ones who know how it feels."

I see the picture of a stunning female on the wall. "What about the girl?" I do not yet remember her name. "Where is she?" I remember her name. It is Peace.

"This is for her, Lawyerman. I'm counting on you to let her know. Tell her she was the pain that wouldn't go away."

I'm getting to my feet now. "Let's have a drink," I suggest. He looks past me. "I'm not ready for this," I say.

"I am," he says.

His hand comes up from the side of his leg. He is holding a gun. I stare at the length of the barrel as it disappears into his mouth.

I rush towards him.

He fires. The blood from his brain sprays. I recoil from him and the explosion with the physical force of fear. A camera clicks. Light flashes surround us, blinding me.

When I can see again, there is new blood on the painting. JD's last work is complete.

CHAPTER TWENTY-NINE

I hold JD's bleeding head in my lap, and blood is coming out of his mouth. I tell myself I never really had the chance to do anything.

I try blowing air down his mouth. His chest rises and falls. I try pumping his chest, just as I learned when I was a lifeguard with Joel in the summers. After each five compressions, I try to fill his lungs again. I can taste the blood from his mouth, and it just keeps coming.

The door opens and Peace walks in. She rushes over and cradles his head as I work. After five minutes, I look up at her.

"You can stop now. He's gone," she says.

"I tried to stop this," I say.

"Well, you didn't do a very good job," Peace says. She bursts out crying, as if saying something mean gave her permission to grieve. Then she raises her hand and brings it down on his chest as I had been doing, but instead of a fist, her hand is limp, her fingers like string.

"You stupid, stupid man," she says.

"I really did try," I say.

This is about her, I think. He did this to show her up. All her silly AA nonsense. JD had enough of it. But what good would it do to say so now?

She starts talking like I'm not really there: "He always seemed so strong that it was strange to see him act so weak. He used to lie in this very spot on the floor and weep. He stretched out his arms like Christ on the cross, and the light from the window would come in and shine on him like he was God's chosen one."

The light from the window is shining over her shoulder on his body now. Lilly comes over and curls under Peace's hand, which hangs loosely at her side as she goes on:

"He tried to show me he could take sobriety seriously. But he really couldn't do it."

We stay silent for a while. Then she decides to keep talking. "Did he tell you he started an AA group for atheists? It lasted two weeks. The only other guy who showed up drank himself to death at the end of the second week. Then he decided that the devil was his higher power. Of course, some days he thought he was the devil."

"I thought AA was okay with atheists."

"No, it's not."

"He told me Lilly was his sponsor."

She talks directly to JD: "You just couldn't accept that you had to give your life over to God. Though you told me so often enough. Just to sleep with me, goddammit. I would have slept with you anyway. I did sleep with you anyway. Maybe this is my fault."

I look at JD's painting of Peace. She probably doesn't have much trouble getting men to tell her whatever she wants to hear, but all this talk of God is making me uncomfortable. I don't see God making an appearance right now. A good god doesn't let things like this happen. But maybe there's something I can do to help.

"I think what was really bothering him," I say, "what was really getting him, is that he had to kill two people."

She looks at the new painting. I nod. "There is not to be a word about that. His parents don't need that. You don't need that. I don't need that."

"I won't need to tell them. He drew it all out for them on that wall. He finished it off with his own blood."

"Trust me, they won't figure it out. First of all, it's too obvious. And as I kept telling JD, once you weld all that junk onto your paintings, no one believes the scene is real. He wouldn't listen. It was like he needed to deface what he had done by pasting all that junk to it."

"He told me he was building on the path of assemblage artists."

"And I'm sure he also told you that was a bunch of phony bullshit. And in exactly those words."

"Yeah, almost exactly."

"Get me the phone."

I bring the phone and Peace calls 911. Her voice is matter-of-fact: "My partner shot himself."

She looks at my bloody face and clothes. "Go get yourself cleaned up."

As I leave her with JD I think of one thing:

"You were coming back, weren't you?" I say.

"Oh, what can you possibly know?" she says.

I wait in the doorway, looking at her for more of an answer.

"I always came back."

"He must have known that," I say, trying to be helpful again. Lawyers think lying helps, at least sometimes.

"I thought he was the powerful one. I guess he was really the weak one. Because I'm alive. And he isn't."

"He took a picture of this."

"Of course. The picture was for me. So I could see it all. He'd want me to wallow in my supposed responsibility. He could be vindictive. Or maybe he wanted me to sell it as his greatest work of art. The ultimate finger to the phony art world. Well, you senseless, silly man, I'm not going to look at it."

After a while, she looks up at me, and says again, "Better get cleaned up. And put this painting in the back room."

After stowing the painting, I find the camera. I take it from the tripod and put it in the freezer. Back behind the Stoli. JD's secret is Peace's secret now.

CHAPTER THIRTY

The paramedics call the coroner. They push us away from the spectacle of JD's lifeless body.

We stand in the kitchen. Peace leans back against the sink, her shoulders hunched. She is shaking.

I look over at the open bottle of vodka.

"Don't you dare," she says.

"Okay, okay," I say. "For God's sakes."

"Oh, go ahead. I'm not in charge of you. I wasn't in charge of him either. It was up to JD to save JD."

I put away the warm vodka and go into the freezer for JD's frozen vodka supply, showing her where I've put the camera behind the bottles.

"That was there?" Peace asks. She's talking about the vodka.

With nothing good to say, I pour a glass of the clear cold syrup. While

I am in mid-sip, Detective Elizabeth Endel enters the kitchen. She speaks directly to me without saying a word to Peace.

"Come with me, Mr. Straight." She turns, and I follow another of her thick, taut wool skirts out into the general area where the coroner and assistants are bustling around. Booker Reed is there.

"It's not even noon," Reed says.

"Let him have the drink," says Endel.

"Imagine our surprise, Mr. Straight," says Reed. "We're looking for you in connection with one shooting, and we find you next to another one." I take my gaze off Endel's skirt and look at Reed, buttoned up as usual. His hair was short last time, but it looks even shorter now, freshly combed with a wet tonic. His blue, latex gloves nearly match his shirt. His khaki pants are starchily crisp.

"He committed suicide. That should be obvious. The paramedics will tell you that. She'll tell you that," I say, gesturing with my head towards the kitchen.

"Apparently you were the only one here at the time," says Reed.

"Why don't you tell us what you saw, Mr. Straight," says Detective Endel, sweetly.

I look around. No sign of Professor Schiller. At this point, of course, I don't need Professor Schiller to tell me it is best to remain silent.

"Aren't you going to read me my rights?" I say.

"You're really not much of a lawyer, are you?" says Reed.

"I've read the Constitution," I say bravely.

"Well, you missed the case where it was held that Miranda only applies in custodial situations. You're not under arrest." I hate how Reed has the answer to everything. After all, I'm the lawyer here.

"Then I guess I'll leave," I say. That's how Schiller always told us to react to this line of argument. But now, only one of two things can happen. I look at my glass.

"No. Mr. Straight, you won't leave," Endel says. Her voice is even. "Go ahead and finish your drink."

"You win, Counselor. You are under arrest." Reed's voice booms from the platform of his pectoral muscles. "Bettie, let's go ahead and read him his rights. Apparently, he slept in that day in law school."

Detective Endel gives me her best apologetic look as she reads. It's good to hear the Miranda warning. I knew JD for two days. He saved my life. I am accountable for doing nothing to save his, for collapsing in a seizure instead. I need a reminder not to say so.

But Reed isn't done trying to get a rise out of me, and as they're taking me away, he says, "So, where's your buddy? Green, your partner."

I keep from saying anything, but my look tells him what he wants to know.

"Yeah. Some chick checked him out of the hospital. Any idea where he might be?"

PART FIVE:
LOS ANGELES
HIGHLIGHTS

CHAPTER THIRTY-ONE

You'd think that a stint in the Men's Central Jail would be the ultimate in Los Angeles humiliation. Instead, it's been an oddly redemptive nearly two-week interlude.

The pain has been pure, the seizures solitary, the withdrawal emptying. My only steady companion has been the strangely artistic piece of industrial art that is my cell's toilet/sink. Why has no art critic ever noticed the elegant purity of combining the sink and toilet into one impenetrable block of stainless steel? Its form follows its function perfectly with the simplicity of a Movado watch. It has everything you need for the solid and fluid cycles of your body, with nothing unnecessary that you could use to hurt yourself or others.

The five-sided column into which it is organized, with softened edges to prevent weaponizing, has all the elements of artistic perfection. I pour the waste of my bodily fluids into this marvel, and with each emptying, what is left in me becomes better. I gather new water from the sink, mix it with the filth of my body, and send it down through the bottom. It seems like a friend now the retching is over. There were moments when I worried I was worshipping the monolith, and I've been cleaning it with my shirt. It has begun to shine through the scratches and years of desperate attempts at defacement.

"You want the doctor?" the deputy said on the first day. I just looked at him. I couldn't figure out whether this was the first time I had seen him. He'd be back again. I'd talk to him then.

"Say yes, Counselor. It's better in the medical ward. A few people are genuinely insane, but you don't have to talk to them. You'll get some medicine. I'll be sure you get good treatment."

"No. I'll be alright."

He moved me into this cell, alone with my magnificent sink/toilet. How did I qualify for protective custody? I feel safer than on the outside. I can't be hounded by other lawyers or Oddyssey acolytes, bike-riding, cab-driving, gun-carrying, or otherwise. As painful as it has been here, no one can get to me. Not so sure about the medical ward.

The same deputy kept coming back. He watched me through when the seizures started and when they stopped. Through when the retching started to when it finally stopped. Somewhere in there, I recognized the deputy as Manny Wu, the bailiff at Alberta Emerald's trial. He's working the jail now. Somehow he decided—based on that old courtroom friendship, I guess—to befriend me.

After three days, I was stronger. Now I'm thinking, *Maybe I can live my life without drinking.* At least for a little while. So long as I stay right here.

We all live in a sort of jail. Is the drive on the freeway from home to work really better than the walk from the cell to the yard? Not in LA. That's how I felt on day three.

At day five, I realized I've taken windows for granted. Windows leave an opening for dreams of escape. When there are no windows, you have to confront the real source of your misery. You're trapped in the room with it.

It's been nine days now. When I first came up for arraignment, I told Deputy Wu I wasn't ready. He showed me how to claim a medical problem. The more contagious, the better. In truth, I'm starting to feel better than I have in a long time. My knife wounds are nearly healed. My psoriasis, the barometer of my stress, has dried up and vanished.

A strong man saved my life; then I helped his courage shrivel up in a storm of frozen vodka. Let him take his own life.

Where is Joel? For all I know, he's been abducted or killed by whoever decided that too many people know the secret of what Oddyssey actually doesn't do. Who was the woman who helped him get out of the hospital?

Without the alcohol, I've started to really sleep, even to dream at night. Last night I dreamt a new sort of dream. I was swimming out on the lake again. But this time, I just swam to shore, got in Joel's car, drove back home, and went to bed.

CHAPTER THIRTY-TWO

Manny is not Chinese, but of an indefinable mixed race you run across in LA. It's one of the actually good things about the town. It gives you hope that one day the whole racial thing will be too confusing for people to give a damn about. Everyone will be the approximately brownish color one gets from a weekend at Zuma. Everyone will need to get DNA tests to discover their race. That will be too much trouble, and the whole thing will be forgotten like one of my bad dreams. That time is not here yet.

"Adoption," Manny says. "So I don't really know. My parents are third-generation American. From Mexico and China. Bonanza for me."

"Did it really help?"

"Got this job, didn't I? Step up from the burger joint I was working."

"Seems a bit of a waste, actually," I say. "Watching idiots like me recycle their guts."

"No way. I love this job. Counsel the doubtful and instruct the ignorant. God's work."

"Do you comfort the innocent?"

"No one is innocent, Counselor. Especially not in here."

"I am."

"Really? Then why won't you let me take you to the medical ward? Why don't you want anything for your seizures? Why do you want to do them alone?"

I am quiet.

"Gotta take care of yourself, Counselor. No one on earth is completely good. Bible says so."

"You trying to convert me? Is that why you're always hanging around?"

"No, Counselor. I'm Mormon. Converting anyone in here is too much of a stretch. Can't understand the Book of Mormon enough to explain it to anyone, and anyway, it might get me fired to try."

"Couldn't you make more money somewhere else? I thought you Mormons gave each other jobs."

"I do make more money somewhere else. You know what your problem is, Counselor? You spend all your time doing one job, and then you can't take the second job, which is the one that makes you the money. The way to make money is to have two jobs. Helps to start with a government job. Good benefits. Lots of free time. No extra time without overtime."

"What are you talking about, free time?"

"Know what Cesar Chavez Day is?"

"I know Cesar Chavez is the reason I never drank Gallo wine in college."

"He's got a whole holiday, and if you work for the government, you don't work on Cesar Chavez Day. Or you get overtime. When you work for the government, you have time for something on the side. That's where you make the money. I'm in investments, but I make the most money flipping houses. I don't know why, but people always pay at least $10,000 more for a house after you paint it. You paint a house for $2,000. Easy money, Counselor. The market goes up. This is LA, man. The market is always going up. There's only so much land between here and the ocean, and more people are trying to buy it all the time."

"Why are you wasting your time with me?" I say, looking through the bars, seeing the metallic glow of their neat white paint. No chips on these bars. This cell, for protective custody, is almost clean. Other inmates are sleeping on floors in large assembly rooms wondering which of the fifty other desperate men around them will feel the need to stab them with a sharpened plastic pen when they close their eyes in the hope of sleep. There is no dreaming in those rooms, and no reason to dream. The erratic god who supervises this cruel place has chosen me for safety.

The god of Los Angeles always behaves with incoherent, random munificence. There is no logical reason why LA prefers some people over the hordes of similar people around them. There are plenty of actresses waiting tables who are just as pretty and witty as the ones pulling down $25,000 an episode for the mindless sitcoms everyone in Nebraska is watching, and it isn't because they won't sleep with the fifty-something overweight agents and producers.

Why should I question the divine order? For some reason, the LA god has decided, in light of my temporary status as a facsimile celebrity, to ordain that I may live through this stint in the county jail with a deputy who has decided to be my personal bodyguard and confidant. Sure, we became acquainted during the Alberta Emerald trial, but it doesn't explain why he has decided to care so much about me. I want to know why.

"I like you, Counselor. There's something about your face. You look like you want to help somebody."

"Thanks, but that doesn't sound like a compliment."

"I also need a lawyer to help me figure out the foreclosure market."

"There's probably five of them in here right now who know the right guy at the courthouse to pay to get ahead in that game. You know, Manny, you can go ahead and think I stabbed my partner, or shot that sleazy gangster, but I'm not interested in advising you on how to pay bribes."

"Okay, Counselor. I guess I deserved that."

"So. Tell me the real reason."

"Oddyssey."

"I got fired from my firm. I've got nothing to do with it now."

"The offering goes out in a few days. The stock went up to $30 last week after that press conference, after you got arrested. Personally, I don't think you've got it in you to murder the gangster, or that artist. But the stock market is starting to think Oddyssey is legitimate and maybe you are guilty."

"Why should I care about this?"

"Look, Counselor. I can get you better treatment than this. I can get you outside for two hours a day. I can get you medicine that will make you feel better. You'll think you're still drinking. You can work out. You can stop looking like you're so goddamn guilty."

"You want to know whether to buy."

"Or sell. Or sell short."

"You know, Manny, you're asking a couple days too late. Couple days ago I would have done anything for some kind of drug that would make me feel even a little better. But now I'm actually feeling like I might be okay. I didn't murder anybody, and even without a lawyer to help me, I should be able to prove that. There's photos to prove it. And I'm in enough trouble without insider trading."

"Nobody's listening, Counselor. No need to pretend."

Yeah right. The sheriff can record anything, anywhere in this building. I turn and go to the back of the cell. But I wonder.

Richard fired me. I am no longer an automatic insider. And I know things. Things maybe even Richard doesn't know. Like the fact that Oddyssey is nothing more than a cover for a criminal enterprise. That the real profits come from laundering money through computer data. That the whole "search" thing is just a cover. No one could ever make money on that sort of thing.

Maybe what I know isn't really inside information. I got it from JD. And he isn't talking.

I come to a decision. Whatever people think now, I am going public with what I know as soon as it proves necessary for me to defend myself.

What the hell. No, let's say it right. What the fuck. Manny's a nice enough guy.

"I'm not greedy," I say. "I want 10 percent."

"Done."

I could have gotten fifty-fifty on this deal. But that kind of money would be too much for me to deal with. I just need enough to pay off Xanthe's credit cards. Get out of the latest hole created by my relentless attraction to women.

"Short it, Manny, all the way down. Move now. I'll try to time it for you."

"That's what I thought."

"So what are you going to do for me?"

"I'm going to tell you the secret to staying here for a while. Which you might want to do in view of the fact that everyone seems to be trying to kill you."

"Okay, I'm ready."

"Represent yourself."

"I thought you had something real for me. I don't have any experience in criminal law. I don't even know how to plead not guilty."

"O. J.'s down the hall, Counselor. He knows how to plead not guilty."

"I'm going to learn from O. J.?"

"Look, here's the deal. You ask to represent yourself. Then you ask for backup counsel, advisory counsel. You get access to the library. Time and money for phone calls. You get out of your cell for almost the whole day and you can call anyone you like. It's a racket, and the people who know it have the best time here. Stay with me, Sam. I can keep you safe while this Oddyssey shit goes down."

I'm beginning to wonder. Maybe I can learn something about criminal law. Xanthe won't miss me.

"If you get in too deep, you can always ask for counsel and they'll give it to you."

"Still sounds like baloney to me. Why doesn't O. J. represent himself?"

"His lawyers are too high profile, Counselor. Shapiro. Weitzman. That

Kardashian guy? Those guys don't let you act like you don't need them. For O. J. it's too transparent. But for you it makes sense. You're a lawyer. The judge will have to allow it."

This still sounds wrong to me. But I'll consider it. In the meantime, I don't want to have Manny entangle me in his trading scheme. "Don't try to pay me. Don't try to contact me. I'll call you."

"I'll be ready."

Why am I always trying to be nice to people?

Two large sheriff's deputies show up outside my white bars. They are the same height, easily six foot six. Could be twins. Identical bodybuilder biceps. Names tags: Williams. Kowalski.

"Manny sent us," says Williams.

"Your lawyer is here to see you," says Kowalski.

"I don't have a lawyer."

"I think you do now."

"I don't want a lawyer. I'm going to represent myself."

"I think you want to talk to this young lady. I will if you won't."

Valerie. But why would Valerie be claiming to represent me? C&C fired me. I was the cancer on Oddyssey. I've been excised. They'll want to keep it that way. Unless they know. Unless Richard has already figured out that Oddyssey is fake. In that case, he needs to keep me from talking.

Richard can be a dark arts sort of lawyer. But how dark? As black as his heart may be, I still can't think of Richard as a murderer. He'd find another way to take care of me. Like sending Valerie.

I remain quiet, castigating myself for ever telling Joel I would get involved in all this. I always seem to go along. Joel used to call me "the man who wouldn't say no." So why did he ask, knowing that?

Kowalski is right, though. Under any circumstances, Valerie in the right outfit is worth going through the getting on and off of the chains, and the walking down to the attorney meeting room.

Williams stands outside the cell while Kowalski gets the chains on me. Then we shuffle together down the hall, going by the cell where they say they're keeping O. J. Even in this context, it's my LA instinct not to stare or whisper about a celebrity, but I catch a glimpse of his powerful shoulders from behind. He is staring at the blank wall in the back of his cell.

"Dude is still pretty trim, huh?" says Williams after we pass.

"You guys could take him," I say. "Why weren't you guys in the NFL?"

"We were."

"Let me guess. You have another job."

"Well, we pose. We lift with Schwarzenegger out in Santa Monica," Williams says.

"We do some bodyguard work for him too," says Kowalski.

"Does it pay better than here?" I ask.

"Yeah, but you can't beat those county benefits," says Williams.

"We retire in five more years."

"You don't think there's any future working with Arnold, do you?" I say. "What happens after those muscles turn to mush?"

"You don't know Arnold," says Kowalski.

They bring me into a room with a seat that is a shiny round circle on the end of a metal post, not enough to actually sit on. But that's what it is: the place where you sit while you try to talk to your lawyer through the window. More minimalist art, form and function perfectly matched.

Sure enough, the lawyer on the other side of the Plexiglas is Valerie, and, as always, the first thing I notice is her blouse, with the cloth of the first two buttons softly curled over like the waves behind a motorboat. The third and fourth buttons reveal just enough to make me wish she had stayed that night when she brought me home. I pick up the telephone.

"Sam" is all she says. She puts her hand on the Plexiglas surface that separates us. I put my hand there too, covering hers. I manage to keep myself from heaving with a tear at the memory of what the touch of someone who cares for you actually feels like. Maybe I've been wrong. Maybe Valerie and I really can be, be . . . together.

"Valerie." All I can add is "I'm sorry. You don't need this."

"Sam, it's going to be okay."

"I'm not sure there's anything you can do," I say.

"It's not going to be just me," she says. "The firm is going to represent you."

"Nobody there knows anything about this type of thing."

"Richard was in the US Attorney's Office."

"That was a decade and a half ago, in New York City. That's not going to help. State court judges in LA will hate him."

"Then they'll get you somebody. They told me they would do anything."

"That doesn't sound like them."

"Two days ago I went in to quit. I told Jenkins—he's the managing partner now—I couldn't work in a place that had abandoned you like they did. Then Total promised me the firm will defend you. They may even reinstate you if you let them. Total is on the executive committee."

"Yes, he rarely fails to mention it. That gives him authority to lie on behalf of the firm."

"It sounded real, Sam."

They've really gotten to her. They must think keeping me under control will help them. Valerie probably thinks she's back on the partnership track. Wonder if she's passed the bar exam.

"I'm going to represent myself."

"Sam, I respect you. You know I like you."

I cut her off. "Where did you go when you left my place?"

"I got called out to the printer on the Oddyssey deal."

"Thought you were a litigator. Thought you were going to call me."

"I'm not anything yet. They brought everyone in that night. They were anxious to have the offering ready to go out on time."

"Why didn't you tell me you were working on the offering?"

"It seemed like the first time you'd slept in a week. You just needed some rest. Look, Sam, I believe in you. But you have to let someone help."

There is something about the swell in Valerie's upper body that makes me want to be the tough guy, a guy she would look up to, a guy who can take care of himself and take care of her.

So I say, "I know I'm not guilty, Valerie. And I think I know who is guilty."

I'm about to say the Kid's name. She must know that. She can't really believe he's legitimate after that stunt in the steam room. Her big eyes swell behind her contacts, and I see pools of tears forming in them.

"Sam, do this for me," she says.

They know my weakness. I really can't think in the face of this onslaught of everything I idolize: care, youth, and sheerest beauty. I just say, "Yes."

Valerie brightens quickly. The tears melt away in situ. She seems ready to leave.

"I'll see you in the courtroom tomorrow. We won't talk there. Too many people can overhear."

"Won't you need me to say something?"

"No. I'll just enter a plea for you. And then we'll get you out—on bail if necessary, but we think we can do OR."

I don't even know what OR is, though I guess it's good. *Who is we?* But before I can ask about these things, she is gone.

I wanted to tell her I've quit smoking. At least for now.

CHAPTER THIRTY-THREE

Something is different about this trip to court.

I don't mean the chains and the orange clothes, or the black-and-white sheriff's bus.

I don't even mean my traveling companion, courtesy of Manny.

"This kid, Sam, I need your help. You're coming with me to East LA. You'll do better there anyway." *Oh great*, I think. Now I'm doing favors for him.

"Kid's name is Timmy. He's seventeen, and he's off his meds. Schizo. I got him in the medical ward. They give him the meds, but he must be spitting them out or something cause he had a break last night. We can get him to the bus alright, but I'm afraid he's going to get crazy on the ride."

"Okay, and . . . ?"

"I need someone to sit next to him on the bus who won't kill him if he gets nuts."

"Can't he get his own seat?"

"Bus is full."

"Can't you transport him separately?"

"Budget cuts."

Always the budget cuts. Every year they raise the taxes in California, every year they spend more money than the previous year, and every year they seem to be saying they need to cut something. They're always cutting something you actually need. And expanding the things you don't actually want, but somebody thinks you should have, like extra instructions on why you should stop smoking.

"Can't he wait till he's feeling better?" I ask.

"His bail is too high. He's got five petty theft charges. Not much on their own, but it adds up when they charge them all. Family can't get him out till the judge knocks down the bail."

"Why do you care?"

"I know his mother." So, Manny is no different from me. It always comes down to a woman asking you to do something. Manny seems to know I'm that kind of guy. Maybe someone told him about all the damsels in distress in my pro bono files.

"Remind me what you're doing for me," I say.

Manny raises an eyebrow on one side. "*The Wall Street Journal* is covering your arraignment."

"Stay short. Today's the day."

"I'll make some more calls. Your tenth could be big." I pray he isn't wearing a wire. There will be a price for this, as there always is for me.

Manny brings Timmy on last and sits him down by me. Timmy isn't too bad, it seems. He's young. His beard seems barely there, full of blanks where nothing can grow yet, if it ever will. Frail, barely about 120 pounds. I say hi. He just stares.

"Sam," I say. "That's my name. You okay?"

"Sam I said. Who is Sam I said?"

Okay, that's a little weird, but I can deal with it.

Timmy panics: "Sam I Said is trying to kill me!"

"It's okay, Timmy." I use my best soothing tone.

"Timmy is trying to kill me too!" Timmy rocks back and forth in the seat. As he strains against the straps of his seatbelt, the veins in his neck begin to bulge.

"Get away from me, get away from me."

"I can't, Timmy."

"Get away from me."

Timmy grows more desperate and loud. The tenor of the other riders on the bus changes with him. Our fellow prisoners rain curses down on him. "Shut the fuck up, you little loco mother," is the least crude and most comprehensible.

"No one's going to hurt you," I try. "Manny will take care of us."

"Manny sleeps with my mother. Manny is the devil."

Oh, God. Looking down, I see he has turned his hips towards me. There is a yellowish pool of liquid flowing from his darkening orange jumpsuit across the vinyl of the seat towards me. I try to move, but I can't. My thigh feels wet.

"Please stop, Timmy."

Timmy doesn't stop. He spits at me. I duck away, but it hits the side of my head, and drips down onto my neck. "Please stop, Timmy."

Finally, Manny walks up the aisle of the bus. Behind him, another deputy draws his gun. Manny's hands are covered with blue plastic. With a strong motion connected directly with his stride, he swings back, and hits Timmy directly on the face with his open hand. There is a crack, and Timmy is quiet. He sobs, slowly at first, then uncontrollably, the tears flowing, the face contorting back on itself as the skin of his cheeks turns red.

"Sometimes, you just gotta hit somebody," says Manny.

Manny strides back up the aisle. They are all talking trash to him now:

"That's federal civil rights, Wu."

"My lawyer pays me a finder's fee for cases like this."

"Your career is over, baby."

Manny has not been as much help as he thinks. Timmy lays his head down on my lap. Pretty soon my orange jumpsuit is wet with an assortment of Timmy's bodily fluids.

Although Timmy isn't the biggest difference from all my other trips to court.

CHAPTER THIRTY-FOUR

"**N**ot gonna be no lawsuit," sighs Manny. "I know his mother."

Manny gets me a new orange jumpsuit. The old one goes in a plastic bag. He has stopped observing the strict formalities of my custody status. He walks freely in and out of the cell. The chains are gone. He has no backup.

"Sorry about that, Sam."

"He could have AIDS."

"Aren't you the tender liberal? He's crazy, but he likes girls. Sometimes little girls. Look, I appreciate what you did watching out for him."

"You hit him."

"I didn't hurt him. He's fine. Except for the fact that he's completely out of his mind."

Timmy is showing just how fine he is by climbing all around the bars of the cell next to me, as if being chased by goblins. He seems to defy gravity, spreading bodily fluids everywhere. Thank God for the wall that keeps him from spitting directly on me.

"You could have hit him," Manny suggests.

"Don't think so."

"You're a good man, Sam. But now I've got something invested in you. So I guess I'd like you to start taking care of yourself." Manny puts his hand on my chin like he's measuring it to level a big slap. But he just wants my attention. "Sometimes it's okay to hit people, Sam."

I can't say anything. Maybe he's right.

Manny returns a few minutes later. "Judge Carrey is coming down here, Sam. You lucked out. He's soft."

Timmy is the problem, of course. He's too uncontrollable to send upstairs to the courtroom.

"We're trying to get him seen right now," Manny tells me.

On television, the arraignment judges are all exhausted civil servants who look like they haven't left their chair for twenty years. Judge Carrey can't be more than forty, his long blond hair hanging on his robe. *What kind of hippies is the governor appointing these days?*

Leaving the twenty-something lawyers behind him, Judge Carrey approaches Timmy's cell.

"Timmy, I'm the judge of your case. Do you know what a judge is?"

Timmy says nothing, appearing catatonic. Then, frantic movement. Judge Carrey maintains his idealistic calm, then flinches. Timmy's spit lies on the shoulder of the robe the judge has bravely worn into the holding area.

"They're trying to kill me," Timmy screams.

"Timmy, here is where we try to decide whether you have done anything to break the law. The charges against you are misdemeanors. Even if you have done them, we're not trying to punish you as much as we are trying to just get you some help. No one in the courtroom will try to kill you. Manny here will make sure of that."

"It's not right to kill me."

The court reporter and the young lawyers stay behind Judge Carrey, out of spitting distance.

"Timmy, did you speak to Miss Roberts here?" Judge Carrey gestures to the petite twenty-something with a brusque bob of brown hair now hiding behind him.

"Miss Rooboo. She's no miss. She's a witch. She's trying to kill me." Judge Carrey looks back at Ms. Roberts. She shrugs.

It goes on like this for minutes that seem like hours. Finally, Judge Carrey has enough. "Alright, let's go. I'll declare a doubt." I have no idea what he's talking about. I had doubt the moment I laid eyes upon Timmy.

Judge Carrey and his entourage decamp with a flip of his robes.

"We're going up," Manny says. He takes me up a cell elevator. I shuffle in chains to a holding cell. I stand there in the completely blank space—the walls a dull-gray metal color.

———————

A little square window opens. I see part of the face of Ms. Roberts, the prim public defender.

"I'm the public defender."

"I saw you downstairs. Is this how we confer? Standing up? Don't I get to see the documents?"

"I looked at them outside."

"Maybe I'd like to look at them."

"It doesn't happen like that."

"I don't get to see the evidence?"

"I've got seventeen other people I have to talk to right now. Some of them in here. Some of them out there on bail. There are two private attorneys here who say they want to represent you. You want to try them?"

"What do they look like?"

"The girl's a real number. Her blouse is looking for action. The other one's got a nice suit, but he looks like some sort of very hungry animal."

"Like a wolf?"

"Kind of a vulture."

Richard. And Valerie, of course. The blouse still open. For my benefit. Or Judge Carrey's.

The window clangs shut. Apparently, this is the end of our attorney-client consultation.

I try to estimate the time passing. It could be twenty minutes or an hour of emptiness going by. Just staring at the wall.

The metal window opens again. This time it's Valerie. And her nicely positioned blouse.

"Sam, we can help you."

"I'm going to represent myself. At least for now."

A voice I almost don't recognize comes from behind her. The cruel and uncompromising voice that recently excised me from the partnership of Cohen & Cranston with precise verbal surgery has been replaced with a soothing contralto almost as pleasing as Valerie's husky tone.

"Sam. I'm sorry about the tough way I talked to you a couple weeks back. The partners have told me to put the resources of the firm to work for you. I know what I'm doing in this kind of court. You know, from when I was with the US attorney. We can get you out today, and then we can figure this out. I've learned a couple things lately."

I've been sober for a week now, and I don't feel quite as weak as I'm supposed to in the face of Valerie's bosom and Richard's Mephistophelean charm. I have something to say out there, and I need to represent myself to say it. I sit down with my back to the door.

Valerie continues talking plaintively. I imagine her looking at Richard commanding her with his wicked face.

Then, Manny's voice. "Do you want them to leave, Sam?"

"Yes," I say.

I hear Richard's more familiar voice.

"Don't be a fool, Straight. No one should be their own lawyer."

"You have to leave now," Manny says, taking them away. For once in my life I have some protection from the Richards of the world.

A minute later Manny is back. "I'll get Ms. Roberts back. Tell her you want her to be your advisory counsel."

When Ms. Roberts comes back, she shuffles a three-page form filled with stiff, legal language through the small opening for me to sign. I'm used to reading through this sort of garbage and within a few seconds can understand how I'm basically being told just what Richard said: I would be a fool to represent myself. Manny has checked off all the boxes in which I'm agreeing I am a fool.

"Should I sign this, Manny?"

"Sure."

I sign.

A few minutes later I stand in the dirty courtroom, just beyond the metal door of the holding cell.

"People v. Straight," Judge Carrey says. On television, the judges have clerks to call the cases. Here, they do it themselves.

Judge Carrey fumbles over the form I filled out. He looks very tired.

Ms. Roberts stands away from me, almost at the middle of the counsel table. She crosses over into the prosecution side. The orange jumpsuits that pass through on this side of the table have left a smell. *No, wait. The smell is coming from me.* Timmy's urine must have dried on my skin.

The young prosecutor's shiny and somewhat long black hair is slicked into a wave and combed back over his head. I try not to stare at the redness of his live acne. These lawyers are practically teenagers.

Both lawyers roll their eyes as the seconds turn to minutes and Judge Carrey continues to puzzle over my file. Ms. Roberts gives me a look that says "We might be here a while." The battered plastic clock hanging crookedly on the wall says it's 3:30 in the afternoon. I am the last case. It is evident that everyone but him is anxious to get home. Must be union rules.

Judge Carrey, however, seems naïve enough to want to do the job to which he has been appointed. Ms. Roberts makes her way over to my side of the table, and whispers into my ear, "This is his first Faretta waiver. Hasn't the faintest idea of what he's doing."

She decides to take matters into her own hands and begins instructing Judge Carrey.

"It's usually sufficient to go through the form with the defendant, Judge," she states, straining to keep the boredom from her voice.

"Well, counsel, I'll tell you, it's not always sufficient for me," Judge Carrey says defensively, without looking up. I can tell it bothers him, but he does not remark about her demeaning use of the term *Judge*. Ms. Roberts is too young to know how judges detest this.

Finally, he stares at me with his tired, puzzled expression. "Have you ever read *Faretta v. California*, Mr. Straight?"

"Maybe in my casebook." Every lawyer's vivid first impression of the law comes from the excerpts of famous cases included in the "casebooks" that used to be the staple of law schools. For some lawyers it's the first and last law they read. I've never heard of this case. Must post-date my law school days.

"Well, I took the time to read it this afternoon. It's filled with the idealism of the seventies. We were supposedly guarding against the excesses of the Star Chamber of nearly 300 years ago by giving every criminal defendant a bright, freshly minted right to represent himself. The problem, and you should know this, Mr. Straight, is that it's never really a good idea to represent yourself."

He's actually looking up cases in the chambers library to help him with routine business. I'm starting to feel sorry for Judge Carrey, stuck in a courtroom where none of these young lawyers have any respect for him, struggling to get by with what he can remember about criminal law from law school. Of course, that's the situation I'm in too, and I am in a bit more danger.

"I understand your point, Your Honor, but I feel this is best for me. If it makes you feel any better, I'll take the public defender as an advisory counsel."

Richard lurches through the gate to the counsel table, with Valerie in tow.

"Your Honor, Cohen & Cranston is willing to act as backup counsel without cost to the defendant," he says.

"I appreciate how you're used to being in charge of whatever room you're in, Mr. Total. But in my courtroom, you need to wait to be told it's your turn to speak."

"Of course, Your Honor," Total says. He retreats verbally, but settles into the smelling range of Timmy's urine. I can't believe the skills of the man. He can go from an obnoxious asshole to an obsequious toady in seconds without a facial tic or grimace.

Carrey gets back to me. "Do you want your firm to represent you?"

"No, Your Honor. I do not want them." I am surprised by the clarity of my thoughts dictating unambiguously, crisply. That's new. It feels good to have a clear head. It's been years since I've walked around without a hangover, and the difference exhilarates me.

"Is there any reason?"

"I'd rather not go into details at this time, Your Honor. But in general, it may be necessary to expose facts confidential to the firm's clients, especially Oddyssey.com, for me to conduct my defense. The truth may be that Oddyssey is not what it purports to be, and that may be the real reason someone else tried to kill my partner Joel Green. It may be the real reason behind the other killings of which I'm suspected. The truth is, the truth is. . . "

"Yes, of course," says Carrey. "I did not mean to invade the privacy of your thoughts," he says. "Or the confidences of your clients. You will need to give full consideration to that."

He seems almost embarrassed. Judge Carrey exhibits signs of actual pain when intruding, in even the most minor way, on a constitutional right. He's never going to last in this job.

I look around. A few of the short sellers have runners in the courtroom, young lawyers trained as observers. They've been waiting to hear whether I intend to make allegations against Oddyssey sufficient to send down the stock price. One by one, they look at each other and begin to leave. They've heard what they needed to hear. Then there is the sound of their footsteps as they start running for the phones. I've hardly said anything, but I've said enough. They know. Something is seriously wrong at Oddyssey.com.

Judge Carrey takes a turn: "Just looking to determine whether your decision to represent yourself has really been fully considered. Mr. Total is a bit pushy, but he looks like he could be a pretty good lawyer."

"And, Your Honor," Total injects, "we are uniquely positioned to both defend our client and guard our client's secrets."

"Mr. Total. In this court we do not interrupt each other. And most especially, and you of all people must know this, we don't interrupt the judge."

"Of course, Your Honor." Total returns to his obsequious tone.

The pimply prosecutor breaks in. "Your Honor, Mr. Straight was about to tell us the truth."

"The truth is . . . Joel Green is my best friend. I could never. . . " There is no strength to go on with this thought. "This is not about Mr. Total's skill," I try. Judge Carrey gives me the eye. I know this look. He has heard as much as he can keep in his mind and doesn't want the lawyers to keep talking as if he isn't there.

"I'm worried that what you may actually have, Mr. Total, is a conflict of interest. Your clients and Mr. Straight have very different interests at this point. Have a seat in the gallery," Judge Carrey says with finality.

"Your Honor, Mr. Straight is not in his right mind. He's a drug addict. He's an alcoholic—"

"Have a seat, Mr. Total." Judge Carrey has learned a tiny bit of toughness in his few weeks in the criminal courts. Total hurries out, allowing the hip-high gate between the lawyers' area and the courtroom gallery to slam in his passing. Valerie stops before following and faces me. She spreads her arms plaintively and looks at me as if to say "Come on, Sam. What are you doing?" I don't move. She shrugs reluctantly and follows Total into the gallery and out the door.

Judge Carrey's clerk speaks up. "Judge" is all she says, but she glares at him, then at the clock. Her hard face is eloquent: "We have to get this done, sometime. . . "

"Look, Mr. Straight, I'm going to allow you to represent yourself, and appoint Ms. Roberts as your backup. I'm not going to take you through every element of this form today," he says, looking back at his clerk to let her know he received her message.

But now the prosecutor wants his word: "Your Honor, Mr. Straight is an accomplished lawyer. There is no reason to appoint backup counsel at the expense of the county."

"Mr. Ramirez, argument is over," Judge Carrey says patiently to the prosecutor.

"Argument over? You just gave a lawyer who isn't even in the case a chance to talk and you're going to dismiss my argument?" Mr. Ramirez's shirt is unbuttoned at the neck and his tie hangs loosely, as if he is hanging out at the other kind of bar.

Judge Carrey collects himself and musters the discipline necessary not to respond. He meets my eyes, and we communicate nonverbally. This is one of those lawyer skills for which there is no box score. The record does not reflect that his eyes say, "These kids are trying to run all over me." Nor does it reflect that my eyes respond, "Don't let them."

"Do you waive reading of the complaint, and a statement of your rights?" Judge Carrey says to me.

"I would actually like to read the complaint," I say.

Now everyone starts rolling their eyes. "You'll get plenty of time to read it, Mr. Straight. I'm just asking if you'll do me the courtesy of not reading it to you. That's not really necessary, is it?"

I look at Ms. Roberts. She makes no effort to move from her place at the middle of the desk. But she mouths, "No."

"No, Your Honor," I say.

"Thank you, Mr. Straight. How do you plead?"

"Not guilty," I say.

"People ask for remand," Ramirez, the pimply prosecutor, says. "This was a violent knife attack."

I look blankly at Ms. Roberts. She shrugs with impatience, and finally comes near me. "Ask for the schedule," she says.

"Could I look at the schedule?" I say.

Ms. Roberts is going nuts. With a glance of her own at the clock she says, "He's trying to say he'll accept bail at the normal schedule."

"Let me see the police report," Judge Carrey says.

"We object to that," says the pimply prosecutor.

"You should object too," Ms. Roberts whispers to me.

"Why?" I say, apparently loud enough for Judge Carrey to hear.

"Yes, really, why?" says Judge Carrey. "How do you expect me to determine how dangerous this man is if I'm not allowed to consider any facts of the case?"

There is a momentary standstill in the court, and finally, with a disgusted sigh, the pimply young prosecutor walks up to the front of the judge's bench and throws the police report at the judge's bench. Judge Carrey ignores the disrespect and intently pages through the report, again ignoring how everyone except me is looking huffily at each other and the clock.

Judge Carrey reads on. The clerk flicks her pen rudely as the minutes tick off. Finally, he says, "Mr. Ramirez, the police can certainly put Mr. Straight in the same place as his partner on the night in question, but he was severely wounded, so severely he wasn't even conscious."

"Thing is, Judge," says Ramirez, "we didn't find anyone else."

"This happened weeks ago. Have they looked?"

"Your Honor, you're not seriously considering putting this man on the street, are you? Have you read the part about the gloves? This would be like letting out O. J. Simpson. The defendant is a killer, and once a killer starts killing, it's likely he will kill again. He's been present at other mysterious deaths since the attack on his partner."

"I'm considering the strength of the evidence of this crime, counsel." Then after a pause, he adds, "Bail will be $50,000."

"Your Honor," wails Ramirez. "I would like the court to state its reasoning. I'm sure the public will want to know if this defendant kills someone while out there on bail.'"

"I don't have to state any reasons, counsel," says Carrey, "but you've barely got enough information here to get you past a preliminary hearing. If that."

"Mr. Straight is also a suspect in the murder of gangster Jacky Real, Judge."

"Well, when you have some evidence of that, you can charge him. When are we going to set the preliminary hearing? Mr. Straight, do you waive time?"

I looked at Ms. Roberts, who shakes her head emphatically.

"No, Your Honor."

Judge Carrey sets the preliminary hearing for next month. But first, he has to look over at his now very unhappy clerk. Is she the person who's really in charge? Then, without a further word, he gets up and walks off the bench.

Manny leads me back into the cell. He's light with anticipation. "It was perfect. Low key, natural, but definite. I'll bet Oddyssey's stock is going down for the count. Actually, that's a bet I already made."

I could try to tell Manny I was just trying to defend Joel's good name. And trying to give a voice to JD. But I decide to let him think I'm trying to make him rich.

And then I realize the biggest difference between this and all of my other trips to court: I haven't fallen asleep and haven't even felt like doing so. I haven't even pretended to fall asleep. I've been awake and alive and alert to every movement, every expression in the court by everyone. Maybe that's the way it's supposed to be.

The elevator has a separate compartment for the prisoner, but Manny leaves open the gate between us. It feels like one of those science-fiction movies where the prisoners are being sent down into the bowels of the earth.

I'm suddenly anxious to get back to the job I thought I hated, anxious to put this new clarity to work. Of course, I don't have any more clients, except for the pro bono ones Richard is dumping on me. I would be surprised if those files have not already been delivered to my home. I wonder if Xanthe has put them in the garbage. Or maybe she called a recycling company. She is big on the environment.

CHAPTER THIRTY-FIVE

My Chinese-Mexican Mormon jailor looks worried. "You did too good a job. Somebody named Peace made your bail."

"The artist who committed suicide," I say. "She's the girlfriend. You should see his painting of her."

"Well, I've got her address and phone if you need it." Manny hands me a little piece of paper, then takes out a pen and writes his own telephone number on the plastic band fastened to my wrist. Hospitals, jails. I'm collecting wristbands.

"I get off shift in four hours. It'll be about 6 a.m. Call me and I'll come get you."

"Are you sure you can put me up?"

"I'll find a place for you."

I've made Manny his money. I'm just his paper trail. I form an intention of not calling.

"I'm going to stop by her place," I say.

"Why?"

"I don't know. I just feel like I should."

"I can get you some money," he says.

"I just want to go," I say. I've stashed some money in crevices of my house. Xanthe doesn't know all of them.

With my clothing marked as evidence, I will be leaving in the baggy orange jumpsuit. Sackcloth and ashes, I suppose. They're looking at the blood spatter from JD. I suppose another brilliant criminal complaint is on its way, courtesy of Ramirez, or one of the other geniuses in the district attorney's office. I hope Peace has disposed of that painting.

I walk through the gate to the front of the jail. Even in the night darkness, there is a crowd. Prisoners just being released mingle with those who have been waiting for them, who have no one better to love. Of course, there is no one here who loves me. No one at all.

A row of pay phones lines the front of the building, every one of them occupied. The phones are so stoutly posted they could stop a truck. I move away from the crowd.

With the LA River not far away, I feel an urge to get to it, to find the one place where no one in LA ever wants to look, to find one of JD's tents and convince the tweakers to hide me for a few days while the wreckage of the Oddyssey public offering plays out. Find my own Sparrow. But then I long for the clean, dark room in JD's condo.

I make my way away from the prisoners and families, forging my way up a street lined with chain-linked fence. The fence bounds only empty land, sparse desert weeds coming through the remains of concrete. Here in a city filled with land pumped to ludicrous notions of value by silly human ambition, there is still empty rubble, abused and spit upon, good for nothing other than collecting the trash that falls on it.

Coming up the concrete tunnel of Vignes Street, I see it sitting there.

A yellow cab. The lights off. Ali's dark, hirsute face gazing down the ramp at me. With JD dead, there is only the dark side of Oddyssey left, and the bad Oddyssey knows I'm out. The *LA Times* probably covered my bail hearing. Ali's lights turn on and his cab approaches. I'm fucked.

Nothing to do but turn and run. Out of the tunnel. Through the crowd in front of the jail. Running freely. My wounds have become cuts, stretching but not breaking. Stronger sober, I can feel the runner within. For the first time in as long as I can remember, my lungs fill and empty freely.

There is an MTA bus, something almost never there when you need it. I board with other inmates. We flash our wristbands, good for passage.

The bus pulls away. Ali's cab has been blocked by the milling crowd. He'll call the rest of the Oddyssey goons. With JD gone, they will be his only constituency. How many cabs, or even sheriff's deputies, are on the Oddyssey take? I should have realized how my defense has put their dreams of a quick fortune at risk.

The stock market means nothing inside this bus. No one know or cares who I am or who is chasing me. Half the people on this bus are taking advantage of the free-ride wristbands. They look at me blankly, in unison, as if to say, "You have to be kidding."

The bus stops at Pershing Square. I thank the driver and jump out. I need to see Peace. But my intestines will not go that far. I go down the stairs to the square's underground parking lot.

I try the bathrooms. Locked: *See attendant for key.*

"You're not parking here, friend. We can't let you," says the security guard in the office. This damn orange jumpsuit.

"In one more minute, this orange suit is going to be brown. Someone is going to have to clean it up."

Rolling his eyes, the guard goes over and unlocks the door for me.

I just stay in the stall, not wanting to move. There is a strange sense of safety here. I sit on the toilet and sleep.

What time is it? A businessman stops in. Then another. Some of this traffic must be from early risers, fresh from their long drives into LA, getting in for the market opening. There will be a new day soon. More commuters stop in, two or three at a time. Somehow there is safety in a new day. I can leave.

CHAPTER THIRTY-SIX

Up from the bowels of Pershing Square, I walk west through the streets of downtown Los Angeles. The morning light comes up over Pomona, illuminating another dirty day in a dirty town.

The new papers will be out. I go to one of the clanky *LA Times* machines, and see that today's paper is there. But I have no quarters, and it takes a few. I step back and try to disappear behind a lamppost.

A tired, hurried young commuter tries for his paper. It takes his quarters, but when he tries to lift the front cover of the machine to retrieve his paper, it catches. His quarters are gobbled up. He starts banging the front cover, but it still doesn't move. "Goddam these fucking things." Finally, he inserts more quarters, and this time the cover opens. I move up behind him to grab a paper after he does. "Be my guest," he says. "As usual, I paid for two."

There it is. Under the fold is a smiling picture of the Kid pumping iron in front of a poster of Nancy Reagan saying "Just Say No."

INTERNET DARLING ODDYSSEY GOES ON STRANGE TRIP
Trading Stopped.

The NASDAQ halted trading today on Oddyssey.com, the Internet sensation helmed by teenage business wunderkind Kid Cauer. The stock has been haunted for weeks by rumors that something was not quite right with the firm, which markets messenger and concierge services world-wide, while answering questions using the Internet as a database. Three earlier suits had been stymied by the company's lawyers, but new allegations of sexual impropriety and a violent incident inside the law firm that had been defending the cases raised new questions two weeks ago. Joel Green and Sam Straight, partners at Cohen & Cranston, the white-shoe New York firm that has acted as counsel to Oddyssey, were taken to the hospital with stab wounds, claiming they were victims of a late-night office invasion.

Police sought out Straight after he left County Hospital against medical advice when police tried to question him. Then surveillance cameras captured Straight at the scene of the murder of gangster Jacky Real, who had also been linked by sources to Oddyssey. The LAPD arrested Straight after they found him at the home of artist J. C. Darrow. They also found Mr. Darrow dead. Although it appears Darrow died from a self-inflicted gunshot, police are investigating his death as a homicide.

According to LAPD sources, police began investigating the initial incident at Cohen & Cranston differently after partner Joel Green, who was the closest lawyer to Kid Cauer, disappeared from the hospital. Initially, it was thought that Mr. Green left the hospital voluntarily, but suspicion has grown about the mysterious woman who accompanied him. He has been reported missing by his wife, Ellen. "I'm just afraid that Sam Straight may have killed Joel too. He's always around when someone associated with Oddyssey disappears," she told the Times.

Yesterday, at his arraignment on charges that he assaulted his partner, and inflicted wounds on himself to cover up his responsibility, Straight took the unusual step of representing himself, rejecting assistance from Cohen & Cranston, and presumably from Oddyssey. In the course of pleading not guilty to the charges, he hinted that he might have to reveal Oddyssey secrets in order to defend himself, and that the company would not come off well as a result.

The combination of these events has caused the value of Oddyssey to collapse in after-hours trading, leading to the halt in trading of its shares before opening of the market in the morning. Richard Total, the Cohen & Cranston partner who has taken over the account after the initial incident, stated yesterday, "Oddyssey was the client of Mr. Green and Mr. Straight. But the company has asked this firm to do a thorough internal investigation. We expect this will take at least two weeks, so we ask for patience. We are fully cooperating with the SEC to assure that investors have complete and accurate information. The company has endorsed the halt in trading so that the true facts of the situation may be given a chance to emerge."

There is a nice graphic showing the ups and downs of Oddyssey's stock value over the last few weeks. I think it's preposterous to suspect me of involvement in anything nefarious, but I have to admit that Endel, Reed, the *Times*, and Joel's wife, Ellie, all have a point: Whenever someone is killed, there I am.

Urgent souls pace through the streets, tired young men and women from law firms and investment banks, the anxiety from yesterday still written in their eyes. They hurry past me to another day in the sinful towers surrounding us. They have no reaction to my unusual clothes, and surely do not recognize the author of the morning's most infamous stock market flameout. Even so, I feel naked out on this street.

I have clearly violated the minimal rules that govern the vermin-ridden State Bar of California. I have violated the law, federal law, punishable in discrete little portions at ten years per piece. My only hope is that no one notices how much one of my jailers is making in his third job.

Suddenly I need a drink even more than I need clothes.

I'm seeing the frozen Stoli in the freezer at JD's condo. I'm at least ten days post-seizure. No reason I can't have a drink. What comes next can always be figured out better in the glow.

A tired figure turns away from the crowd, and strides purposefully to the front door of the condo. He enters the ten-digit code on the outside gate and walks in without looking back. I grab the doorknob just before the door closes and walk in after him. He whispers to the towering security guard, who lets him pass.

It's my turn: "Tiger," I try. Tiger smirks. *Yeah, okay. Be nice if all it took was an animal name. JD loved those.* "Here to see Peace," I say. "She made my bail."

"Yeah, recognize you from the other day. Peace told me you might be by."

He pauses, thinks, then says, "Couple guys and a girl, nice looking by the way, they went up a while ago. Might've been lawyers. Said they had information about property JD left to her."

He lets me go.

The elevator opens on JD's floor. His door is ajar. I knock anyway. No answer. How pleasant it would be if Peace is out. And the path to the refrigerator wide open.

CHAPTER THIRTY-SEVEN

"Hello, Sam. I think I have what you came for."

Valerie's soft girlfriend voice. She emerges from the kitchen with a short glass, frost on the inside and the out, the alcohol climbing in tiny, clear waves around the inside of the glass. She's thrown in a couple olives that have dropped to the bottom.

Her chest is bursting, even more than usual, from a tight white shirt. An extra button is undone. Actually, she seems a little disheveled. How this has happened can be figured out after the first big sip, which I take. Pause. Drain the rest.

"You were thirsty."

"The Men's Central Jail can have that effect on you."

"Let's get you another."

We walk into the kitchen, and I follow her hands as they pour the next drink. Her hands are shaking. *I can find out why after I finish the next glass.* She only gives me about an inch, so it takes a second to drain it.

Raising her eyebrow, Valerie turns and pours yet another. This time, as she hands it to me, she puts her hand around my waist, and hooks it tightly around my pelvic bone. She holds on to the drink. "It's okay," she says. "You're going to just do what they say. I'll try to keep you alive."

She puts down the glass and reaches over to touch me with her other hand, puts her finger right on the site of the knife wound in my thigh. The deepest, most unhealed point.

"How is it?" Valerie's voice has gone lifeless, almost drugged, as if she has been drinking with me.

Something has dulled Valerie. There is no warmth or welcome to her face. She seems to be sleep-walking, a Valerie zombie.

"Where's Peace?" I say, breaking away.

"She went out for a while."

"How do you even know her?"

I have been dreaming of Valerie's touch since that night in my home when she left me to sleep. But that was fantasy. This is reality and none of it makes any sense. Her eyes are blank. She graduated from Harvard, as I recall, but now she cannot answer a simple question. Valerie's arm snakes around my back, and I feel the strength of her biceps pull me close. We are face-to-face, and I see dark bruising near her left eye. A heavy mark on her neck shows redness even through her dark skin.

"Valerie, what's wrong with you?"

She pulls me close. "Sam, I'm sorry. They've drugged me with—"

"That's enough, Ms. Valerie."

The voice is behind me. I try to turn, but Valerie holds me tightly, arresting me with her arms. She seems to want to say something more. A pain I lost days ago returns to the back of my skull. She tries to say something else, but her eyes lose focus and roll away. "There's a gu—"

"That's enough," the voice behind me says again. I recognize that voice. I've heard it recently, but it has a strange new quality that keeps me from immediately realizing the speaker. Turning around, I see that it is the voice of Richard Total's craven sidekick. Eddie Guarnieri.

Like Eddie's voice, his face has a new commanding confidence to it, as if he has just been to a Tony Robbins seminar. I think of Eddie as a bottom-feeder, a phoronid organism, a parasite supporting itself in the wake of the predatory killer that is Richard. But Richard is not around, and here is Eddie with a new posture and voice that says he's in charge. There are more new things about this Eddie. He's standing up straight. The weird ass and the tent pants are gone. Was that an act? Even the boogers? And he has a gun—a very gentlemanly sort of pistol, but an actual weapon. He is pointing it at Valerie and me.

Valerie lets me go. "I'm sorry, Sam. They have . . . leverage." She leans against the counter, like a robot that has lost power.

"Eddie?"

Eddie smiles, confident. "As one of the partners, or should I say former partners, of the firm, you probably don't expect much of me. So I can see how it could be surprising for you." And then he laughs, as if he has told a joke.

Even when behaving as a sycophant to Richard, Eddie has a way of talking that expatiates pretentiously, dismissing the thoughts of others as beneath his Mensa IQ. This is followed by a laugh that suggests you join him in laughing at the inferiority around him.

"I don't really feel that way, Eddie. I've always felt the rap on you was mostly jealousy. Of your intelligence. I always thought Richard led you on, took advantage of you."

"Actually, I admire Richard in some ways. He's the only one in the firm who would even try to eliminate the dead weight like you and Joel."

"We were the best thing about that stupid firm," I try weakly.

"You forget the all-nighter Richard made me pull to digest your files. What a complete load of crap. The widows. The helpless. The broke. That insurance verdict was your only good case, and it looks like you just got lucky when your prostitute client lied her way to a verdict."

"What could you have against me?"

"You got the partnership I worked for years to get. Because they took you two losers on, they had no room for me. The notion that you and Joel should be partners in a firm like C&C was always ludicrous. The notion that you should be partners anywhere was ludicrous."

"I guess I underestimated you, Eddie. But I never intended to take anything away from you."

"You act like you're some sort of nice guy, but you're just like the rest. You think people are valuable because they are beautiful, like Valerie here, or young, like the Kid. None of you really value intellect for intellect's sake. Did you know I was the one who designed the computer tracking of the artificial monetary units? I can change dirty American cash for drug supplies in Mexico or Chinese manufactured goods. All through computer entries."

"John Darrow told me it was his idea."

"Thinking of things isn't the same as doing things. Do you think that dreamer could program a computer?"

I guess he's been dying to tell me this. After all, if it's true, who else can he tell? Even after what I've been through, the news has an astonishing and dreadful quality. Astonishing as if Eddie were telling me he is the Messiah. Dreadful because he doesn't seem worried I will tell anyone his secrets.

"Hell, Eddie, people respect your intelligence. Though I don't think they really appreciated . . . the extent of it."

"You walk by me every day, Sam. You think you're different, you think you're so 'nice.'" Eddie makes air quotes. "You don't even look me in the eye. You usually can't wait to get away from me. You think I'm sitting there burning with envy. Well, you should have been envying me."

"Eddie, I'm just in my own world, my own cases. I've got no dislike of you."

"I don't dislike you, Sam; I just dislike stupidity. You're the kind of idiot who takes law school at face value. You probably think being a lawyer is about the law, about the cases, about the clients. It's not about any of that. It's about the money. But in the end, it's a pretty stupid way to make money isn't it? No matter how high you push the billing rate, it's still about th drudgery of putting in the hours, and there are only so many hours before you die. You're just keeping track of the slipping away of your life. Look at you. You're ten years older than me, and you don't have any money."

Being nice isn't working. In fact, it seems to be pissing him off. But I remember that Eddie needs to win any argument, about anything, be it his latest case, something in the news, or an event of everyday life. Now, completely in character, he apparently wants me to know the whole story and is willing to retell it until I agree he is the hero. Making this my lucky day. So long as I can find a way to take him on before this is all over.

"So, let's accept that you really are smart, Eddie, but if you're so smart, how come you're not rich?"

"I am now."

"You realize the stock just tanked."

"This isn't just about the stock."

I remember a back hallway going into the area of the bed and bathrooms. It's in the other direction, away from Eddie. That's where I somehow have to go.

"Have you brought Richard in on this? Is he working for you? Or are you working for him?"

"The strange thing about Richard, Sam, is that he isn't really that bright. What he's really good at is being cruel, which allows him to act when being cruel is the smart thing to do, instead of being crippled by some inner sense of doing the right thing. Like you."

I've been backing, ever so slightly, to a position behind Valerie's tranquil form during this rant. Eddie can't be oblivious to what I'm doing, but he doesn't seem worried about it.

Needling him again I say, "It was Joel who brought in the Kid, and the Kid who brought in Oddyssey. Without Joel your brilliant plan would never exist."

"It was brilliant that the Kid reeled in Joel. He was the perfect foil for the Kid's little stock play, just respectable enough to make the Kid credible with auditors. Just desperate enough from his impending divorce that he didn't want to know the truth. Just romantic enough to believe that a kid could have all the answers. Of course, he got moral on us, which is why we're having all these problems. So we had to . . . to take him out."

"You took out my best friend," I say.

"No. I took him out." The voice comes from a man with a black leather mask who moves around the corner of the hallway behind Eddie. The leather mask worn by Joel's attacker. It is the attacker. Once again, he has a big knife. He takes off the mask and laughs, twirling the knife with loving fascination.

It was the Kid all along.

He looks somehow different than he did in the gym. I suppose I was dazed by the hospital drugs and the steam as well as the urge to keep my distance from a naked man with a whirling penis. My eyes travel up his bare arm to the knife, and I see the brutal bulges constructed by the weights, and some steroids certainly, but now, on his exposed shoulders and back, for the first time I see the acne damage from the steroids, the same acne I saw on the neck of the guy stabbing Joel and me that night.

The Kid is moving towards me. I move behind Valerie, and towards the hallway. I need to find that stairwell.

"Joel cared for you," I say.

"I liked him in a way," says the Kid, "but you can't respect anyone that pathetic." From the way the Kid says this, it's obvious there was never anything but contempt for Joel. "He was ready to do anything for his next drink," the Kid continues. The Kid looks around. "I hear you met my friend, JD. Nice apartment he's got here, huh? Nice girlfriend too. Just got a chance to find out how nice. She put up a bit of a nasty struggle, though." The Kid wipes a little blood off a cut just above his eye.

"JD believed in Oddyssey. He thought it could really be something important."

"What a pathetic dreamer. Nice that he did himself in for us. As it is, we still have to deal with his Bible-toting girlfriend," Eddie says.

"You seem to have a lot of hatred for people who've helped you out," I say. It could apply to both of them. I want to keep the argument with Eddie going.

"Is it really so wrong to detest stupidity?" says Eddie. Then there is that conspiratorial laugh. The Kid is right there with him.

"You two are finished. That public offering is never going to happen," I say.

"So what if Richard and the partners don't get their money? Oddyssey has already given us more than the public offering," says Eddie.

"What are you talking about? How?" I ask.

Eddie still doesn't mind explaining: "We have the first offering. All those suppliers who were paid from it . . . don't exist. It's disappointing not to have the second offering, but you don't understand the San Fernando Valley, my friend. It's filled with little old ladies with $100,000 or so in the bank. They live off social security and the interest, but if there's a rumor that 18 percent is out there somewhere, they'll empty their insured savings account and go after it. They're suckers for any good-looking young man who will actually talk to them. I showed the Kid how to charm all those blue-haired ladies and swept up all their cash hoards. Now, that's just for the two of us. Isn't even on the books."

Here the Kid laughs at the memories: "The little ladies think they're all pre-invested for a public offering. It was simple, and easy—just $20,000, $40,000 a pop. Pretty soon it's a cool number. Enough to disappear forever."

Eddie wants the floor back: "You did us a favor, Sam. Sure, it would have been nice to have the second offering, but there would be an endless SEC investigation to find that money. No one's going to help these old ladies—they'll be too embarrassed to admit what happened. No one will even know how much we've got. This way, we head out tonight. Tomorrow morning the Kid and I will be drinking margaritas in a place where no one will ever find us. You'll be back to filling out time sheets. If you can still practice law after this."

"And all the messengers? And all the dealers looking for the money you're laundering?"

"The messengers have had a good ride. They can go back to being messengers. All the other accounts have been balanced. There was a little misunderstanding, but that was taken care of when the Kid took out Jacky Real for us."

"I suppose you're thinking of killing me too?" I say to Eddie.

The Kid, usually voluble to the annoyance threshold, continues to defer to Mad Eddie, the alter ego of the cowardly associate I thought I knew so well.

"All those disgusting bodily fluids everywhere? I'm not inclined, unless you make me. Our getaway is clean. No one will find us. If necessary, of course, the Kid here will be happy to oblige."

Valerie seems to be receding into a faraway, drugged state. She begins to shudder, as if she is very cold. I'm almost completely behind her now. Time to bolt. Maybe Eddie really is reluctant. Maybe he will hesitate just long enough.

The Kid walks around Eddie and starts towards me, twirling the knife.

"Eddie may not care," the Kid says, "but I'm not particularly happy to be moving to Mexico. That country is a toilet."

"Jesus, Kid. Did you have to tell him where we're going?" complains Eddie. He seems to be contemplating the untidy necessity of making a mess of my bodily fluids.

From the kitchen counter, the Kid picks up a hypodermic needle loaded with clear fluid. I didn't notice it when Valerie poured the drinks that are making me feel better, like myself again.

I relive the knife entering Joel, entering me.

"Valerie, you're not really part of this are you?" I plead. Her eyes are dead, dreary. She is looking beyond me. At the Kid. This is my last chance. I make my break.

CHAPTER THIRTY-EIGHT

The door to the stairwell looks close by, but I only have a few seconds to reach it.

"He's your responsibility, Kid," says Mad Eddie. "Better get him." Eddie has authority now, like the Kid did with his weightlifters. After a few steps, I turn and see the Kid coming after me. I reach the door to the stairwell, but as I reach for the doorknob there is a sinking feeling—it's just too far. The Kid catches me quickly from behind with a diving tackle that buckles my knees. He is about to drop on me, but Valerie comes behind him, and tries to pull him off.

The Kid throws Valerie against the wall. Now he's on me, twisting my arm behind my back, tightening to the point of breaking. He seems poised to inflict more pain.

My stomach turns over, and I retch, coughing up hot, clear liquid.

"My old friend JD has a fantastic welding unit," says the Kid.

"For what?" says Eddie.

"I'd like to know where his sloppy drunk friend Joel has gone. As I recall, he's the only other one with the passwords. Maybe there's some more loose ends."

"Alright, but make it quick. I figure we have an hour to clean up here."

"Let me get the welder."

"Tie the guy up first."

"Tie him yourself. I can't do all the work," says the Kid.

The Kid climbs off me. Before I can move, Eddie jumps on my back, grinding his knee into my spine. His efforts at sadism seem laughable after the Kid's handiwork. But he gives it his best, twisting my left arm hard and wrapping thick rope around my wrists. He pulls to tighten the rope, wraps the rope around my ankles, and connects the two bindings. I struggle to breathe as my sternum grinds against the hard floor. Yet, Eddie has done a bad job, which I may be able to exploit.

Turning my head, I see Valerie slumped near the hallway wall. She must have hit her head. Eddie returns from the kitchen. He walks up to Valerie—and sticks her with the hypodermic needle I thought was meant for me.

"Kid?" Eddie calls to the next room. Then to me: "I'm going to let the Kid figure out where Joel is. Because it'd be nice to know."

"I have no idea where he is. He left the hospital. That's all I know."

"Really? I think we better be sure. Consider just telling us. It'll hurt less. The Kid's a kind of animal—not appropriately domesticated."

He wanders away to see how the Kid is coming with the welder, leaving me facedown and struggling for breath.

Valerie is adjusting to the hypodermic, struggling to keep her eyes open. She sprawls against the wall, her powerful legs splayed out.

"I'm going to work on something truly special for you, Mr. Straight. But I want it to be a nice surprise. So I'm going let you have a time-out with the little lady who made your bail."

One-handed, the Kid lifts me by the rope stretched between my ankles and my wrists. He walks me into the back bedroom and tosses me down on the bed. "By the way, she's got quite a pretty mouth," he says, loudly.

The mattress has some give in it, so I can get my diaphragm to pull enough air into my lungs to breathe. If he had left me on that floor much longer, I might have blacked out.

"You strike me as somebody who doesn't really like pain. I'm guessing you're not the courageous type, either."

CHAPTER THIRTY-NINE

A couple weeks in jail makes me appreciate being dropped on JD's guest bed. There is a fresh smell from laundry softener. Morning fresh, or some such scent.

It's dark. As my eyes become used to the light, I see her lying on the floor across the room. Peace is hog-tied too, but she has managed to flip over on her side. She is wearing a pair of bikini panties. The elastic is tortured into a limp curl. Her face lacks the composure of JD's painting. Her expression is . . . smeared. Except I know she wears no makeup. Her shirt has been torn, and the pieces hang from her shoulders, exposing her.

"That goddamn Kid," I say, trying to assess what must have happened to her in this room.

"He stuck his—"

"You don't need—"

"Oh yes, I need. He tried to stick his stupid cock in my mouth."

There's nothing I can say.

"I've been through AA, so I can accept a lot. But I'm not going to accept that."

"Is there any way out? Maybe we can untie each other," I say. I flip over onto the floor, landing on my shoulder. Something jams, and my shoulder nearly dislocates, but pops back in. We are face-to-face.

"There's a door back there," she says. "JD called it his secret passage. You can get out that way if we can get free."

I start to loosen Eddie's inept knots, then look in the direction Peace indicates with her head. The door to the supposedly secret passage opens. Miraculously, in walks Manny, my friendly house-flipping, short-selling sheriff's deputy. He is dressed casually, in a polo shirt and jeans. More importantly, he's wearing a brown jacket that bulges in a way that makes me confident he is carrying a concealed weapon.

"Sam."

"What are you doing here?" I ask, with incredulous gratitude.

"Protecting my investment."

"How the hell?"

"Tiger is an old friend from the sheriff's department. We've bought a few houses together. I told him to call if he saw you. Like I say, protecting my investment."

"Let me guess, another Mormon?"

Manny moves towards me.

"We come in bundles," Manny says.

"Get her first," I say, indicating Peace with my head. Manny turns and looks at her. He hesitates for a moment, set back by the sight of her. Then he unties her.

Once freed, she moves to all fours. Her head is down. She rises up and says, "Before we get started, there is something I need to do."

Manny and I just look at her as she strides into the bathroom, not bothering to cover herself or close the door. She sticks her finger down her throat until she vomits.

Wiping her mouth, she pronounces, "There is some form of shit in every fluid that comes from that pig." She reaches for a bottle of Listerine.

Coming out of the bathroom, she waves to a closet across the room. "The guns are in there."

"How many guns?" Manny says.

"Plenty," says Peace.

I've freed my hands, but I need to move. Manny comes over to help. "Hurry, Manny."

"Any chance they're just going to leave?" Manny asks.

"I'm not going to let them leave," Peace says. She hasn't corrected her shirt, and she seems not the least self-conscious about it. Then to me: "You want a gun, Counselor?"

"Better give me something simple," I say.

She hands me a pistol with a long barrel. "This should be easy for you. It's loaded, ready."

"Just point and shoot?"

"That's it. Can you?" she asks

I am a product of an education that taught me guns are evil. I look at Peace's destroyed face, what little remains of her shirt. "I think I can."

But I don't think I can fire first. Even at the evil that is the Kid.

I turn to Manny. "Look, I think we can get this. You need to get out of here. There's going to be some gunfire. The last thing either of us need is to be together at a crime scene."

Peace pulls something that looks like an AK-47 out of a drawer and clicks in a magazine. She looks ready.

Manny must be thinking about how this girl looks like she can handle anything. I can see he's also thinking about the profit he has made over the last twenty-four hours, and the insider-trading investigation that could easily destroy it, along with all three of his careers. He takes a look at the stock of weapons in JD's closet.

"I've got this, Mr. Manny," Peace says. "Whoever you are." No, the right thing is for him to disappear without even telling Peace who he is.

"Get out and call the cavalry," I say. "You know how to get them here better than anyone else, and you know how to do it without getting traced."

Manny is persuaded. "Okay, you two buy some time. I'll call it in," he says. He looks at Peace. "Don't do anything you'll regret. Let the lawyer talk to them for a bit. He can stall."

Through the door I hear Mad Eddie say, "Wake up, Valerie dear. And bring in our fool." Manny raises his gun and points it to the door.

Valerie stumbles in. She's walking slowly, but she has absorbed enough of whatever was in that hypodermic to get her eyes open. They bulge when she sees Manny's gun leveled at her face.

"Don't say anything," Manny says to her very softly, but very powerfully.

I hear the *whoosh* of one of JD's acetylene torches.

CHAPTER FORTY

Peace pushes Valerie down on the bed and points the machine gun at her.

Valerie is looking at the points of two guns now. She can see that I'm holding a third. But the drugs have her stunned. She looks like she'd like nothing better than to lie down and go to sleep. But I have some things I need to say.

"Did you really try to kill Joel? Did you change the orders at County?" I ask her.

"The orders were already DNR. I came back and told them it wasn't worth the risk. Then he had some sort of heart attack or something, and I had to get out of there."

Her eyes are dead, like the eyes of a reptile.

"Why would you get involved in this?" I ask.

"It started because I wanted things, Sam. I've never had anything. The Lexus is on payments. The firm was about to drop me. In case you haven't figured it out, I'm not cut out to be a lawyer. Eddie promised me a way out. Then there was Richard. He promised to help me if I didn't pass the bar."

"You know what, Valerie, you do have what it takes. You just have to work a little more and work out a little less. And if you want to pass the bar exam, you're gonna have to study."

"But then there was that day we went to see the Kid. When I saw how . . . good you were."

"Then why didn't you stop? Why didn't you tell me what was going on?"

"I've been trying to help you, Sam. I really have. Richard has figured it out now, I think. But you haven't let us help you."

"Why don't you help us now?" I say.

"Hey, what are you thinking?" says Peace.

"Joel just walked out of the hospital," Valerie says. "I wanted to make it up to you, Sam. I went back to find it. What you told me to find, Sam. The checkbook. And I found it. It's got all the checks to the phony suppliers. But the Kid jumped me. In those showers."

I am silent at that horrifying scene. She is too, remembering it. Then she goes on: "You know what? That complaint from the teenager? You know . . . Exhibit A . . . It was him. Him all along."

Valerie's voice trails off, and she grows quiet. Then I realize she is sleeping.

"Let her sleep," says Manny. "I'll call help." Manny has made a decision. He heads out the door.

"You should go too," I tell Peace.

Peace grips the AK-47. "Oh, I'm not going anywhere."

I look down at Valerie. I still have more to say to her: "Sometimes you just have to do the right thing, Valerie, even if you need the money."

"She can't hear you anymore," says Peace. "The drugs have her now."

"Hurry up," yells the Kid from the other room.

"I'm going first," I tell Peace.

CHAPTER FORTY-ONE

"See if you can bring our patient out to talk to the Kid, Nurse Valerie," Eddie yells out.

I walk out into the open area of JD's studio.

Eddie steps up from behind me and places his gun directly in the back of my head; I feel the muzzle pointed upwards into my brain. He must have figured we were up to something. Eddie has a lot of experience listening outside partners' offices.

"Where'd you get the gun?" he says.

"JD had an extra. Does that surprise you?"

"Drop it."

I throw the gun on the floor out ahead of me, thinking I don't want Eddie to retrieve it right away. Also, I'm a little afraid it will go off when it hits the floor and want it to be away from me.

I turn to a point of sound, the sound of chemically created, rushing fire coming out of a torch. The Kid is over in the corner where the tanks are. He has taken off his shirt and strapped a large tank of fuel onto his back. He wears a helmet with a safety visor flipped up.

He stands there holding what must be JD's biggest welding torch like some kind of warrior-king. He smiles broadly as he turns the flame on and off, watching it with fascination as it flies out and recedes.

"It's like a flamethrower, Mr. Straight," the Kid says. "Serious fun. Naturally I have fully equipped myself with proper safety equipment. Unfortunately, JD doesn't have a matching set for you. I fear you may have to report me to OSHA. Yeah, that's what you should do. Of course, if you need some legal advice, Eddie's here to do some research. I hear he's good at that."

The Kid stalks towards me.

A gun fires, and I flinch downward.

I'm still alive, so it wasn't Eddie who fired. This is my chance to duck away, my whole body jolted with the rush of adrenaline. Startled, Eddie is looking around when I turn and kick him hard in the groin. He doubles over. A second shot goes by our heads.

I look towards Eddie, worrying he's ready to point the gun at me again. I catch sight of his back as he darts into the kitchen, bent over from the waist.

The Kid seems frozen. His eyes dart back and forth around the room. The same gun that fired the first two shots fires a third and a fourth, quickly, automatically. It is Peace's AK-47. She's firing from just beyond the doorframe of the bedroom, using the wall of the room for cover. The shots ping off the fuel tanks behind the Kid. A frown of worry appears at the top of his frozen smile.

I scramble on the floor to the gun I dropped out ahead of me. I bring it up, and fire. The gun kicks out of my hand and goes flying across the floor. My shot misses the Kid but hits the tanks squarely. Two of them explode in an iamb with a fatal backbeat: la DOOM.

The air shifts with a rush, and the thump of the explosions lifts me off the floor and sets me down flat on my face. A body falls on top of me. I catch a glimpse of a dark hand. Valerie wraps her arms around me.

The Kid screams as the blast throws him towards the kitchen.

Valerie has protected me from the blast with her body. Debris falls, and I feel the vibration as a couple pieces hit her in the back. My hearing briefly shuts down. Lighter debris settles. Part of the wall behind the tanks has fallen. At least two of the tanks are gone, exploded or sunk through the new hole in the floor. The floor around the hole is burning. I hope Manny made it to a phone.

An alarm sounds. The ceiling sprays water.

A warm trickle of blood comes out of my ear.

From the center of my being comes a surge of adrenaline that flows through my whole body to the ends of my fingertips. The explosion has freed me. I'm done running away. Time to strike back. I throw off Valerie and get up to go after the Kid.

The Kid has landed across the large open area, not far from the kitchen. He bounces up, throwing off the tank and welding torch, though the visor stays securely in place. He runs into the kitchen, then reappears with the knife, the same knife, his favorite knife, raising it over his head.

Valerie reaches her feet, runs in front of me, and plants herself. She holds a bloody hand out protectively. My eyes focus in the crook of her neck, fixing on the drops of sweat. From beyond I see the Kid's knife. It comes down, headed past Valerie to my chest. Valerie raises her arm, and the knife slices like a guillotine across the lower half, going an inch into it, before thudding against the bones of her lower arm.

Valerie cries out and slumps to the ground. For a moment, the Kid draws back. I look down at Valerie's arm. It has split open in a great gape. The incredible whiteness of the flesh below her skin stuns me, like milk shining in the sun. Then bright red flows over it. Valerie looks down in shock. The Kid stares at the hole he has made in her arm. Then he looks up and starts coming again. At me. Raising the knife above his head again.

Another shot. Looking up, I see Eddie aiming past the Kid and firing from the kitchen. He fires again, suddenly, shockingly, seemingly at me. I flinch and duck my head. Eddie disappears back into the kitchen.

The Kid's arm drops uselessly. His face staggers into me, and he exhales on my cheek. I draw back, shoving him away. He has a puzzled expression. He staggers into me again, and this time I catch him in my arms, as if he is a fallen comrade. My hand around his back feels the warm blood spilling. He is limp, and I lay him down.

I survey myself. No bullet has hit me.

"You stupid idiot," the Kid rasps, turning his head to the kitchen. "You fucking shot me."

"I guess I'm not a very good shot," Eddie says from around the corner.

"Let's see if you're a good target," the Kid says. Somehow, the Kid pushes himself into a sitting position with one hand. The other hand hangs limply at his side. He reaches with his one good hand into his belt and pulls out a pistol. He fires twice into the kitchen. Then the pistol drops to his side. But he is still sitting there.

Eddie cowers, half in and half out of the kitchen, his head poking out, then disappearing. I survey the rubble and smoke around the room from the explosion. I'm on my knees, feeling helpless. But I'm the one who is intact. For now, the Kid's sitting body gives me cover.

Hoping that Eddie and the Kid will keep shooting at each other, I crawl on all fours over to Valerie. Blood flows from her arm into a pool on the concrete floor. The sight of the dust particles floating on top of it fills me with certainty that Valerie and I are going to be eliminated as soon as Eddie can summon the courage to come out of the kitchen. He may be new to his gun, but we are right in front of him, and he can't keep missing us forever. We have to get up and move.

I try to get to my feet, hoping to drag Valerie with me to safety, wondering, briefly, why I'm not just saving myself.

Gunfire again. Shots come from the kitchen ahead of me and the bedroom behind me. Peace and Eddie must both be firing. Another shot hits the Kid. His torso flattens, his remaining breath emptying out without protest.

"That was going to be a lot of baggage to take to Mexico," Eddie says. He thinks he has killed someone, syrupy bodily fluids and all, and he seems proud of it.

"You've made a mess now, Eddie," I say. "This is just too much for anyone to cover up. You can't get away from it anymore. Don't make it any worse."

"Oh, here comes the advice. Thanks, Sam, but I don't think I need advice from you. I think I've just discovered something quite invaluable."

"What's that?" I say, still thinking Eddie won't be able to kill me until he's had the last word.

"You know what, Sam? Sometimes being a good lawyer means that you have to kill the client."

Okay, you win, I think. I look down at Valerie's body and at the pool of blood beginning to surround her. The bleeding needs to be stopped.

Eddie continues his lecture on being a good lawyer. "And sometimes it means eliminating the other lawyers in the room."

I look up. Eddie is less than thirty feet away, safely under the cover of the kitchen. I can see the muzzle of his gun.

If I'm going to leave this world, I don't want Eddie to be the last thing I see. So I look down at Valerie. She has tried to push her left hand down on the shocking white gap in her forearm. Her eyes are closed, and there is hardly any pressure coming from her hand.

CHAPTER FORTY-TWO

I've stopped caring, except about what death will be like.

But Peace, wearing only panties and the flying, tattered remnants of her shirt, walks purposefully out of the hallway, through the smoke, pointing her AK-47. Beside her is Manny. His jacket is off, and he's holding his revolver. They look like they know what they're doing. Eddie sees them. His momentary bravado vanishes, and he rushes back into the kitchen.

Manny crosses the room quickly at an angle, strategically until his gun is pointing to the kitchen door from an angle that will be difficult for Eddie to address. Eddie's gun and head emerge from the kitchen and he fires wildly. Manny dives towards the kitchen, taking yet another angle, and rolls.

Eddie's head pokes out again. He appears watchful for Manny, but he hasn't accounted for Peace. She has moved fearlessly into the middle of the room, and now she stands, legs apart, braced and ready and focused. Her next bullets hit Eddie neatly on the side of his head as it sticks out from the kitchen. He topples over in the kitchen doorway, brains and blood spraying.

Peace lowers her gun.

For a minute or more I stare back and forth at the dead bodies of the Kid and Eddie. And the burning hole in the floor. The spraying water from the fire sprinklers sounds loud now.

Every aspect of their being has simply stopped. The Kid is on the floor, on his back, with his head tilted in the direction he had twisted it in an attempt to ask Eddie for his life. Or just to say "Fuck you, Eddie" again. Pretty depressing final words those would have been. He never got a chance to get them out. The blood flows from his body towards us, a river of death.

Eddie was upright when Peace fired at him. He has slumped down, his legs collapsing underneath him. As with the Kid, there'd been no struggle for breath, for life. Two minutes before, he'd been trying to tell me how to practice law.

Moving with purpose, without emotion, Peace approaches the Kid's body. She kicks his legs apart, and carefully places one more shot in his crotch. Just one. Then she turns and walks back to the hallway.

Manny reaches my side and says, "Glad I came back. To protect my investment."

"Me too. Now get going. Get clear of the building, and then make that call." Manny heads back into the bedroom, with its back way out to the stairwell. I'm hoping our secret is safe.

Valerie is on the floor next to me, her eyes open but rolling back, the blood still flowing from the laceration in her arm. I rip off my shirt and use it to apply pressure. It is soon soaked.

Peace appears from the hallway with a towel. She hands it to me and says, "I'll get the first aid." She emerges from the bathroom with a couple more towels. I use my shirt as a tourniquet. Valerie is breathing faintly.

"I think she's alive. Call 911," I say. "Hold on, girl," I say softly to Valerie.

Looking up to see Peace disappear into the kitchen, I behold a vision of JD. He has on a fresh Façonnable shirt—blue and red stripes. His white board shorts look like they have just been starched and ironed for a Fourth of July picnic. His blond hair is clean, soft, and billowy, blowing in a nonexistent wind. How can he be so clean in the midst of all the blood, rubble, and dust caused by his exploding welding materials?

I hear Peace in the kitchen, talking to 911: "We have a deep bleeding wound here. You need to get here now . . . Yes . . . Yes . . . We're doing that now . . . Yes . . . No need . . . Just tell them to get here . . . Tell them to come in the front door . . . The guard's name is Tiger. He will meet you there . . . I'm going to hang up now. You can call me back at this number if you need me. There was an explosion here, so the police are probably already on their way."

JD has some words for me: "The girl keeps her head in tough spots. How are you doing, Counselor?"

"I'm better. I'm going to take charge more. Tired of just drifting along in the crisis."

"You know you're going to have to quit that firm."

"That's no problem."

"And that marriage."

"There's not much for her to take."

"And that stupid way of making a living."

"I've got bills to pay."

"Watch out for Peace. In about an hour she's going to understand what it feels like to kill someone. Don't let her do what I did." *He doesn't know*, I think. *He hasn't been watching.* She was always the strong one. But I owe JD.

"So I was the one who shot these two guys?" I try.

"Yes, you did," says JD. "Excellent work."

Peace comes in with blankets. "I called Tiger too. He's going to meet people and get them up. Who are you talking to?"

I think about just telling her, but I say, "Let's try to help this girl."

JD is moving, saying, "Gotta travel, brother."

Peace untangles Valerie's legs, and covers her torso with blankets. I make one into a pillow and put it under Valerie's legs.

JD walks over to Peace. He bends down, covers her with his huge arms, and realizes that he and his body don't work anymore. After a brief, despairing pause, he kisses her hard on the top of her head. He tries to cover her by pulling the remnants of her shirt, then looks at his hands, again in despair that they no longer work. I am the only one who can see him. Even Peace doesn't know he's here. "Check on the black chick," he says to me. And then he's gone, even to me.

I look at Valerie's body stretched out in front of me. Her face is peaceful. She is strong, young, and exquisitely striking. Everything I idolize about human life. Except that her life is running out. I feel for the big artery on her neck. There is nothing running through it. Valerie is not breathing.

I hear Peace breathing hard, her chest surging. I hear my own breath. We are kneeling on either side of Valerie now. We look at each other, wondering. Should we let this be? And then I don't.

"Start pumping her chest," I command.

Peace doesn't move. "Now," I say, and pinch off Valerie's nose, push down her jaw, and start breathing. Peace pumps her chest.

After a few minutes of this, the door bursts in and is thrown across the room. Reed and Endel follow their revolvers into the room. Tiger trails them. He has a key in his hand. Reed could not be deprived of the drama of kicking in a door.

"Clear. It's just the lawyer and a girl with half a shirt on," announces Reed, his spine as straight as ever.

Paramedics rush past Reed and Endel as the cops go to "clear" the rest of the place. Peace and I lean back and let them take over. They don't even ask us any questions. The nature of the emergency is obvious to them. They shout directions to each other. There is a rushing in my ears, and I stop hearing the noise. Time is suspended. Soon Valerie is out the door.

Peace and I are still kneeling, still facing each other.

"What, were you in love with her or something?" she says.

"I couldn't help it."

"She wasn't as nice a person as her body was telling you she was."

"You would know about that. Listen, Peace: I shot these two. Both of them. JD wants it that way."

"How would you know?"

"He told me."

Peace looks at me but doesn't say anything. I think she decides to believe me. Maybe she has seen JD lately too. He's one of those spirits who does not leave the earth quickly.

Reed and Endel have given us just enough time, but now they're back.

"Lay facedown on the floor, both of you," Reed commands. He kicks the guns away from us. He handcuffs us, probably because it feels good to him, but he has put away his gun. He knows he has nothing to fear. "Jesus Christ, Straight. What the fuck happened here?" he says.

"Get me a drink and I'll tell you everything," I say. "There's some Stoli in the back of the freezer. That will do."

EPILOGUE

There is no painless way out of LA, though most agree that the pain is worth it. An exit through LAX is certainly one of the most excruciating paths. I can endure the awful torment of creeping cars and the enervating exhaust that makes its way through the air-conditioning system. I can endure it all. Because my exit date has finally come.

The last two years have led to this moment, to my being stuck in traffic on the airport loop, inching towards the American Airlines terminal. Right now, I'm passing the International Terminal, wading through the endless automobiles and the confused stare of an occasional exhausted international traveler wandering from the sidewalk and onto the road, wondering why there is no oxygen in the hot, dry air of what is supposed to be paradise. My passport is in my backpack, which is the only luggage

I am taking. That feels good. I feel free of what I'm leaving behind. A lot of things have felt good today.

One person has defined these two years: Richard Total.

Total is now the head of the Los Angeles office of Cohen & Cranston. It's the job he always wanted, the job he was made for, the culmination of those long hours of drudgery in the humorless New York office. He brought more than a bit of discipline to the task. He quickly convinced two partners they needed to find another firm. Then he fired the four associates who were billing less than 1,500 hours per year. The remaining associates started billing more than 2,000 hours a year, and the New York partners now think of the LA office, which they were about to close, as an exemplary profit center.

These two years, however, have demonstrated how Richard's wide range of talents extend far beyond mere law firm management. Previously, he was viewed as good at cleaning up messy situations for the firm's clients. But he has outdone himself on the biggest legal mess ever to cross the thresholds of Cohen & Cranston, a mess for which all of the partners, including even me, might have had to pay out of their pockets: Oddyssey.

Richard was at the jail the morning after my second arrest to explain that he wanted me to return to the firm. He admitted I would need to work with him on the Oddyssey cleanup but told me he could not explain my role until we were in a secure and privileged environment. I would need to accept his offer to find out the precise contours of what it involved.

I was willing to view my first trip to Men's Central as a needed stay in purgatory, but I had no interest in a second stay, even with Manny's protection. Manny and I needed to steer clear of each other anyway. This time, I decided to listen to Richard.

I still wonder whether it was my claim to have shot Eddie that earned me Richard's respect. Other partners could claim to dress down associates, but I had actually killed one. Talk about the sting of discipline. Richard agreed that I would be reinstated as a partner, with a yearly compensation of $500,000, which was about one and a half times what I had ever made. He had a contract with him that guaranteed the compensation for two years. A cool million. All I needed to do was sign.

"What about Joel?" I said.

"I think we have to assume that he is gone. Courtesy of Jacky. Or Jacky's friends."

Richard saw the crestfallen look of responsibility in my eyes. An instinctual salesman, he realized that I was blaming myself for stirring up the Jacky situation. Richard has contempt for this sort of guilt, but at that moment he needed me. So he tried to soften the blow:

"It could have been the Kid. Or he might have sent a bicycle messenger. Or a cab driver, or some other sort of lowlife. But look, if Joel turns up, I'll give him a guaranteed deal too."

I thought of Joel, finally peaceful, with a million dollars in his account. It might be enough for him to finally throw off Ellie and find a woman who really loved him.

"And my pro bono clients?"

Richard was prepared for my bleeding heart: "We'll take back the files. You can work on those cases as much as you want. Just don't use associate time."

"What about Valerie?" I asked.

"You know there's evidence she was working with the Oddyssey crowd, with Eddie. Before I came out from New York and cleaned up this mess."

"You worked with Eddie. You even worked with the Kid for a while."

"It took me exactly nine days to figure out the Kid was a fraud."

"You know we can save her. She was raped. She was drugged."

"I suppose, but she has absolutely no talent for being a lawyer." Richard could see me withdrawing. Before I said anything, he said, "Oh well, you're right. We won't get anywhere pointing the finger at one of the LA office's few minority hires."

Richard and I were exchanging ideas as if we were equal. A deal was coming together. Was I selling my soul? I decided to take the risk. Those clients needed me, and I had no ability to help them from behind bars. Even if I got out, I had no office, no secretary, no Xerox machine. I didn't even have a non-metal chair to sit on. I was unemployed, and like everyone in LA who hasn't received this week's paycheck, I was on the verge of going broke.

Just this one time, I told myself. *Just this one time, I'm going to take the money.* I told Richard he could bail me out.

"We are not going to screw around with bail, my friend. I've already discussed this with an upper-level district attorney, who just happened to be my roommate at Yale Law. You're going to have to plead to a littering charge, but the rest of the state charges are all being dismissed. Without prejudice at this point, but they've really got nothing on you. Of course, you and your friend Peace are going to have to keep telling the story I have been telling for you, about how Eddie and the Kid tried to kill you, how they masterminded this whole thing. You usually are believable, and anyone will believe a girl who looks like that Peace creature. They don't even want to charge her for the weapons. Darrow owned all of them legally. She shared the picture with me, the picture of Darrow's suicide. You're clear of that."

I really appreciated what Peace was doing. It must have been difficult for her to get that picture developed, and then to look at it. But I had a question: "Littering?"

"I had to give him something. There's some statistic involving the ratio between convictions and arrests, and it was really on his mind at that moment."

"Okay, but littering?"

"Do you know how many cigarette butts we had to clean out of that stairwell where you used to smoke?"

At that moment I needed a cigarette to contemplate just how crazy this all was. I didn't need to wait long. I was out within the hour. Richard whisked me to the Bonaventure Hotel, and installed me in one of its pie-shaped rooms. Smoking was allowed in this particular room. Richard was still at the Beverly Wilshire.

For the next two days, Richard completely controlled my life. Richard and/or at least one of his little asshole associates was always with me, even taking me to the pool and making me swim laps. There was good food from room service, long showers, and sleep. Plenty of alcohol in the minibar.

The key to cleaning up complex legal chaos, Richard explained, is to design and control the narrative. Although government enforcement entities and news organizations portray themselves as investigators and discoverers of information, they almost always function as receivers of information that is fed to them. Information requires analysis and sorting to form a narrative. Except in matters where the narrative is set by political diktat, or the reporters' political bias, law enforcement and the media lack the ability or the energy to appreciate the context of the information in the time frame they have to act or report. Richard believes that the media and law enforcement are therefore hungry mostly for a narrative. "They need to tell a story. With a beginning and an end. With a hero and a villain."

Richard believes that in an apolitical case, law enforcement and the media will adopt the narrative fed to them first—so long as it can be rationalized with their preconceived prejudices. After that, new information will bend to the narrative.

Within twenty-four hours of the deaths of Eddie and the Kid, Richard established himself as the deliverer of the narrative he and the little assholes had designed and outlined. He took the initiative in planting the narrative, calling the authorities instead of waiting for them to call him. He used his Yale contacts to set up meetings with the FBI and the US Attorney's Office in Los Angeles, as well as SEC enforcement and the bankruptcy trustee. Bankruptcy trustee? Yes, within that first day Richard had filed a chapter 7 bankruptcy petition on behalf of Oddyssey.com. The trustee would have to get his narrative from the same source as everyone else: Richard. As it turned out, it was the only narrative anyone would ever need.

Still, lawyering alone is not evidence. As Richard explained, every story needs a storyteller, a connection to the evidence. Richard needed a controlled, somewhat omniscient witness, one who could put the pieces of the story together so that it would not become fragmented and confused by multiple perspectives. The storyteller would need to be available for weeklong depositions, to be somewhat articulate, and strong enough that he would not be easily bullied by leading questions designed to further a counter-narrative.

Richard's somewhat improbable narrative was that Cohen & Cranston, the firm that had been the principal outside counsel for Oddyssey for nearly two years, had somehow managed to be completely innocent of the fact that Oddyssey was a giant fraud on every level.

Richard explained that the storyteller in his narrative would be me.

I was the perfect storyteller to tell, to sell this narrative. I had been the best friend of the partner managing the Oddyssey account. I had actually met with and interviewed the Kid. And yet, until after Joel and I were attacked, I knew absolutely nothing about how Oddyssey really made its money. Thus, I was the perfect person to explain how a partner at a major law firm could perform extensive legal work for a client without realizing that it was a criminal enterprise. The greatest bonus of all for Richard was that I could be at least somewhat convincing. Because I would be telling the truth. Of course, as Richard explained, I was in for some embarrassment. Headlines such as "NO LEGAL EAGLE: Lawyer slumbered while client pilfered" were in my future.

The truth was nice, of course, but the truth itself would not be enough. As Richard further explained to me, narratives are not believable simply because they are true. Many true narratives do not succeed. Rather, they are believable because they are like other narratives that the listeners want to believe or have been conditioned to believe by watching movies and television. For these reasons, the financial markets were willing to believe that a teenager like the Kid was the legitimate leader of a public company. For these reasons, I believed everything Valerie told me because she was so beautiful I couldn't look her in the eye. Here in LA, youth connotes wisdom, beauty connotes virtue.

In this case, my narrative would also match the narrative of every partner at every law firm when things go wrong: the associate screwed up.

Four days after my preparation began, we were ready to walk down the street to C&C's offices to meet with the SEC.

The first thing I noticed was the new receptionist. She was pretty enough. Probably another aspiring actress. Her hair was cropped short in the way directors were after now. There was a pang in my heart because she was not Sandra. Sandra probably should have cut her hair, but she could never bear to. I, for one, wouldn't have wanted her to. Sandra had given two weeks' notice. Maybe she finally got a part, a real chance to leave the waiting room.

There came a blinding flash from one of the couches in the waiting room. Xanthe, dressed all in the sleekest white. Her short hair was bleached so severely that it seemed translucent. It made every feature of her face flash. The effect stunned me, putting me back in the place I was when I first met her.

"I haven't been able to reach you," she said.

"Richard has kept me to himself."

"So I've heard. Funny. After, we need to talk." She gave me a tiny kiss on the cheek. "I'll wait for you in Richard's office."

It sounded a little strange. *Why not in my office?*

"Beware of the dog," I called after her. She turned and smiled.

I didn't know what else to say to her. Nothing in particular was called for, I suppose. For a moment, I just looked at her walking away, her thin legs high and strong under the tight white pants. *Maybe now*, I thought, *now that she sees that the life we aspired to can turn to this kind of shit in a minute, maybe now she'll give up her desire to be someone well known, or at least rich.* We could sell the house, live in Fresno, or one of those other very hot or otherwise very uncomfortable and very small places where normal people live on less than $200,000 a year. *Sure, sure. That's what her new look is surely saying to me.*

Richard had decided to start with the SEC because they would be the easiest. We'd get them to join us in retelling the narrative because they could add a part where their assiduous oversight and quick action brought the situation under control. Richard and I entered with our cell phones (he had issued me one of my own) and placed them down on the table like pistols in a saloon card game. These new phones were a significant advance over the bricks Richard had been using. They opened like switchblades. They were about as heavy as a baseball, which immediately made me think about throwing them somewhere.

We sat down across the table from Francis Cudahy, a junior SEC lawyer. He was an obviously lazy man, ruddy faced, overweight, and resentful that he was working on a Saturday. He had brought a breakfast burrito from Lucky Boy, on the Arroyo Parkway. This was all a part of Richard's plan. Richard had called precisely at a moment when he knew some deadweight like Cudahy would be assigned. He wanted someone who would be amazed by what he was going to say, and grateful to be chosen to hear it.

Once, over martinis at the Yale Club in New York City, Delbert Cranston, our hoary name partner, expounded on some of his ancient wisdom about the SEC to Richard and me. "It's as if they take a shotgun, and point it at your kneecap, and then make you promise to sign something saying you're going to be a good boy. So you just sign. They're very happy, and they go away. And then you go back to doing whatever you want until they come by asking you to sign some other ridiculous piece of paper. So once again, you sign."

Cranston was forever insisting that laws of general application didn't apply to him or one of his friends. Usually it was because the law had been enacted when he was in the Eisenhower administration. But he was right in this case. It would be easy to get the bankruptcy trustee to agree to a consent decree and shut down the company. That would help us in wading through the rest of it and give me a chance to practice my narrative before we got to the tougher audiences at the FBI and US Attorney's Office. Oddyssey was classic securities fraud. And a criminal enterprise. And about a thousand other federal crimes. Richard wanted the US attorneys to feel that they didn't need to go all out given that the SEC was already handling the problem as it related to the securities market.

Another great thing about the story Richard and I had put together in the Bonaventure: all of the really guilty parties were now dead. Unless you believe that Joel is still alive. There had been no sign of him since he left the hospital in the company of the mystery woman.

When Richard looked into Cudahy's eyes, he saw an animal need, and he decided he better fill it before getting to the rest of the meeting.

"Holly, may we please have the coffee service?" Richard's tone was even. He didn't want Cudahy to think that he needed to shout after coffee. Holly came in, accompanied by a woman dressed in a white waitress uniform. There were cups and saucers of real china, and spoons of real silver to stir the real sugar. New York touches Richard had brought to the LA office. When the sugar from the pastries began to reach Cudahy's bloodstream, Richard knew that it was time to begin.

"We've called this meeting to disclose a criminal conspiracy. Sadly, we have found that one of our publicly traded clients has been engaging in a criminal conspiracy and drew one of our marginal associates into the conspiracy."

What is a marginal associate? I wondered to myself. *Oh yeah. Eddie.*

Richard continued: "Francis, I want to assure you that we intend to cooperate fully with the SEC and other law enforcement authorities in making sure that all that there is to be known about this conspiracy becomes known to you first, and then to the investing public."

Richard paused. He took in the wideness in Cudahy's eyes. The hook was in.

Cudahy felt it appropriate to say something, seeking to let us know he wasn't dumbstruck.

"You meant Mr. Guarini?"

"Mr. Guarnieri's career had topped out here, and he became resentful. Apparently he had other talents that were not of use to a law firm."

A greedy heart is of great use to a law firm, I thought. It's just that they never made him partner so that he could take full advantage of his greed in the context of the firm's compensation structure. So he found another way.

"Don't you have a problem with the attorney-client privilege?" Cudahy asked.

Richard looked down at his outline, which Holly had left in just the right position on the desk. "We have carefully reviewed this matter and are confident that the attorney-client privilege is not a bar to our disclosures to you today. We rely, principally, on the crime-fraud exception, which I presume you know well. Additionally, the board of directors—as much of it as is still alive, that is—has met and given us authority to make these disclosures to you."

Cudahy nodded, as if this were normal. There's nothing normal about a law firm laying out a case against their client for law enforcement consumption.

Richard laid out the story, which began and ended with his own heroic role in coming out a couple weeks ago to see what was wrong in the LA office, and then single-handedly uncovering the fraud that had since become apparent to us all. Of course, the picture Total painted showed that he, and the really serious lawyers at C&C, were now back in control and prepared to turn over a tailor-made case to Cudahy and help him present it in court. He painted me as a hardworking, trusting innocent, which I suppose I was.

When it was done, Cudahy realized that he needed to ask a few questions.

"What did Oddyssey actually do?"

"Really nothing. The search service and cellular concierge service they claimed to be running were really just fronts—obviously these are impossible strategies for actually making money. There was some money laundering at work to keep the cash flow going. It was all on Edward Guarnieri's personal computer. None of it on his firm computer. We will have it for you shortly, including a printout of everything we could find. But the main business was pretending to be in business for the purpose of convincing people like our law firm that they were in a real and profitable business. There may be other books, but they have not been found."

I was silent. I had no doubt there were other books. Joel may be the last person alive who knows the passwords. If he is alive. At the Bonaventure, Richard and I had agreed that I would not point the finger at Joel.

"Although," Richard said, dropping his voice, "we did find a very interesting checkbook. Millions of dollars were paid to"—Richard made air quotes—"'suppliers,' who don't seem to exist. That's probably the money for you to follow."

Valerie had paid the price for that checkbook.

A nerdy coterie of computer workers from the New York office had been walking the hallways when I came in that day. I wondered whether Richard had cleansed the computers. I have absolutely no evidence that he did, so I will assume as fact that the computer data from Oddyssey was being fully produced. I feel better that way. And I was right about the checkbook.

Cudahy looked bored by talk of computers. This was good. Richard changed the subject. "The major end and aim appear to have been the public offerings, which is why you were our first call. They planned to abscond with the cash."

"So it was a complete fraud?" Cudahy asked.

"A Ponzi scheme in the classic mold, but of modern proportions," said Richard.

Richard had taken the lead, as he would for the next two years. I would only provide the background, the first-person authenticity to illustrate his points. Ultimately it would be enough to verify the essence of his narrative.

Cudahy felt he needed to ask me a question: "So, when did you know?"

I looked him in the eye and was careful not to blink: "Really, not until I realized that Eddie and the Kid were trying to kill me," I said. "Up until then, I knew mostly what I was seeing on television, or reading in the *LA Times*." I was trying out my answers for the first time with the intended audience. Richard and I had agreed that during these early days I would be vague so that my statements could not be impeached with references to emails or collateral documents I hadn't had time to review. Richard had reviewed the entire universe of producible documents, so I had to rely on his instincts to align my testimony with known facts. But at its core was a story, and I was telling it.

"Eddie was the kind of guy, well, when he did something brilliant, and he really thought this was brilliant, he felt like he had to tell somebody. I guess that was me."

"It really is sort of brilliant," Cudahy said. "Most of the money in the world is just a notation in a computer anyway. He decided that might as well be his computer. What about your partner Joel Green? What did he know?"

"Joel was doing his job as a lawyer, just believing what the Kid said. When you met the Kid, he impressed the hell out of you, just like he did the media. So just like the auditors, just like the *LA Times*, just like MaryLee Lacy, Joel believed him. He was doing the legal work. He thought the lawsuits against Oddyssey were the usual nonsense. He asked me to make them go away."

"So where is Mr. Green?" Cudahy asked.

I had been thinking about how I was going to answer this. It was the one question that Richard couldn't coach me on. Because he didn't know the answer. I had seen my clients tell the truth when they needed to lie, so I fell into that. "I haven't heard from him since he disappeared," I said. My best friend was gone. There was a good chance he had met with a death that had debauched his spirit and despoiled his body. But I did not say that. Because I wasn't completely sure it was true, and thinking of him alive made me feel better. My eyes welled with tears. My demeanor was enough to gloss over the question, as it would be for the next two years.

Two of the little assholes who worked for Richard appeared, fresh from an all-nighter. They carried in boxes of freshly copied, freshly two-hole-punched papers stacked neatly in manila folders and red welds.

"Here is the firm's complete file on the Oddyssey matter. We have withheld nothing. Everything is exactly how it appears in our original files, Bates stamped for verification. If you need any of the originals, just let us know, but we have carefully examined these copies to make sure they are faithful. The checkbook is on the top."

This too was brilliant. Cudahy readily accepted that he had the full file, the legitimate documents. There would be no search warrant, and no question as to whether anything had ever been removed. This file, prepared and culled by Richard, would be the official record for the next two years of investigations. No one ever questioned the narrative it supported. It had the credibility of a law firm exposing its own client. That was an unusual narrative, except in the movies, where such things happen all the time.

By the time Francis Cudahy left the conference room, he was Richard's best friend. I noticed that the fake yellow skin color from Richard's tanning products was completely gone, replaced by real sun darkness, as if he'd been sunbathing in the actual sun for a week. As I would later learn, he had been doing just that. Richard's brilliance was about to pay off, and he was done working so hard.

When Cudahy had gone, Richard told me that he wanted to keep me close. He had rented me an apartment at Bunker Hill, "for the time being." He would have my things delivered. "There's another thing," he said, "another reason." The ever-prepared Richard was almost stuttering.

I can't repeat what Richard said after that because I was lost in the shock of it. Xanthe was in his office for a reason. She wouldn't be coming home with me. I remember he said something to the effect that he loved her, that he wanted to marry her, and that he would make it easy for me.

Through all of the shock, I didn't say anything. I just kept saying to myself, "This is good; this will be for the best. You have one million in checks you need to cash, and this means you don't need to give any of it to her."

I looked at Richard in a different way after that conversation. For one thing, he really was quite handsome when you took away the yellowing from the fake-tan product. And he could be quite charming, especially when his own economic interests were at heart, as in his dealings with Cudahy. But Xanthe could not be said to be within his economic interests. He was capable of love, even if it was only for a being like Xanthe, who was nearly as shallow as he was.

The meeting with Cudahy was not the end, of course. There would be a few follow-up calls and requests for interviews. I sat through hours of boring questions that Cudahy read from his legal pad, questions that would be repeated by FBI agents, US attorneys, and plaintiffs' lawyers.

I held up my end of the bargain with respect to Richard's narrative. Oddyssey's trustee signed a consent decree closing the company down. There were no indictments out of the US attorney. I sat through several FBI interviews, but they seemed uninterested from the start. Their eyes seemed to say, "Why is there even any meeting here? We haven't indicted anybody."

In the end, absolutely nothing significant happened.

There would be a need to pay off the civil suits by Oddyssey shareholders, but that would be no big deal. Richard won his usual 12(b)(6) motions, and the plaintiffs' lawyers, sensing they might actually have to work for the money, went away for $50,000 each. Nominal money to them. "Fifty thousand?" one of them said to me. "I couldn't wipe my ass with that." Two days later, he accepted the offer.

With Richard's help, the bankruptcy trustee actually tracked down a couple million dollars of bank accounts or other assets. The firm's entire bill, including all time dutifully billed by the little assholes, got paid as an administrative claim. There was even some money for the blue-haired ladies from the Valley, at least the ones who were willing to come out of their assisted living facilities and admit how they had been duped by the Kid's easy charm.

Two years later, I agree with my partners that Richard saved the LA office, and he saved C&C from a major scandal. Richard's partners are appreciative, including me. They often tell each other that he might be a total asshole, but he is also, without a doubt, a very good lawyer.

Richard and Xanthe were good for me too. The divorce was swift and painless, unlike my first one. I didn't have to pay any alimony. I even got half of the equity when our house was sold, which certainly hadn't happened in my first marriage. Richard picked up the attorneys' fees himself because he actually wanted to marry Xanthe. Really, I can scarcely appreciate my good fortune.

Xanthe moved into a new home Richard bought on a cliff in Beverly Hills. I'm told she spends most of her time by the infinity pool Richard installed for her, but she has managed to become a sort of Westside socialite. She's friends with a couple minor television stars, and she was even photographed with one of them on page forty-three of a *People* magazine. Everything she wanted.

I hadn't realized it, but she was everything Richard wanted. At this point in his life, he needed to stop working so hard and have some fun. Now that everyone else in the LA office is working hard, he could coast for years on the credit he got for that, as well as for the brilliant hours in which his strategy saved the firm. Richard hardly ever comes into the office anymore. He does his work by his infinity pool so he can keep an eye on Xanthe. It's a nice view.

As for me, the "time being" stretched into the past two years. My few possessions are still at the Bunker Hill. Each night, I do laps in the pool. The butterfly stroke can be a good outlet for frustration. After about four laps, I stop, looking up at the gap in the sky between the tall buildings, my smog-scarred lungs heaving. The dull gray of the empty Los Angeles night leaves me longing for the black of the Northern Michigan sky, rich with its bounty of starry jewels.

Of course, I wish for someone to share the blankness of that sky with me, to keep me from feeling so alone.

Valerie would not be that person. Richard was true to his word, and we saved Valerie. She did not return to work for months, during which we portrayed her as too emotionally fragile to sit through interviews. By the time she was better, the SEC and the US attorney had lost their interest in talking to her. They had their narrative. New evidence would just be confusing.

I told myself to be Valerie's aging asexual gentleman friend. But I couldn't help my attraction to her. The nerves on her arm had been damaged by the Kid's knife, and the arm hung loosely at her side. But the flaw seemed to make her even more beautiful.

My nightly swims made me feel strong and alive. In my mind, I was twenty-four again. I waited, patiently, almost a year. She was well, her eyes clear. She was back at the office, though Richard continued to complain that her work was not saleable to clients.

"Guess what? I'm leaving the firm," she said.

So now she had the chance to say those happy words.

"What brought this on?" I asked.

"Remember Richard's assistant Holly? Turns out they paid Holly off for Richard's harassment, sexual and otherwise, so they had an insurer in place to pay me off too."

"Pay you off?"

"Oh, I slept with him too. At the fabulous Beverly Wilshire. He was a little amazed by it. Even locked out the dog, for once."

She saw the look of anger in my eyes.

"Don't feel sorry for me, Sam. I knew what I was doing. I thought I had to in case I flunked the bar exam again. Turns out I did pass the bar exam after all. Kind of ironic, isn't it? I feel kind of stupid about all the things I did because of that bar exam. I never said anything. But Richard must have said something. Or maybe he just wants me gone because he thinks I'm not a good lawyer. They offered me quite a package. On condition I leave the firm."

"Let me stop this. I'll—"

"No, Sam. This is what I want. I want the package." The look in her eyes told me the question was settled.

"Is Holly okay?" I ask.

"That girl had her act together. She had pictures of Richard with his hands all over her. They paid her, and they paid her very well. She's at law school now. She's going to be a helluva sexual harassment lawyer."

I turned away. Valerie understood why. "This all happened before he settled on Xanthe."

"Really?"

"Well, I think it was before they got really serious. Now she keeps an eye on him." Although I'm not proud of it, I often think Richard and Xanthe deserve each other.

"And you're okay with this?"

"Look, Sam, it's actually a lot of money. I'm leaving in a couple of weeks. I can afford to work without pay for a while. If you still want to start a firm, I can help you get an office started." Valerie came up to me.

"We can really do some good," I said.

I took her hand. It had been months since I had held a woman's hand. I realized, from deep inside of me, how lonely I was.

She put my hand back at my side.

"Jesus Christ, Sam," Valerie cried out. "We're friends. I need you to be my friend. I appreciate all you have done to keep me out of it, but I don't want you or me to think we need to sleep together to keep it that way. Besides, we might be working together, right?"

"I guess I'm no better than Richard."

"No, Sam, you are better. Although I don't deny he's a pretty good lawyer."

She pronounced "lawyer" the same way Richard did, so that you could say there was something of an East Coast accent, or you could just admit that it sounded a little like "liar."

"But you are different. You have a chance to be good," she told me, letting go of my hand for the last time.

I told Valerie I had another year of working out the Oddyssey situation before I went out on my own. She looked at me for a second and then said, "Well, you know, by then I'll probably have *my* own office. You can join me."

A couple months later, I heard she got married. It turns out she had been seeing one of the in-house lawyers who had been trying to date her. He was a pencil-necked, narrow-shouldered kind of guy. Valerie's limp arm made her just flawed enough that someone less than perfect could love her. And it made her just humble enough to love him back.

────────

No one could believe that Peace was anything other than a victim. After all, she was beautiful. There was physical proof of rape. She was questioned only once, and with extreme sensitivity. Everyone accepted I was the shooter. There were no ballistics investigations of the firearms, and Peace quickly disposed of the rest of JD's extensive arsenal. His surfer friends dropped them off at sea, the same way he had dropped off the weapon he used on the messengers.

Peace had her faith, and her meetings, and she believed in them more than anything in the world of the living. I envied her these things, but I could not understand them. She incinerated JD's *River Painting*, which she had taken to calling *Three Bodies by the River*. We both felt it was a shame, but there was no other way. JD left her a million or so in the bank, and his loft was worth another million. Somehow insurance covered the damage from the blast. Peace would not be worrying for money. JD had seen to that. I don't think I need to worry about her much. She seems to have the Peace that passes all understanding.

Everything about JD said muscle, power, force. In the end, however, he was weak. He could not kill and go on. Peace was the strong one, and she stayed strong. He was right about one thing, though. There was no reason not to drink after a day like that.

Dr. Rosa told me she wouldn't see me anymore unless I stopped drinking. I got Peace to take me to a couple meetings to get her off my back. It worked for a while. Actually, I don't drink that much anymore. But the meetings were too damn serious. They say that you should give up drinking completely. Forever. That still seems like overkill to me. And a lot of those people seemed addicted to the meetings, just like they had been addicted to drinking, so I started to wonder whether any of it really made any difference.

My own theory is that my drinking got bad when my life got bad. I'm not so much an alcoholic as someone who logically decides that life is better when experienced with substantial impairment. My life isn't so bad now, thanks to the steady flow of income, and Richard's removal of Xanthe from my life. So I don't drink as much. I feel a bond to JD, and, like him, I can't buy into the whole religious thing. I didn't start my own atheist AA meeting. I didn't kill myself in despair. I just stopped going to the meetings.

I saw Manny once or twice in court. He got himself transferred back to bailiff duty. We had a hard rule that we wouldn't talk to each other. I decided to let Manny keep all the money he made shorting Oddyssey stock. With what the firm was now paying me, I didn't really need it, and

I certainly didn't need any loose ends. As far as anyone knew, Manny had never been to JD's loft.

After about a year, I didn't see Manny anymore. He slipped away. Probably retired to Utah. Three jobs had added up to an early retirement. Good for him.

After two years, most of the pro bono cases had settled. Of course, it helped that I had the firm's resources and letterhead to pursue them.

I can't say I learned to like Richard, but I learned to learn from him. Most of all, I learned to be a little tough, to put the sting of a bit of discipline into opposing counsel. That was when my pro bono cases started to settle.

I stopped pretending to fall asleep. I'm okay just being here. And I don't see dead people. JD doesn't appear to me anymore. I guess he is at peace with how things turned out.

As I sit in LAX traffic, it's been two weeks since I cashed what I figured was my last check under the deal that Richard and I negotiated that day in the jail. I stopped in to see him before heading to the airport. Of course, I had to wait while he harangued another travel agent on his cell phone. Richard's cell phones are smaller now, but he could still exhaust the batteries. His latest secretary is always ready to hand him another one.

This time, I had an outline.

"The last check has been cashed under our deal," I opened.

"I know. I've been putting together a new package."

I thought of asking whether the deal would be adjusted upward or downward. But I knew the answer. I stuck to my outline.

"I'll still be available for depositions and such," I said. That was the way I decided to say I was leaving.

"Shouldn't be much more need for your testimony."

"It doesn't matter. All I've ever been doing is telling the truth," I said. Mostly.

"Take your time, Sam."

"Leaving today." Last point on my outline. I got up and left. I took my freshly charged, firm-issued cell phone.

"Can you track these things?" I asked at the door.

"I track them all."

So I guess that rumor's true. Still, cell phones aren't all bad. You can reach someone or they can reach you at times when you used to be out of the reach of a telephone. Of course, the very fact that people can reach you means that people expect they can reach you, which means you can only fulfill their expectations by having one of these devices. The world was a lot better without them.

Not sure I fully believe that your location can be traced as long as you have your cell phone with you, but I don't want to take any chances. On the way to the airport today, I stopped at the bridge over the cave where JD shot the Oddyssey messengers, where they lie with Sparrow. They have never been found.

For once, it had been raining in Los Angeles, and the water flowed through the concrete channel. I wound up, and tossed the cell phone in. I was proud of the arc of it in the sky, like a Raul Mondesi throw from right field to third base. It sure felt good to see it fly. Maybe the cops will trace it and finally figure out what happened to Sparrow and the messengers. It's time to give those poor souls a decent burial. It will be some fun to see Richard explain that without my help.

I didn't tell Richard, but I had checked out of the Bunker Hill apartment. My little pile of stuff is in a storage locker. Haven't told anyone where I'm going. Because there is one other thing I didn't tell Richard. Or the SEC. Or the US attorney.

I know where Joel is.

CODA

"Aguila," I say to the short guy crowding me outside the airport. He motions for me to follow him.

"Aguila," I say again. I am worried he will trap me in a time share, a fate befalling dazed American tourists all around me. He looks at me quizzically. "*Eres chistoso*," he says. I try English. "Rental car."

"Ah, rental car. You do not want a rental car."

"You speak English."

"Yes, always," he says. He is dressed neatly, but very cheaply. His shirt is plain white Fruit of the Loom. He has shaved, this morning probably. His skin is a dark brown, dry in the late-morning sun. He is sweating, but there is no swarthiness to him, just the clean hopefulness of a young man with his own car.

"What's your name?"

"Ernie."

"Why don't I want a rental car, Ernie?"

"You want me to drive you. I'm a good driver."

I have my credit cards with me, but to avoid using them, I brought enough cash to keep me for several months. "Okay, Ernie, you drive me. I'm on a bit of an odyssey."

"What is odyssey? What does it mean?" *Thank God*, I think. Odyssey is just a strange word to him. *Of course I don't want a rental car. What was I thinking?* I don't want credit card receipts going back to a bank in the US.

"A long strange trip."

"Luggage for this trip?"

"No bags. Let's just go."

"Where?"

"I'll show you."

Ernie's car is old, the paint seems worn by the coast and the sun, but it is clean. There is no air-conditioning, so we drive with the windows open, and the hot, humid air surrounds us.

I tell Ernie to head west out of the airport. It is a long ride along the coast. At first there are hotels, and then, after we pass through a trashy town, we head north. Soon there is nothing but brush and a few small trees between the road and the mountains on our right, and nothing but brush and sand between the road and the ocean surging on our left as we drive. I sit in the back.

"Are you sure this is what you want, señor?"

"Just keep going."

An hour passes. The road is good in some places, and we pass work crews working in the sun to widen it. But there is hardly anything on either side. We pass a crude cantina, and then the remains of attempts at crude cantinas. I see the occasional isolated homes at some points along the coast, vestiges of dreams of the impossible getaway, the paint worn off, the glass long shattered. Mostly the coast is the same as God made it.

This is how it must have been in LA, I think, *before all the people got there.* No wonder they decided to come.

Then I see it, rising into the sky on a promontory along the Pacific coast, the soaring of a bell tower that should be in a church. "That's where I'm going," I tell Ernie.

"Ah, no. I cannot drive this car there. I must take care. This car is what feeds me."

"You can leave me. I'll walk."

Ernie stops by a dirt road pocked by pools of water and gibbous mounds of dust. "Are you sure?" Ernie asks. "It's a mile and a half."

I look at my watch. It is two in the afternoon. "I'll meet you here tomorrow. This same time."

"Okay. Fly straight, my eagle."

"My eagle?"

"That's what *aguila* means. Rent-a-car is *auto de alquiler.*"

I'll never remember that.

Trudging over the dusty road towards the beach, I sweat, but the wind from the ocean is already cooling my body and soul. My shirt, which soaked into the small of my back during the long car ride, begins to dry. I reach the pavement for the hotel on the bluff, and I climb up the narrow road to the yellow building with the four-story tower. Inside the doorway, the word *hacienda* enters my mind as I look at the bright flowers surrounding the walls of the courtyard. There does not seem to be anyone here.

The back of the building opens out to the ocean and the endless sky. There is a bar, but no one is there drinking. A small infinity pool seems perched in the sky. As I sit, I notice the bartender at the far end of the semicircular bar. His gnarled hands patiently chop limes.

"Margarita?"

I hesitate.

"Fresh," he says, pointing down at the board of limes.

"Coke," I say. He shrugs and digs a worn bottle of Coke out of a cooler below the bar, snapping it open. It breathes in the sunlight. I taste the real sugar and am grateful for it after the flight, the ride, the walk through the dust and up the hill. I light a cigarette, and the bartender shoves an ashtray to me. Free country.

A group of women enters and sits by the bar. They are dressed as I would imagine women kept by drug dealers dress for the beach: in bikinis that barely cover their curves, yet draped with diaphanous coverups that endow them with modesty. Their faces are made up, and colorful jewelry decorates their ears, necks, and arms. Waves of perfume reach me in the breeze. My humble bartender has found a market for his margaritas.

What was I thinking? That Joel would just be here? Drinking all day long? Well, sure. Why not? He's got nothing else to do. I gaze out at the ocean and think about ordering some food.

When I turn back, I realize that one of the women has moved away from the group and to the seat nearest me. She is still turned away, and I see her long, sleek hair, down to her waist. It is red, with long, sun-bleached strands of blond. She finally gave up on dying it black to look like Liz Taylor. It seems a little like the end of the world here, but they apparently have lots of hair conditioner. Her bikini and her coverup are bright white, setting off her hair. She is still looking at the other women, who are chatting fiercely. Her face is turned away from me. Then she says something.

"He knew you'd come."

"What are you talking about?" I am surprised at how my voice shakes.

The woman turns to me. "How are you, old Sam?" she says in exaggerated Londoner. It's hard to see through the dark brown of her skin, and the swirling abundance of her hair, but it is Sandra, the aspiring actress who had been our receptionist, the woman in charge of the drugs in the coatroom. She folds me in her arms with abandon, her whole body pressing up against me as I realize she is the mystery woman who got Joel out of County against medical advice.

"You are stunning. More than you've ever been," I say. I am just telling the truth. My lawyerly reserve has faded in the Mexican sun.

Sandra's coverup falls open. She's been working out. No one would guess she is in her forties anymore.

"But there are no movie parts down here," I say.

"Joel is here."

"And he's okay?"

"He's waiting for you."

"Really?"

Listen to me, acting like I'm surprised. I know he's waiting. More than twenty years ago, Joel and I drove down here after the bar exam and before we started work in LA. We surfed for days and slept in the car, or right on the beach, watching the whales dance out on the ocean. We were one of the first to ever drink at this bar, and one drunken night decided it was our favorite place in the universe. It was just another idiot, drunken thing to say. But I had the feeling that we both really meant it. I knew that if we ever couldn't find each other, we had decided, without saying so, to meet here. I knew it because we were brothers, and almost part of the same person.

"Wait," Sandra says, and then rushes away. The bartender is not the same guy who once cut limes for Joel and me, but he cuts them the same way, slowly, carefully. I remember how Joel and I stared drunkenly at the old man's practiced fingers, cutting and squeezing the fresh limes. I decide to have a margarita.

I have two before Sandra returns. She is wearing shorts now, not needing to fit in at the bar anymore.

Outside the hacienda we jump in an old jeep. Sandra's hair rushes behind her as we drive north along the dirt roads at the beach. We stop at a grouping of brown rocks that seem to protect a beach. Sandra and I walk to a break in the rocks, which leads to a cave.

"He's in there." She hugs me deeply, warmly. "Watch your head walking through, Sam."

"What, you can't come?"

But she is already walking away. I take one more look at her hair dancing in the distance.

I bend over and see beyond the end of the tunnel where it breaks out into the ocean. The water rushing through the tunnel scares me. But I go through.

At the end of the tunnel is a small beach, protected by the surrounding rocks. The waves come in hard, and the beach looks terribly small, and in the middle of it is Joel. In a speedo. His skin is as brown as it was in the summer gleam of the lake in Northern Michigan. The layers of fat are gone; the muscles are bulging again. The top of his head is bare and flecked with dark-brown spots. If that hair were not gone, and the face were not hidden beneath a long, straggling beard, he would be no different than the young man who saved my life on the lake. It was like LA had formed a layer of unhealthy flesh all around his spirit, and now it had melted away.

Joel moves swiftly to gather me in, saying, "Brother Sam."

"How did you know I would come?" I say.

"How did you know I would be here?"

"We never talked about it."

"We never needed to. We are brothers."

Joel is right. We had both known we would meet this way. We walk over to a paper bag near the rocks, and he pulls out a couple cans of Tecate. We crack them open like kids celebrating our first beer. The margaritas have worn off, so I feel grateful for the feeling that used to make life worth living. I open a second beer.

"You finally did it. What we always talked about."

"Didn't have much choice," he says. "I should have done this sooner. I could have done this sooner. I just didn't have the guts."

"Have you learned any Spanish?"

"I started with *cerveza*. You can too. My name is Miguel, by the way." He hands me another Tecate.

"Gracias, Miguel. Don't you miss . . . I don't know, people?"

"There are people here, but without the hidden agendas, the layers of duplicity, or strategy. They'll get you a beer. Or steal from you. Or shoot you. But they aren't in the least conflicted about which one it is they want to do. They don't pretend they are being nice to you while they remove a vital organ."

I pull out my pack of Kools and offer him one.

"Gave it up," he said. "Damn unhealthy. You should too."

I decide to light up anyway. It's my life now, I guess.

"I'll tell you one thing I don't miss. Traffic." He goes on: "And I don't miss Richard. I don't miss courtrooms and judges. I don't miss lawyers. I don't miss clients. I don't miss the fucking law. I do miss Trader Joe's."

"I miss you."

"Yeah, I miss you. But I knew you'd come."

"I miss the man you were."

"I was never that guy, Sam. You were always the different one. The one who cared about the law. The one who cared about the clients—even when they were lying whores. The one who cared about being good. I got tired of trying to live up to what you wanted me to be."

"You look like you again. Without the hair of course. But this, this all, it looks like giving up. Like you think you've got nothing else to do."

"A lot of shit has been left behind." He looked around. "Clean beer. Clean water. Only other thing I need is a clean woman."

"Looks like you have one."

"Sandra's gonna go back. She's got an offer for a sitcom. Somebody liked a picture she sent with the red hair."

"And you're okay with that?"

"She still wants the illusion. It's been a good two years. I gotta let her go or she'll start to get miserable. I'll live. The girls who make it this far, to this beach . . . well, you remember don't you?"

"Is that all this was about? Giving up, getting drunk, getting laid?"

"What else do you think there is, Sam?"

I think of my pro bono clients. Some of them are entitled, sure, but most are humble, grateful. Some even tried to pay me. I think about my new law firm, about how Valerie and I will start jousting with the insurance defense lawyers. I am a better lawyer now than I used to be. I could really win some money now.

Joel knows what I'm thinking. "I wish you were like me. I wish you could be happy here. I wish you weren't one of those people who always thinks there is something more important than just getting laid. I wish you'd stay."

"And live off money from the Kid?"

"It doesn't take much to live here."

"Some of the people you stole from were just little old ladies in the Valley," I say. I start to feel the moral outrage that has boiled in me for the last two years. The resentment that made me wait to be the one to find Joel.

"Mostly I stole from sharpies trying to steal from little old ladies," Joel says.

"It wasn't your money."

"I think I paid the price."

"He tried to kill me too, brother. You're the one still living off the money."

Joel takes another drink. "I don't really have trouble sleeping here," he says.

The tide is really coming in now. It washes over our toes. Time to get what I came for.

"What was he doing?"

"The Kid? You mean really? Oh, you guys got it right. It was mostly money laundering."

"The Kid did try to kill you. Did you know I saved you? There was a DNR."

"Thanks, brother. I would have done the same. I did do the same. Once upon a time."

"So now we're even. A life for a life."

"I don't think of brothers as having balance sheets."

"I was protecting you from the Richards of the world. Did you know I was sharing my draw with you?"

"I figured as much. I would have got you back if this all hadn't crashed down on us."

"You should have been straight with me. You could at least be straight with me now."

"The Kid did have a format where he could get anything done."

"Anything?"

"Murder, extortion. The worst of things."

"And you knew?"

A whale breaches out in the ocean. We are standing in the water now, and it surges from our knees up to our thighs. My pants are getting heavy with water.

I turn back to walk up the beach. But the beach is almost completely gone, covered in water except for a narrowing strip between us and the rocks. To the right and left of us, the sand is entirely underwater, and we are being wedged into a narrow opening. I look for the tunnel but can't see it.

"I knew a little. I could live with that. And then I knew a little more, but I could live with that too because I needed a little more than I thought I did. Oddyssey became my way out. Out of all the traffic, all the shit."

"Was I part of the shit?" I ask.

"Sam. You're not the kind of guy who lives with things, who just makes compromises. You drink, sure, but you wake up the next day looking for the next damsel in distress. You try to make the bad things stop. And, you know, I didn't want this one bad thing to stop. Because it was going to make money. I didn't want it to end this way. I was just the last guy alive who knew the passwords to the Mexican bank accounts. It was luck, but after all I went through, well, it was luck I deserved."

I think of the compromises I've been making. Of all the money in my bank account. I haven't turned into Richard, but I've started to understand that always being the nice guy can limit your effectiveness.

"Who did order all the killings?"

"Oh, it was the Kid. He started to believe his own publicity. Didn't want to share. Not with Jacky. Not with me. Not with Eddie, really, but he figured he needed Eddie. Jesus, did you really shoot the Kid? And fucking Eddie?"

"I guess I got mad. I've decided not to sit around and watch bad things happen anymore. At least not to people I like."

"Well, thank you, Sam. I was getting pretty tired of those guys."

"It was the Kid who stabbed us."

"Figured."

"But it was you who killed Jacky, wasn't it?"

"Yeah. Jacky was the one guy who could have found me here. And he cared enough to do it. Also still bothered me that he never paid our bill at Green and Straight."

"How did you do it?"

"A couple of the Kid's messengers. The Kid conditioned them well. They're still with me."

Joel looks up at the top of the rocks. Two dreadlocked men stand there, looking down. Both holding AK-47s.

"They work for you?"

"Same two. That's all I need these days. You can't really have money down here without a little protection."

"Shouldn't we get going? While we can still get through the tunnel?"

"The tunnel is flooded, Sam. You better take off some of your clothes and get ready to swim with me."

Joel points to the tunnel. The water surges in and out of the opening. I bend over and try to see my way through, but there is no way to walk through anymore. The only way out is to swim for it and try to land further down the beach.

The water heaves as high as our waists now, and a narrow strip of sand is only visible between waves. I let this go too long. I've grown used to thinking of myself as the smarter one, yet here I am trapped in surging water that he has been expecting, counting on.

The waves crash against the rocks now. They look strong enough to toss my body and slam my skull on them.

"Let's go back together, Joel. If you didn't kill anyone, you can face up to it."

"I'm not going back, Sam."

He takes off his shirt, and I see the muscles rippling again as they did that summer in Michigan. He comes up and hugs me, pressing up against the electric recorder taped inside my shirt. "You can take off your shirt now."

We are backed up almost to the rock wall. I toss my shirt and tape recorder into the surf.

Joel shakes his head in the sadness of betrayal. "There you go again. Always obsessed with what you think is the moral thing. Don't you know? There is nothing like the right thing?" He doesn't wait for me to answer before he says, "See you, brother." He turns, and then turns back, pauses as if he has forgotten something, and adds, "Love you." Then he nods up to the messengers. "Always loved you."

He swims out then.

I have to decide whether to move. He was always the stronger swimmer. I look around for a place of purchase on the rock wall, somewhere where I can catch on, climb up and over to land. I make a few tries, but my hands keep slipping.

The sand pelts my bare skin. I look out at the billowing ruction of the waves—so unlike the peaceful surfaces of the Michigan lakes where Joel and I used to swim. I start to swim. Yards ahead, I see Joel's muscular shoulders rise up out of the pit of a wave as they did so long ago. His back humps over in a smooth, undulating coil like the back of a killer whale. His immense arms flick out in a butterfly stroke, and the back of his hands flick upwards from his wrists in a final, skyward gesture of grace. His arms dive swiftly into the water in front of him and pull him up and over the foam and the crest of the wave. His head points down into the water beyond. His legs snap one last vicious kick towards land. There is a glimpse of his toes. And he is gone.

Goodbye, my brother.

The dreadlocked messengers begin firing. One of the bullets splashes in the water in front of my eyes. I gasp for air and dive, searching again for the flowing hair of the girl I fell in love with. In Northern Michigan. So long ago.

ACKNOWLEDGMENTS

I n Michigan, so long ago, I had good friends. My summer running mate, Joseph Lampe, became my sixth brother. My roommate, Norbert Chu, stayed up late nights to talk me through the demons that might have led my life to an early end. Joe and Norb read early versions of the book, which gave us the chance to realize that time and distance had not diminished our friendship.

Nancy Morgan, a lawyer who can really write, and knows good writing from bad, read and commented on numerous drafts, encouraging me to tone down some of the less admirable parts of Sam.

My colleague Judge Kenneth Freeman told me to keep going, that I really could write even if others thought I couldn't.

Mary Logue, an accomplished author of many books, told me what to leave in, and what to leave out, at a time when there was a lot to leave out.

My brother Dr. Michael Kralik and his wife, Shannon Kralik, slogged through the novel during the COVID scare and made many important improvements.

I am indebted to author and attorney Melanie Bragg for bringing me to Koehler Publishing, and to Koehler for taking this chance.

My wife, Catherine Beyerle Kralik, was the first person to read any version of this, and without her help I would not have lived to write the last version. She kept me alive and gave me a reason to live.